THE DEEP VELVET BLACKNESS

The two Cubans didn't have the time to become suspicious. The Death Merchant burst into action with the suddenness of a hidden hand grenade exploding. A high leap, his right leg shooting outward and upward in a TNT *Mawashi Geri* roundhouse kick, the automatic rifle in his right hand coming up simultaneously and with equal speed.

Bartolome Predes and Orlando de Rivera were not the only ones surprised. So was Colonel Bin Maktum. Because of Camellion's incredible speed, the Saudi intelligence agent didn't even have a chance to go into action.

The muzzle of the AKS-74 A-R stabbed into Orlando de Rivera's throat, just below his chin, the hard steel of the barrel going three inches into the flesh. The Cuban was as good as dead. With the top of his Adam's apple crushed, he couldn't even scream. All he could do was shriek within himself at the intense pain and at the horror of the situation in which he found himself. Helpless, he found the ground rushing up to meet him and heard the roaring of the velvet blackness bombarding his brain.

Bartolome Predes wasn't much better off. The heel of the Death Merchant's right foot had fractured Predes's breast bone and slammed him into a state of shock. Before he could even let out a groan, Camellion's right arm moved to the right and the barrel of the assault rifle crashed against Predes's right temple—a sound similar to a large twig being snapped . . .

THE DEATH MERCHANT SERIES:

#49 in the incredible adventures of the

DEATH MERCHANT

NIGHT OF THE PEACOCK

by Joseph Rosenberger

PINNACLE BOOKS   NEW YORK

DEATH MERCHANT #49:
NIGHT OF THE PEACOCK

Copyright © 1982 by Joseph Rosenberger

An original Pinnacle Books edition, published for the first time anywhere.

First printing, March 1982

ISBN: 0-523-41645-8

Cover illustration by Dean Cate

Printed in the United States of America

PINNACLE BOOKS, INC.
1430 Broadway
New York, New York 10018

Technical advice for all the
Death Merchant books is
supplied by
Colonel George E. Ellis
of
Le Mercenaire
(Aurora, Illinois)

"In a sense, human history and human destiny are determined by sheer weight of numbers; yet dying gods and sacrificial victims have always attended the rise and the fall of civilizations, and within this soaring to greatness, followed by the plunge into dust, there is always the death of countless millions. Death feeds on life just as life needs and demands Death to have meaning. Because this is so, the grandeur of Death is lost in a world of timid hypocrites, in a world in which mass murder is excused within a framework of impermanent "morality."

—Richard J. Camellion
Votaw, Texas

This book is dedicated to
Saad bin Tafl

(It wasn't Allah who
saved you, my friend.
It was a well-machined
Safari Arms .45 Match-Master.)

☐ ONE ☐

Since Death always favors the man who is not only proficient but who also makes a virtue of necessity, Richard Camellion was positive that the two Yemeni guards, sixty feet ahead of him, were not aware of his presence. Sitting with their right sides facing him, the two *Dasni*[1] devil worshipers could have been two big black rocks, dressed as they were in *jellabas*, hooded black robes. Across each man's lap was a Soviet AKM assault rifle. In front of the guard—the one closest to the Death Merchant—was a curved, metal warning horn.

Camellion, as flat as a postage stamp among the rocks, reflected that he must be patient—*one blast on that horn, or one shot, and the entire camp will be alerted.* Very slowly, he brought up his right arm, his right hand filled with a stainless steel "Alaskan" Auto Mag pistol, to the barrel of which was attached a Lee E. Jurras noise suppressor. To the lower outside butt was attached a custom-laminated, wood-stainless steel stock, or shoulder attachment. There was no moon and the Death Merchant could barely see the two guards. Camellion wasn't concerned about the darkness. A Neumann Night-Site infrared scope was also attached to the AMP. Nonetheless, one mistake now, one tiny noise, and three weeks work would dissolve under the brilliant blue-white stars of the south Yemen sky.

Getting to within shooting distance of Rabadh Yahya Tabriz's camp had been extremely difficult—"Impossible!"

[1]. Actually members of the fierce Zaidi tribe—Arabs. These devil worshipers call themselves *Dasni*, but to other Arabians and Yemenis they are known as *Yezidis*. Utterly ruthless, they delight in torture. They number between 30,000 and 40,000.

Colonel Bin Maktum of Saudi Arabia's General Security Directorate had said—*But we did it!*

Disguised as knife and sword selling Anazah merchants from north Arabia, the Death Merchant and the twenty-three other men—all Arabs—had departed from Riyadh, the capital of Saudi Arabia. The thirty camel caravan had crossed the treacherous Jabal 'at-Tuwayq, a tremendous area of low rocky ridges and steep escarpments, and had finally entered the blast furnace hot Rub' al-Khali, the "Empty Quarter," although the Bedouins called the fantastic expanse *ar-Ramlah*—'The Sea of Sand."

As long as he lived, Camellion would never forget the Empty Quarter where some of the dunes were as high as 400 feet—mountains of sand that took the shape of domes, pyramids, huge crescents, and other weird shapes. With a daytime temperature as high as 130 degrees, they had travelled by night and slept and suffered under black goat hair tents by day, taking salt and potassium tablets and drinking water only when they were forced to—which was often.

They had met only three other caravans . . . long strings of camels whose Bedouin masters had been careful to keep their distance. Arabia is a savage land and one never trusts strangers, especially in the desert.

There came the time when the Death Merchant and his people had entered the *sabkhahs,* the broad rocky plains of the southern Rub' al-Khali. Soon they had crossed the border into South Yemen, or The People's Democratic Republic of Yemen, the first and only Marxist Arab state in the Middle East, and were in the Ramlq as-Sab'atayn desert, in the north section of the country. Twice they were stopped by jeep-driving *Shurtat al-Badiya,* the Police of the *badiya,* of the desert regions of South Yemen[2] and, as was customary, forced to identify themselves, state their business and their destination. All their papers were in order, the documents identifying them as citizens of Arabia, including Camellion, who was travelling under the name of Ibranim Ghazi, and who, because he did not speak Arabic, was posing as being deaf and dumb and retarded.

2. North Yemen is known as the Yemen Arab Republic. Ruled by a nine-man council, the Yemen Arab Republic is violently anti-Communist.

2

"Ghazi has been cursed by Allah," Bin Maktum told the police, then added that "He works for me."

And where was the caravan going? To the town of Ar-Rawuk, to sell firearms.[3] The *Shurtat al-Badiya* were satisfied, and the caravan was allowed to proceed.

Several days later the caravan made its way through one of the passes of the Hadramawi, a treacherous range of mountains whose ugly forbidding peaks were called the Fingers of Sheitan (satan) by the Arabs.

"We really have no proof that the police believed us," said Hussain i'Qujd, the North Yemeni Royalist agent. "We are taking a terrible risk."

"Suppose there was a millenium and no one came?" laughed the Death Merchant. "We take our chances. Nothing is certain but death."

"And heat," added Muhammad al Auf, another north Yemeni.

A day and a half passed and, when the sky was filled with stars and the *shamāl*, or hot wind, was only a breeze, the caravan turned and began to move in a southeast direction. The encampment of Rabadh Yahya Tabriz, the leader and the high priest of the Dasni, was only 96.54 kilometers, or 60 miles, away.

Extreme stealth and extreme security now became an ultranecessity. They made no fires. They ate their food from tins, then buried the cans (and their fecal matter) deeply in the sand. During the day, on the last stretch of their journey when they were only 12 km. from the Tabriz's camp, they stretched sand-colored netting over the kneeling camels and camped by dunes.

On that last night, they had left the camels five miles north of Tabriz's camp, and the Death Merchant and eight of the men had gone the rest of the way by foot. They were now in extreme danger. But there were safeguards, for the Death Merchant firmly believed in the ancient Arabian proverb that: *The chameleon does not leave one tree until he is sure of another.* By like token, he wasn't going to assume that the assassination of Rabadh Yahya Tabriz would go down without any complications. It could, in which case, fine. If it didn't, he would be prepared.

3. There is no "gun control" in Saudi Arabia.

Camellion, Rashid al-Khaima and Muhammad al Auf had proceeded to creep in closer to the camp in which numerous campfires could be seen. A mile behind the three, other men planted a dozen small land mines that could be detonated by remote control and, still farther back, set up five Famas rifles on bipods. Three other men waited with Israeli hand mortars.

The Death Merchant, with al-Khaima and al Auf eight feet behind him, belly-crawled across the rocks with all the stealth of a stalking tiger and with all the silence of back alley shadows. The first to die were three guards a half mile from the north perimeter of the camp. They fell without so much as a short muffled cry, .44 AMP slugs tearing enormous bloody tunnels through their bodies.

Carefully, the Death Merchant and his two companions crawled closer to the camp that was actually a village composed of scores of one and two room mud-brick huts and goat hair tents. To all appearances the village was a normal Arab settlement—if it hadn't been for the monstrous stone structure in the center of the camp. Made of black and brown streaked stone, the building was 175-feet long, 75-feet high and 62-feet wide. Shaped like an overstuffed "T," the cross-arm was, of course, wider than the longer section of the building. The cross-section was domed over and painted Chinese red; the point or apex topped by a metal peacock with tail feathers spread and coated with vivid colors. The Dasni had larger camps than this village but Danikil was the most important settlement of all. It was the "Rome" to the 35,000 devil worshipers in South Yemen, the holy of holies because Danikil contained the temple of Melek Taus, the Dasni's name for Satan. Danikil was the "St. Peter's" of the Dasni religion and the temple was the very heart of the tribe's evil and cruelty, a diabolism and an inhuman ferocity that was feared throughout the Arabian peninsula—*Which is why Colonel Qahtan al-Shaabi wants the Dasni on his side when he attacks north Yemen!* thought the Death Merchant as he moved his right arm and, with his left hand under his right wrist, brought up the AMP. *And the Soviets are going along with the scheme because they know they don't have*

4

a chance. They need al-Shaabi and his Marxist goons in their ultimate move against Saudi Arabia.

Expertly, Camellion raised the Alaskan Auto Mag, put the wooden part of the metal stock against his right shoulder, and carefully sighted through the night vision scope. The two guards were sitting side by side, crosslegged, Indian style. A head shot?—or aim for the right side of the man closest to him? Even through the Nite Site vision scope, it was difficult to ascertain whether the man closest to him had his arms folded or hanging loosely at his sides. The hood of the jellaba was down but the rest of the robe was draped over the back and the sides of the Arab. A .44 magnum bullet was tremendously powerful—*But suppose it strikes the man in the arm? It will go all the way through his arm and enter his body. But it's possible that the projectile won't go all the way through and hit the other joker. I'd better make it a head shot. Once the first man's down, I can pop the other sand crab anywhere.*

The Death Merchant focused the open ring in the center of the crosshairs of the scope just above the Dasni guard's right ear and gently squeezed the trigger of the Alaskan AMP.

PHYYTTTTT! SPLATTTTT! Traveling at 2,000 feet per second, the 265 grain flat-nosed bullet blew apart the Arab's head as effectively as if a stick of dynamite tied to his skull had exploded.

Stone dead, even as parts of his skull and brain were dousing the freak next to him, the headless corpse—blood spurting upward a foot—started to topple. The Dasni guard next to the dead man, totally unprepared for what was happening, tried to pick up his assault rifle and jump up, all at the same time. He failed miserably.

Camellion's .44 projectile bored into the left side of the Arab's chest and blew open a hole in his body large enough to permit the passage of ping-pong balls. The Dasni devil worshiper died so quickly, he didn't even have time to realize he was no longer a part of the land of the living.

With a feeling of satisfaction Camellion lowered the AMP, turned his head and called out softly, "Come ahead. The two have been terminated."

Soon, Muhammad al Auf and Rashid al-Khaima had crawled forward and lay prone on either side of the Death

5

Merchant. Both Arabs carried silenced MAC[4]/Ingram machine pistols, and like Camellion their faces had been smudged with dark camouflage paint.

"We are almost in the laps of the devils," whispered Rashid al-Khaima. "May Allah smile upon us."

In his early thirties, al-Khaima was a fierce-eyed man with carmel-colored skin, thick, curly black hair and an enormous mustache. A Muslim of the moderate Shai sect,[5] he was also a valued member of the Yemishu 'fi, the small but efficient intelligence service of the (north) Yemen Arab Republic.

Camellion turned his head to the left. "That ridge ahead, about a fifth of a klick away. From bottom to top, it's about sixteen meters tall. From the top we can view the entire village and see Tabriz when he goes to the temple at midnight."

" 'Klicks?' " echoed al Auf, puzzled by the U.S. Army euphemism.

"Kilometers," explained the Death Merchant, turning then to al Auf, who was also a North Yemeni and a member of *Ibn'u alib Saqr*—The Sons of the Falcon, the underground organization in south Yemen that was trying to overthrow the Marxist regime of Colonel Qahtan al-Shaabi, the strongman of The People's Democratic Republic of Yemen.

"Muhammad, get on the walkie-talkie and tell the men that we've made it and what we're going to do. As nervous as they are, they need some reassurance."

"I could use some assurance myself," al Auf said seriously. With his left hand he pulled a Tadiran PRC-601 palm-held transceiver from his belt, extended the antenna, switched on the set and pushed the four-channel button. Then he started speaking in Arabic.

After al Auf finished talking and replaced the PRC-601 in its case, the three men began to crawl, began to slither over and through rocks mingled with cushion-plants, thistles, coarse grass, and hogweed. Like some kind of

4. Military Armament Corp. The inventor of the Ingram was Gordon Ingram.

5. The Arab Muslims are divided into various sects—the Sunni, the Shi'ites, the Alawis, and the Ismailis.

black robed "creepers," they belly-crept up the incline that would take them to the top of the ridge.

With rest stops and pauses for listening, it took almost an hour and fifty minutes for them to reach the top of the rise. All the while, one worry kept nagging them: suppose other Dasni devil worshipers came to relieve the dead guards? The answer was glaringly obvious—all hell would break loose. . . . Second part of answer: the force would have to retreat, would have to run and hope that the two Saudi helicopters, waiting at the tiny settlement of Kuh-i-b'yda in the Empty Quarter, would arrive in time to airlift them to safety.

Danikil lay spread out before the Death Merchant and his two companions. Studying the village through binoculars, they could see the stone huts and tents illuminated by numerous campfires, generating hundreds of flickering shadows that glided silently into the nothingness of the night.

"There's Tabriz's house," the Death Merchant said, "that four room deal to the east, the one that has a peacock on top of a pole in front of the place."

"*Rahmat sab Ullahi,*"[6] Rashid al-Khaima exclaimed excitedly. "We have an almost unobstructed view from the house to that temple of slime and filth."

"It's eleven-thirty-five," Muhammad al Auf said as if to remind the Death Merchant of the time.

He might as well have kept his mouth shut because Camellion had reached into the pack on his back and was taking out a disassembled Soviet SVD Dragunov sniper rifle, a weapon chambered for the 7.62cm (MI908) cartridge and modified to receive a noise suppressor and a Ramax Night Vision telescopic sight.

Camellion said lazily, "Muhammad, better tell the men we're up here and ready to hit the target." He fitted the wooden stock to the barrel and the firing mechanism, then began to screw the noise suppressor to the end of the barrel.

"From us to the temple is a good half a kilometer," Rashid al-Khaima observed casually, glancing from Camellion to Muhammad al Auf who was speaking in a

6. "Allah is merciful."

low voice and holding the PRC-601 very close to his mouth. "As you Westerners say, it's a 'long shot.' "

The Death Merchant smiled crookedly. *A "long shot!" Bull! Half a kilometer is only one thousand one hundred and forty feet. A cinch with a Dragunov and a N.S.D.*

By the time Muhammad al Auf had finished talking and was putting away the walkie-talkie transceiver, Camellion had the stock of the Dragunov sniper rifle against his right shoulder, was peering through the Ramax NV-T. sight and was adjusting the focusing knob.

Again, Muhammad al Auf consulted his wristwatch. "It is eleven-forty-five. Any moment, we should see that Shaitan-worshiping pig coming out of his house with his attendants. Allah willing, that Ape of God[7] will soon be dead and in hell with his master."

The Death Merchant, testing the NV scope on a Dasni sitting by a fire, barely turned the knob. There! He had it—perfect clearness, the image made bright by the infrared rays, so luculent that he could see the cruel features of the man.

"First Tabriz, then that psychopath of a swine Colonel Shaabi," muttered Rashid al-Khaima through clenched teeth.

"Let's not be too quick to count the chickens," Camellion said. "Tabriz could change his schedule. It's possible, my *Sahib*[8]."

"No, *Sahib* Gardner," responded al-Khaima, using the name by which he knew Camellion. "The evil religion of the Yezidis demands that an animal be sacrificed to the Evil One each night at midnight. When Tabriz is in Danikil, he must officiate. He is the High Imam of the devil tribe. When he is not in the village, one of the lower priests does the killing. But it's law that a sacrifice must be made each midnight."

Muhammad al Auf, peering through 11 × 80 binoculars—so powerful that, to keep the images from flickering,

7. "The Ape of God:" A term used by the early Christians in referring to the antichrist. The disparaging name was also bestowed on Satan after he organized his own kingdom.
8. Means "friend." Unlike the derived usages in Persia, India, etc.

he had to stabilize the glasses on a small tripod—was the first to see Tabriz leaving his dwelling.

"There he is!" he whispered, his low voice filled with hate. As a devout Muslim, al Auf, who only tolerated *nasranis* (Nazarenes: Christians), thoroughly despised Tabriz, considering the high priest of the Dasni a personification of Lucifer himself.

"Right on schedule," murmured the Death Merchant.

Rabadh Yahya Tabriz, dressed in a gold *gandoura,* an ankle-length robe, was preceded by two acolytes, each of whom carried a tall, unlighted black candle in a brass holder. Behind Tabriz, who also wore a gold colored coned headdress, a foot high, were eight other men, all wearing *dish-dashas,* ankle-length white robes without hoods. All eight were carrying a stark naked, desperately struggling black man. Two held the doomed man by the legs, two others grasped the trunk, a fifth walked behind the nude victim, holding him by the shoulders, while the three other Dasnis carried the man by his arms.

"By the sacred memory of Allah!" exclaimed Rashid al-Khaima. "The Shaitanists are going to kill a human victim!"

"Kill them all, *Sahib* Gardner!" Muhammad al Auf hissed. "They all deserve the eternal darkness of hell."

The Death Merchant, who was centering his sights on Tabriz, said softly, "The other men are minnows. Tabriz is the shark. I'll take him out first."

"A'jiz! A'jiz!" ("Shoot! Shoot!") Khaima was so excited that he lapsed into Arabic. He glanced expectantly at the Death Merchant who had his eyes glued to the two rubber cups of the Ramax infrared scope. Before he could pull the trigger of the sniper rifle, Tabriz and his party moved in front of a house, making it impossible for Camellion and the two Arabs with him to see them. There were a dozen mud-brick houses in a row, and Camellion calculated it would be several minutes before he would be able to get Tabriz in his sights again. From the last house in line, it was almost a hundred feet to the temple of the peacock and—*I'll have more than enough time to terminate all nine of the trash.*

Tabriz and the other eight must have been moving in front of the tenth or the eleventh house when a voice called out loudly in Arabic from the bottom of the incline: "STAND UP, INFIDELS, OR YOU WILL DIE!"

If the Death Merchant and his two companions had not been accustomed to the suddenness with which Death can strike, all three might have died within seconds. A flash of thought stabbed at the three men—*Discovered!* Other Dasni had come to relieve the guards that the Death Merchant had killed. They had spotted Camellion and his two companions on top of the ridge.

The Death Merchant and the two Arabs reacted instantly. Capture and/or surrender was not even conceivable, considering the repertoire of hideous torture the devil worshipers used on helpless captives, one of their favorites being to slowly skin a man alive. Roasting a man very slowly, over hot coals, with another favorite amusement.

Bringing up their silenced Ingram machine pistols, al Auf and Rashid al-Khaima rolled away from the Death Merchant and, turning over on their backs, reared up and fired downward in a sweeping arc, in the direction of the voice at the bottom of the incline. At the very same time, Camellion rolled over to his left, jerked his body lower on the incline, swung around the SVD sniper rifle and fired blindly.

Almost simultaneously the three Dasni at the bottom of the long, rolling slope fired short bursts, Adi Shimar and Najaf Qizan, Soviet AKMs, Salah Aulaqi firing a single shot from a World War II British Lee Enfield No. 4 Mark 1. rifle. The roaring of the enemy weapons shattered the silence of the night, the fragments of the echoes bouncing back and forth across the warm sands and rocks.

Several AKM 7.62 ($\times$39mm) projectiles zipped through Muhammad al Auf's woolen burnoose, one bullet going through the left side of the turned down hood of the cloak, the second steel-cored slug cutting through the right side of the material, only inches from Auf's left side.

Rashid al-Khaima came even closer to dying. Three of Najaf Qizan's 7.62mm AKM projectiles burned air within inches of his left temple. A fourth bullet struck the handle of the large, ornately decorated dagger[9] stuck in his wide

9. These daggers are often a foot and a half long and always curved. They are very expensive but the more ornate the dagger, the greater the wearer's prestige, especially in Oman.

belt over his stomach, a dagger that was actually steel overlaid with silver. *Zingggggg!* The projectile first bent the handle, then glanced to the right, cutting its way through the right bottom of al-Khaima's burnoose.

Salah Aulaqi's .303 Enfield bullet struck a rock only a few inches from the Death Merchant's right hip, showering the lower part of Camellion's body with jagged chips.

Camellion's 7.62mm projectile hit the sand at the bottom of the incline. Rashid al-Khaima and Muhammad al Auf's lines of nine millimeter swaged lead massacred the three Dasni guards. Four of the full metal jacketed slugs sliced into Adi Shimar's lower chest and upper stomach, the quadruple impact doubling him over as it kicked him down to the rocks.

Najaf Qizan died with two 9mms that erased his face and blew out the back of his skull. A third bullet tore off part of his left ear lobe, a fourth smacking him in the right side of the neck and cutting through the carotid artery. A bloody mess, Qizan was a cold-cut before he could even begin to fall—and so was Salah Aulaqi, six of al-Khaima's slugs hitting the lower part of his body. Two tore through his colon. Another bored a tunnel through his pancreas. Two more knifed through his jejunum or small intestine. The sixth 9-millimeter slug zipped into his lower groin and butchered his rectum.

"We got them!" snarled al-Khaima in satisfaction. To make sure, he raked the three dead men with the remainder of the cartridges in his Ingram, the noise suppressor made one long, discordant whisper.

"But we've missed our chance at Tabriz." Camellion's low voice was even more serious as he ordered al-Auf to get on the walkie-talkie and ". . . tell our boys we're all right. Tell them not to open fire or detonate the mines until we've joined them. Snap it up. I'm going to take a look at what is going on in the village!"—*As if I didn't know!*

"Make it fast, *Sahib* Gardner," urged al-Khaima, shoving a full magazine into his Ingram and pulling back the cocking bolt. "They will come after us."

The Death Merchant looked over the rim of the ridge at the village below. Men with weapons were running from tents and mud-brick houses, but racing in orderly fashion without fear or panic. Such methodical movement and behavior indicated the worst to Camellion, indicated that the Dasni sadists were both trained and determined.

There was no sign of Rabadh Yahya Tabriz and the men and the sacrificial victim. Even as Camellion watched, scores of men ran toward the area where the camels were tethered—*And those cantankerous ruiminant quadrupeds can run faster than we can!*

Camellion turned and, with the two other men, butt-slid a dozen feet from the incline. He then stood up, slung the sniper rifle over his left shoulder and unhooked the silenced Ingram dangling from the cross straps over his chest.

"Let's move as fast as we can," he said calmly. "By the time the first Dasni get here, we can be three hundred meters to the west. We can take cover in those boulders I remember passing."

"We must do better than that, *Sahib* Gardner," Rashid al-Khaima said firmly. "Should we allow ourselves to be surrounded, we will surely die."

"We will do better." The Death Merchant's feet crunched in the sand, in rhythm with the two other men who were rushing down the slope. "The Dasni will have to come along the route to the left of this slope. We'll drop a modified V40 every twenty feet and wait until the Dasni are riding over them before making a big bang."

"We have six grenades each," Muhammad al Auf said. "That's three hundred and sixty of your American feet. The explosions should disorganize them enough to give us time to reach the others."

"Allah be with us." Rashid al-Khaima sounded worried. "Should those demon-loving sons of whores be able to mount a second attack before we can reach our people with the machine-gun, we'll have to put bullets through our heads to save ourselves from capture."

"We'll succeed," the Death Merchant said, breathing deeply through his nose as they reached the bottom of the incline. "I'm confident we will."

I'm positive we will. But if I told them how I knew, they'd think I was possessed of a dozen djinnis. . . .

Camellion dropped the first V40 grenade twenty-five feet from the bottom of the incline and thirty feet to the left, then called out in a low voice, "Muhammad, drop the second one. Rashid, the third. Call out 'drop' each time. We don't want to drop them too close to each other."

Moving as quickly as possible in the darkness, at times stumbling over the rough, uneven terrain, they dropped grenades in rotation, each man hoping they could reach the boulders in time. If they could, they would have a fifty-fifty chance. The V40s were deadly.

The V40 fragmentation grenade (manufactured by NWN de Kruithoorn, Holland) was the smallest grenade of current known manufacture, its size and weight being roughly half that of most current frag grenades available. None the less, the V40 produced 400 to 500 fragments with a lethal radius of five meters and a maximum effective zone of 25 meters, or an incredible 85 feet, although the fragments did lose velocity after five to six meters.

These V40s had been modified in that each grenade had been fitted with a battery powered remote control detonator that could be triggered by a preset frequency of 7.10 MHz, but only by pressing the master control button four times in quick succession.

None too soon did Camellion and the two Arabs reach the rocks that, scattered about, offered some small measure of safety. The largest were the size of large barrels, the smallest the size of water buckets. As they snuggled down behind the granite and limestone rocks, they could hear the feet of Arabian camels striking the rocks and the sand, some of the cranky beasts snorting in displeasure at being urged, by their riders, to go faster. The "most egotistic beasts" in all the world—Yazid Ahl, one of the Saudi agents, had once laughingly told Camellion. Ahl had said, "*A camel thinks it knows all the one hundred names of Allah and that man knows only ninety-nine. Therefore, he feels superior to us!*"

Taking the remote control device from the small pack on his left hip, Camellion did not feel like laughing now. Belial, the Cosmic Lord of Death, was too close.

"Well, what are they doing?" he asked Rashid al-Khaima who was watching the approaching Dasni riders through the night vision scope of the sniper rifle.

"How many?" inquired Muhammad al Auf.

"A dozen of the swine have stopped at the bottom of the slope. Four are dismounting," reported al-Khaima.

13

"Many more are coming ahead at a trot, and they are spreading out."

"But how many?" demanded al Auf.

"*Haqui!* ("Damn!") Do you think I have time to count them?" al-Khaima retorted angrily. "At least a hundred, perhaps more. Most of the pigs are carrying automatic rifles."

"Spreading out—how far?" The Death Merchant's voice was harsh.

"Now . . . eighteen meters at the most."

"Keep watching," said Camellion. "When the first of the riders is over the last grenade we dropped, tell me."

"*Rafiq'l, Gardner Sahib, su'qa birik.*"

"Speak English!"

"I will tell you, friend Gardner."

Muttered Muhammad al Auf, "Let us hope we are not hammering cold iron. I do not trust electronic devices of any kind."

The Death Merchant waited, not speaking . . . almost hating Courtland Grojean, the boss of the CIA's clandestine section, for getting him into this mess—*On the other hand, I could have turned down this mission, If I had, I wouldn't be with these two sand crabs in this damned desert. The superstitious fools!*

To Camellion, it was illogical that al Auf and al-Khaima, both educated in Europe, could believe in the nonsense of Allah—*"A crackpot, a dedicated fanatic, who thought he could talk to God! And al-Khaima and al Auf believe that bull. They must have the Arab franchise on crapola!*

"Now!" said Rashid al-Khaima hoarsely.

Camellion began to push the master button of the remote control box—one . . . two . . . three . . . four. Eighteen V40 grenades, scattered out in a length of 360 feet, exploded as a single unit, as a solitary bomb, the prefragmented bodies of the V40s, filled with Composition-B, exploding with a thunderous roar and a brief but bright flash of red-orange fire, the wall of noise smashing against the Death Merchant and his two companions.

Roar and flame were followed by the agonized screams and shrieks of men and animals as thousands of steel fragments rocketed upward, outward, and ripped through robes into arms and legs, chests and stomachs, faces and backs, the effect a hundred times worse than being rolled violently in a barbed wire envelope of concertina wire. In a second, scores of camels—the poor beasts making hideous sounds of fear and agony—went down, throwing off their riders, many of whom had already been mortally wounded by the tiny "slingshot" shrapnel.

His ears ringing, Camellion said, "Rashid, keep watching through the scope. "Muhammad and I will hose 'em down with Ingram slugs."

"Ahhh, Sahib Gardner. Most of them are already down," al-Khaima said happily. "They are completely disorganized!"

"Uh-huh, and in a minute they're going to be 'completely dead,' " Camellion said.

Although the Death Merchant and Muhammad al Auf could not see clearly ahead, they methodically raked the area in front of them with Ingram machine pistols, the long noise suppressors hiding the muzzle flashes. More Dasni devil worshippers screamed and fell, the 9mm projectiles ice picking into their bodies. The ones still alive fell to the sand and lay flat, cursing their ill fortune and asking Satan to save them from a hail of lead they could not see.

Camellion and Muhammad al Auf used four magazines each before the Death Merchant ordered a retreat. "We have almost a mile to cover," he said, "and we've got to make it before those devils regroup. Even if they do reform—what's left of the first batch—it's not likely that they'll come after us in the dark. As it is now, they don't know how many of us are out here and what kind of mine field we might have laid."

"I only hope that Colonel Maktum radioed for the helicopters," Rashid al-Khaima said dismally. With Camellion and al-Khaima, he moved out, keeping in line with the larger rocks. "It will take the birds several hours to get here."

"We'll be in the air before daylight," Camellion said. "Colonel Maktum sent out the SOS and the coordinates when he heard the first shot."

They hurried ahead in the darkness, Camellion glancing at his compass every now and then, Rashid al-Khaima

15

turning occasionally to peer through the night vision scope, to make sure they weren't being followed. Behind them lay death and destruction. Ahead lay life and salvation.

But only if the choppers arrive before dawn. ...

☐ TWO ☐

"We must be patient," said Colonel Qahtan al Bin Shaabi. "The cool air will come soon."

For the past two hours technicians had been working on the air conditioning on the roof of the five story People's Government House in the Madīnat ash-Sha'b section, and the unit still was not fixed. The more General Yuri Kasmanovisky thought about the Yemeni lack of efficiency, the more disgusted he became. But not surprised. Breakdowns of machinery and incompetency were considered normal in Aden, the capital of the People's Democratic Republic of Yemen. Even in at-Tawāhī, the "modern" business section, people took it in stride when power failed or water ceased flowing from a tap. They simply shrugged and said, "It is the will of Allah."

It had not been the will of Allah that had brought General Kasmanovisky and the other GRU[1] officials to the hellhole of South Yemen. It had been the bosses in Moscova, the master strategists in the Kremlin, whose longrange plan included the collapse of Saudi Arabia. Part of the plan involved the invading North Yemen, the Yemen Arab Republic, and attaching it to the People's Democratic Republic of Yemen. Once that had been accom-

1. The *Glavnoye Razvedyvatelnoye Upravleniye*, or Chief Intelligence Directorate, is a division of the Soviet General Staff. The GRU, operated independently of the KGB, engages in the collection of strategic, tactical, and technical military intelligence. It is also heavily involved in industrial espionage and guerrilla warfare.

16

plished, infiltration into Saudi Arabia could be increased a hundredfold. Eventually, this infiltration could lead to a takeover; all under the guise of "civil war."

The wind through the open window was very hot, almost scorching. Feeling the sweat trickle down his back and sides, Kasmanovisky turned, walked slowly back across the room, glanced first at Major Rasseikin and then at Colonel al Bin Shaabi.

"I don't like it," Kasmanovisky said harshly. Wiping the back of his thick neck with a handkerchief, he sat down on a chair with a wicker seat. "It's not like the Saudis to make such daring strikes. They're too busy with their damned oil."

Major Arseni Rasseikin, fanning himself with a folded copy of Pravada, said casually, "I don't think that what happened at Danikil was an intelligence probe that backfired. I'm convinced it was an attempt to assassinate Rabadh Tabriz."

General Kasmanovisky looked thoughtfully at the much younger Rasseikin, whom the Kremlin considered an expert on the Arab mind.

"I have been thinking along the same lines," Kasmanovisky agreed, "and if we're right, we're in for serious trouble, even though the attempt against Tabriz was made over a week ago."

Colonel Qahtan al Bin Shaabi's dark eyes narrowed suspiciously. Clean shaven, a man in his middle forties, he was of medium height, muscular, and with skin the color of honey. His hair was very black and straight; his lips so thin as to be almost invisible.

"Whoever it was, they had the help of the Saudis." Bin Shaabi's voice was as cruel as his eyes. "After killing over a hundred of Tabriz's men, they were lifted out by helicopters that came from the north, from Saudi Arabia." His fist came down heavily on top of the metal desk. "*Haqui!* If only those helicopters had not arrived before daylight. If you gentlemen are correct, then it means that our plans to invade the north are known. Whoever it is will also try to kill me. We know it can't be the Israelis."

General Kasmanovisky said coolly, "The invaders were agents of the Saudi General Security Directorate. They were probably helped by the American CIA and Royalists from the north. We all know that Ibn Zarikid is determined to reunite all of Aden[2] and—" He stared at Colonel Bin Shaabi. "—And execute you for treason, Comrade Colonel Bin Shaabi.

"Abdulla Ibn Zarikid's own blood will flow years before mine does," sneered Bin Shaabi. "I beat him once and I will do it again. This time there will be no compromise. Egypt and the Saudis are too afraid of the Jews to intervene. But we can't move against the north until we have Tabriz and his Dasni firmly with us."

General Kasmanovisky and Major Rasseikin considered Colonel Bin Shaabi a brutal savage, yet they grudgingly respected him for his extreme cunning. Bin Shaabi was a master of the triple cross. At one time, Bin Shaabi and General Ibn Zarikid had led the *National Liberation Front* and had triumphed sensationally in 1968 over both the *shaikhs* and sultans of South Arabia as well as their rivals of the *Front of Liberation of South Yemen*.

Once the *shaikhs* and sultans had been ousted, Colonel Bin Shaabi showed his true colors—red. General Ibn Zarikid had wanted a true republic, a genuine democracy. Colonel Bin Shaabi, a secret communist, was determined to turn Yemen into a Marxist state.

Civil war followed, a bitter royalist-republican war which ebbed and flowed across the northern and eastern parts of the country for the next five years. As a concerted move to destroy Colonel Bin Shaabi and his possible Marxist state, General Ibn Zarikid called on Saudi Arabia and Egypt for help. The Saudis were willing, but not if President Nasser sent Egyptian troops.

Nasser did—much to his regret. The Egyptians, inexperienced both in mountain guerrilla warfare and in dealing with fierce Yemeni tribesmen, suffered heavy losses. At length, as a consequence of the 1967 war with Israel, President Nasser withdrew from the Arabian peninsula.

General Ibn Zarikid, in control of the northern part of Yemen, and Colonel Bin Shaabi, in control of the south, continued to battle each other fiercely. Finally, after Colonel Bin Shaabi won a decisive victory at Sanaa, a

2. Under the rule of Britain, Yemen was known as Aden and in 1937 was made a crown colony. Aden became the capital of South Yemen in 1968.

compromise was reached. Zarikid's forces were exhausted. Colonel Bin Shaabi also had his own problems with his own people, many of whom had Maoist views and were arguing with Nasser-type factions.

North Yemen became the Yemen Arab Republic. South Yemen became South Yemen. The formation of the two nations was followed by an announcement of the kind which is only astonishing to those who are unfamiliar with the Arab mind. Both Zarikid and Bin Shaabi said solemnly that they hoped the two nations could merge.

Arab specialists in the West knew why: General Zarikid and Colonel Bin Shaabi wanted to destroy each other. Colonel Shaabi in particular was determined, since Zarikid had brought former royalist leaders, but no members of the royal family, into the North Yemeni government. Furthermore, North Yemen had a population of almost five million against South Yemen's one and a half million. Eventually, General Zarikid would be able to muster a large army and again attack Colonel Shaabi.

Colonel Bin Shaabi requested aid from the Soviet Union.

For its own protection and security, North Yemen moved increasingly into the orbit of Saudi Arabia, while its relations with the militantly left-wing regime in South Yemen—like those with the rest of the Arab world—continued to deteriorate. The entire Middle East bitterly opposed Colonel Qahtan al Bin Shaabi, knowing him for what he really was—a communist.

Colonel Shaabi quickly consolidated his power, first executing the pro-Chinese Communists in his own PDRY regime. In November of 1971 South Yemen changed its name to the *Popular Democratic Republic of Yemen*. Sweeping nationalization laws took over what private capital remained. However, the PDRY was still not a full-fledged Communist state. The new "Constitution" still referred to Islam as the state religion, and there had been nothing in the way of any antireligious crusade, which would have been counterproductive.

Shaabi and his government then introduced a more radical land reform and encouraged the peasants to stage a series of *intifadhat* or insurrections, in which they seized the lands and houses of landowners, arrested them, and set up popular "Justice Committees" to administer their assets.

19

But the private ownership of land was not entirely abolished. Maximum holdings were further reduced, but the new lands were redistributed to individual families and grouped, as in Egypt, in cooperatives.

The rest of the Arab world screamed "Atheists" at Colonel Bin Shaabi and his government, charging that he had rejected both Arabism and Islam for the godliness of materialism. Colonel Shaabi rejected the charges as the absurd propaganda of "reactionary" or "petit-bourgeois" states to denigrate his government's policies.

Colonel Bin Shaabi, dressed casually in light tan trousers and a white short-sleeved sport shirt, got up, walked around the side of the desk and sat down on the right corner, bracing himself with his sandaled feet flat on the carpeted floor.

"The attack against Tabriz has set us back months," he said in a dissatisfied manner. "My agents at his camp in Danikil sent a radio message yesterday afternoon that he's having second thoughts about committing his Dasni to our cause against the North. I contacted Tabriz and talked to him personally. You can guess what he wanted."

General Kasmanovisky and Major Rasseikin nodded.

"More weapons to use against his traditional enemies, the Zaidi tribesmen in Oman." Kasmanovisky sighed audibly. "Where will it end? We've already given him and his men grenades, three thousand assault rifles and six thousand side arms. What did the old swine demand?"

"No doubt a dozen of our latest fighter planes," Rasseikin said drily.

"He wants another five hundred AKMs and fifty thousand rounds of ammunition," Colonel Bin Shaabi said easily. "I told him I'd have to think it over. Comrades, we will have to give him what he wants. We need Tabriz and his people."

"Five hundred AKMs is out of the question." Kasmanovisky was blunt to the point of rudeness. Leaning back in the chair, he began tapping his fingers together. "He asked for five hundred. He probably expects to get several hundred and twenty thousand rounds."

"We might have to give him two hundred and fifty rifles and thirty thousand rounds." Bin Shaabi's tone was as firm as Kasmanovisky's had been. He surprised the two Soviet intelligence officers by adding, "What's the difference whether we give him two hundred or five hundred? His entire army will have automatic weapons when Tabriz helps us attack General Zarikid; and Tabriz can put almost twenty thousand men into the field."

"But how far can we trust him?" Major Rasseikin remarked. "Why that treacherous old son of a bitch couldn't care less about our cause!"

"He does care about land," Bin Shaabi quickly pointed out. He stood up. "I have already promised him that I will double the size of his lands in return for his help."

"It's giving him the land that I detest," Kasmanovisky said bitterly, then caught himself, realizing that his tone gave the impression that the Soviets already considered South Yemen their own private base on the Arabian peninsula. The GRU expert instantly corrected himself. "It's your land, Comrade Colonel . . . your nation. But why waste valuable land on a crazy cult leader, land that can be given to the peasants?"

Colonel Bin Shaabi, smiling slightly, sat back down on the edge of the desk and, for a brief moment, contemplated General Kasmanovisky, who was on the low side of fifty and had a smooth face now dotted with sweat. Mild-looking, he had blond hair streaked with gray, but his movements were quick and decisive.

Bin Shaabi said slyly, "Should Tabriz die of 'natural causes,' with the help of some poison, the matter would be greatly simplified. We could then satisfy his followers with much less land . . . those who don't die in battle."

"That decision is your choice," General Kasmanovisky intoned suavely. "The sole concern of my government is that your government permits the Soviet Union to use Aden as a warm water naval base."

Colonel Bin Shaabi slowly nodded. "We have already agreed—informally—to that proposal by your government. However, there shall be none of your land forces based in my nation." The timbre of his voice changed, the tone becoming a subtle warning. "Under no conditions could my government permit personnel of your army on the soil of the People's Democratic Republic of Yemen. The PDRY will never become the 'Cuba' of the Arab world."

General Kasmanovisky and Major Rasseikin managed to conceal their astonishment at Shaabi's brusque and undiplomatic manner. At the same time both intelligence officers felt that the Arab leader's imprudence was actually a weakness, yet not a flaw that the GRU could exploit. Regardless of his candidness, Colonel al Bin Shaabi was an extremely crafty individual, a desert-conditioned Machiavelli who went through life playing both ends against the middle while chopping at the center as a reserve, in case the plans at each terminus failed; and he was very conscious of personal security. A realist, he knew that the rest of the Arab world would say a prayer of thanks to Allah at hearing the news of his assassination. The only possible exception was the Baathist (or Socialist) Party in Syria.

Qahtan al Bin Shaabi never appeared in public without a bulletproof vest underneath his uniform. He never rode in an open car, nor reviewed troops without being surrounded by thousands of trusted bodyguards.

Realizing intuitively the extreme value of security, when combined with secrecy, Bin Shaabi had sent fifty of his most trusted officers to East Germany to be schooled in electronic surveillance. Thirteen months later, Government House and Colonel Shaabi's residence in at-Wanani were filled with hidden microphones, electric eyes and other monitoring goodies. He even had a device in his home by which he could send telephone conversations to Abdul Jahiz, the chief of security, in total silence.[3]

Major Arseni Rasseikin frowned, his squeezed-together face (like the face of an old child) turned upward toward Colonel Shaabi. "If our theory is correct," Rasseikin said, "that the small enemy unit was trying to kill Rabadh Tabriz, you, Comrade Colonel, must certainly be on their death list."

"We Arabs have learned to live with the threats of assassination." Shaabi smiled without the least trace of mirth. "It is a way of life with us, especially with Arab leaders. Rest easily, my Russian friends. I am well protected."

"Victory Day celebration is only three days away," General Kasmanovisky observed, "and you must appear in

3. A very common device. One writes the message and it is sent instantly through ordinary telephone lines. Since no one can hear the message, nobody can eavesdrop. CCS Communication Control, Inc. sells the device as the SECUR-A-CALL SL 50.

the parade. Your presence will present a golden opportunity to any would-be assassin, especially in the narrow streets of the old commercial quarter."

"I have already discussed the matter with Major Abdul Jahiz," Shaabi explained. "Just as the fly knows the face of the milk seller, so one cannot trap the fox without exposing the poultry."

"I take that to mean you're going to use yourself as bait!" Major Rasseikin said severely, his thick black eyebrows arching in disapproval. "Comrade Colonel, permit me to say you are being foolhardy."

"All too often the fox kills the chicken," General Kasmanovisky warned the Yemeni strongman. He stood up and pulled his sweat-damp trousers and shorts from the crack between his buttocks. The damned heat was almost intolerable. "I feel you're either underestimating your enemies or overestimating your own security—with all due respect to you and to Major Jahiz." He glanced at Major Rasseikin. "Do you not agree, Comrade Major."

"I do, definitely," Rasseikin quickly replied, making a vague motion with his left hand, all the while looking at Colonel Shaabi. "We are not trading wits with unsophisticated desert tribesmen, Comrade Colonel. We must assume that the Americans are helping the Saudis. In its efforts to spread Capitalism, the American Central Intelligence Agency has some of the best killers in the world in its employ."

"Even as good as the GRU'S or the KGB'S?" A warm, rich amusement touched his eyes and played around the corners of Colonel Shaabi's thin-lipped, wide mouth.

"Every bit as good as the Soviet Union's," replied General Kasmanovisky. Thinking quickly, he had decided that while there was a time to lie, now only the truth could serve the purpose of the Soviet Union. It was better not to take any unnecessary chances with Colonel Bin Shaabi. The Soviet Union had a long way to go with Shaabi. First, the Yemeni ruffian had to conquer North Yemen. Only then, and only after the Soviet naval base had been constructed at the eastern side of Bandar at-Tawāhī—Aden Harbor—Only then could Bin Shaabi be eased from the scene . . . have an "accident" and be replaced by a puppet whose strings could be pulled from Moscova. *Da* . . . a very ticklish situation, one that had to be handled with

23

the utmost caution. The irony of it was that, for the present, Colonel Shaabi had to be kept alive.

Colonel Shaabi was suddenly very serious, his features a mask of cold logic and concentration. "My Soviet friends, you have said it yourselves. We are not fighting stupid desert nomads or fanatics who would gladly give their lives to accomplish their purpose. We are fighting educated, highly intelligent people . . . men, who while willing to take enormous risks, still consider their own lives precious.

Confused, Major Rasseikin exchanged a quick glance with General Kasmanovisky, who also appeared disconcerted.

"Colonel Shaabi, what are you saying?" demanded Kasmanovisky, trying to keep his voice casual. "Please be specific."

Shaabi appeared pleased, almost virtuous. "The American CIA is not composed of fanatics. There will not be any attempt on my life when I appear in the Victory Day parade." He stabbed a long finger at General Kasmanovisky. "Unless you're wrong. Unless it was those damned Royalist rebels from the north. Even they are not crackpots!"

"There are still hundreds of those swine hiding out in the Jabal Mahrat," Rasseikin spoke plaintively. "We've been urging you for months to strike against those traitors. I tell you, Comrade Colonel, those Royalists are a cancer in the pit of your gut, an Achilles heel that makes your government appear inefficient in the eyes of other Arab nations."

"Comrade Rasseikin is right," superimposed Kasmanovisky. "My dear Colonel, why should General Abdulla Ibn Zarikid in North Yemen, or the Saudis, or Sultan bin Said of Oman fear you when you can't even clean dirt from the tents in your own back yard?"

Leaning forward, Colonel Shaabi made a great pretense of candor.

"My own back yard?" he repeated, the quality of his voice almost mocking. "I suggest that the Soviet Union first practice what its advisors are so fond of preaching. The entire Soviet Army can't seem to sweep Afghan dirt from the tents in its own back yard!"

Major Rasseikin reddened slightly. General Kasmanovisky nervously cleared his throat, determined not to show his anger at what he considered to be an insult.

"The Soviet army hadn't won in Afghanistan for the same reason I have not ordered an all-out assault on those damned Royalists holed up in the Jabal Mahrat," continued Shaabi harshly. "The area is entirely too mountainous. The entire range is one natural kasbah[4]. And have you gentlemen forgotten the two assults we already made—at your insistence, by the way? We lost three helicopters and almost three hundred men. We attacked a second time. It was another disaster. The Royalists retreated. We were made to look like fools!"

"Sooner or later you will have to destroy them," insisted Rasseikin, refusing to give ground and intensely irked over Shaabi's vituperative remark over Russian failure in Afghanistan. "Even Rabadh Tabiriz hates and fears the Royalist rebels. Many times they have raided Dasni camps for supplies. To destroy the Royalists would be an accommodation to Tabriz and help to insure his cooperation."

"Enough, Comrade Major," enjoined General Kasmanovisky pleasantly. That was Arseni's trouble. He pushed too hard and at the wrong times. "At the moment, let us concern ourselves with Colonel Shaabi's physical safety."

Kasmanovisky's sky-blue eyes moved to the casehardened face of Colonel Shaabi. "We could be wrong as to who attacked at Danikil. We have no proof it was the Saudis and certainly no evidence that the American CIA was involved."

"The helicopters did head north," Colonel Shaabi commented—as if the matter, in his own mind, was settled.

"Comrade Kasmanovisky is saying that we hope you have taken extraordinary precautions when you appear in the Victory Day parade," Major Rasseikin said slowly, wiping sweat from his upper lip.

"Have you?" General Kasmanovisky asked, peering up at Bin Shaabi.

"I have." Shaabi did not elaborate—a clear indication to the two Russians that the clever Yemani considered his own personal security none of their business.

"Let me add," went on Shaabi, "that I don't think you

4. The word means "fortress" in Arabic; usually refers to a building.

25

are wrong. None the less, I'm convinced that if the Saudis—with the help of the Americans—do make an attempt on my life, such an attempt will not be made during the parade. They are much too clever. They will have deduced that we might expct such an attempt during the parade. Let us not underestimate our enemies."

General Kasmanovisky felt like a man who had just made a beautiful landing at the right airport in the wrong country. That son of a bitch Shaabi was far more intelligent than his psychological profile indicated.

Curiosity prompted Kasmanovisky to ask, "Where then? Where do you think they will try to kill you—if they try?"

Suddenly the three men in the office felt cool air coming toward the floor from the vents in two of the walls.

"As you see, gentlemen, all we needed was patience." Colonel Bin Shaabi walked across the room and closed the east side window. General Leonid Kasmanovisky and Major Rasseikin stared after him, despising the Yemeni "president," who was a virtual dictator, hating him the way they hated all Arabs.

☐ THREE ☐

Fry City! thought the Death Merchant. A few fluffs of clouds in the bright sky, a flaming sun as hot as molten brass, the *Bahr as-Safi*—"sea of pure sand"—and heat. All these elements combined to torture the caravan which, as caravans go, was small—the Death Merchant, eight other men and twenty-nine camels. All the men were Arabs except for Camellion and Marlon Clayton, both of whom were disguised as Bedouins. The Death Merchant had darkened his and Clayton's skin with special greasepaint that would resist sun and washing. Hairpieces of long black hair and flowing black mustaches, plus a few battle scars on the cheeks and dark plastic lens over the eyeballs, completed the disguise.

Camellion and Clayton were dressed for the part, wearing ample, loose clothes—a long white Arab shirt, baggy trousers of blue cotton, held up by a decorated leather drawstring and, on the outside, a long *gandoura,* or robe without a hood. Fifteen-foot long veils were wound around their heads, a part of the black cloth covering the lower part of their faces.

No one should suspect that they were anything but simple merchants, Bedouins who had lost their pastoral lands to ARMACO (Arabian American Oil Company) and had been reduced to making a living selling decorated tobacco pouches, whips, brass and wood items, knife blades, and *narghilas* (or water pipes). Twenty of the camels carried the packs filled with the merchandise.

The Death Merchant, second in line, behind Ahmed Shukairy, a North Yemen Royalist, reflected that it was easier to ride a camel than a horse. Camel saddles have a small seat with a high back and a large pommel in the form of a cross, richly decorated in metal and colored leather. The rider crosses his legs and rests his feet on the camel's back, pushing rhythmically at the speed he wishes the animal to move and guiding the beast by a single rein attached to its nostril.

The Death Merchant's thoughts were as bleak as the desert. *We have been lucky so far, but we haven't accomplished anything. All we have succeeded in doing is to warn Colonel al Bin Shaabi!*

The escape from the vicinity of Danikil had been close, notwithstanding Rabadh Yahya Tabriz's reluctance to come after them in the darkness. Camellion, Muhammad al Auf and Rashid al-Khaima had reached the area where the other members of the tiny force, in position with the Famas rifles and an H&K-13 light machine gun, had been waiting.

For hours the force had waited, keeping a vigil through night vision devices, confident that the Dasni—if they did attack—would be slithering slowly and quietly through the rocks.

There had not been any Dasni. No fool, Tabriz had not been foolish enough to commit his forces to the unknown. Nor would he—until dawn.

The east had been streaked with dawn when Camellion and his tiny group had heard the *thump-thump-thump-*

thump of helicopter blades from the northeast and the stamping of many camel pads on the rocks, combined with the war cries of the Dasni from the south.

The two French Super Frelon choppers had arrived before the Dasni could find and reach the group; one of the egg-beaters keeping the Dasni down by opening fire with a French 20mm M621 heavy machine gun mounted on the port side.

The second helicopter had just started to lift from the sand when the Dasni, their honor at stake, had chosen to charge—another mistake on their part. From within the chopper—at the time the bird had been sixty-three feet in the air—Colonel Bin Maktum had detonated the small F-mines by remote control, the series of explosions butchering fifteen of the Dasni.

The two Super Frelon helicopters shot upward into the sun.

Six hours and twenty-seven minutes later, Camellion and the rest of the force were in Riyadh. The afternoon of that same day, the Death Merchant had conferred with Shaikh Qasin Ibn I'nqudi, the boss of the Saudi General Security Directorate, and Burton Webb, the CIA Chief-of-Station at the United States Embassy in Riyadh.

Two days later a twin-engined Douglas transport plane, clearly marked ARAMCO, had flown "Noah Gardner" and eitht other men to Al-Lu-baylah, a small oasis that, on the edge of the Rub al'Khali, was 274 miles north of the People's Democratic Republic of Yemen.

The "Bedouin merchants" and their caravan had left that night, toward sunset. Once again they would cross the Empty Quarter . . . the Sea of Sand.

The majority of the men considered the mission impossible, a probe akin to divine madness; yet not even the cynical Colonel Bin Maktum could argue with the validity of Camellion's logic: Should Colonel al Bin Shaabi and Major Abdul Jahiz, his chief of intelligence, have deduced that the fracus at Danikil had been a botched-up attempt to assassinate Rabadh Yahya Tabriz and that an attempt would also be made to terminate Colonel al Bin Shaabi, neither would assume that such an attempt would be made so soon.

"Even if they do," the Death Merchant had said,

"they'll expect the hit to be made against Shaabi during the Victory Day parade. We'll have to strike from another direction."

As the time, Shaikh Qasin Ibn I'nqudi (who looked and sounded more British than Saudi Arabian) had been very skeptical about the Death Merchant's plan. Burton Webb had called Camellion's plan "A way of committing suicide the hard way. . . ."

Camellion's reply had been simple and logical. "You want Shaabi dead, don't you?"

Ibn I'nqudi and Webb nodded, both looking at Camellion in a strange way.

Webb, who resembled a banker who loved to eat, had stated in a practical manner, "Gardner, I think that you and the man that go with you are going to their deaths. Call it off. We don't expect a suicide mission."

To the surprise of Ibn I'nqudi and Webb, the Death Merchant gave a light, pleasant laugh, then said, "I have things to do in another part of the world. I can't afford to hang around Arabia for months."

"Mr. Gardner, there is something about my nation that you don't like?" Shaikh Qasin Ibn I'nqudi had asked in a soft tone.

I was here a thousand years before your grandparents were born!

"It isn't the country, Shaikh Ibn I'nqudi. It's my own schedule. I have many important things to do, very important to me."

"I agree with Mr. Webb," Ibn I'nqudi said positively. "I can't ask any of my people to go with you. I feel I would be murdering them."

"Suppose I ask for volunteers?"

The Saudi intelligence chief smiled slightly. "Mr. Gardner, you remind me of a man who insists on speaking Arabic in the house of a Moor!"

"And the camel that travels to Mecca will return lame at last," retorted the Death Merchant. He grinned broadly at the sight of Burton Webb's mournful face. "Have faith, Webb. Colonel Shaabi will be in 'hell' before Ramadhan[1]. Even if we should all die in the attempt, it would

1. The Islamic month of fasting.

29

not be any real loss. After all, only lives end. Life goes on. There is only a change from one energy field to another."

Camellion looked straight into the eyes of Shaikh Ibn I'nqudi.

"Do I have permission to ask for volunteers?"

"If they elect to go with you, I shall not stop them," Ibn I'nqudi replied solemnly. "May Allah be with you. . . ."

Thus far, "Allah" has been! Camellion, his lower face veiled, stared out over the sands, his body moving up and down in motion with the camel's. *The real fun won't start until we reach Aden. . . . Damn this desert. . . .*

Except to desert born and bred Bedouins, traveling on the Sea of Sand (larger than the State of Texas) is never a pleasurable experience. In the dazzling glare of the sun, the sands are always whitish, although the colors do vary. One soon discovers that each dune has its own peculiar shape. Sometimes the dunes run together so that one has the impression that he is on another planet. At other times, one comes to individual dunes, some 200 and 300 feet high, each rising in apparent confusion from the desert floor. Nevertheless, all the dunes have one thing in common: On the north side of each dune the sand will fall away from beneath the summit of an unbroken wall at a very steep angle as the grains of sand will lie. On each side of this face, sharp-crested ridges will sweep down in long, undulating curves. Behind there will be alternating ridges and troughs, smaller and more involved as they reach farther down the main face. The surface will be marked with diminutive ripples, of which the ridges will be built from heavier and darker sand, while the hollows will be of smaller, paler-colored grains. It is the blending of these colors that give such depth and richness to the sand: gold with streaks of silver, orange with cream and brick-red, yellows and grays, burnt-browns mingled with various shades of pink.

The desert is never monotonous, changing subtly from mile to mile and with the time of day. At times it will look like ocean waves as seen from a jet airliner—an "ocean" that is strangely pink. At other times the "waves" will become larger, changing into giant dunes, mountains of sands separated by broad white plains.

Now on this fifth day from Al-Lubaylah, the caravan found itself on a flat stretch of sand as the sun began to drop in the west. The caravan was on a *sabkha,* as dry and as flat as a lake bed and perfect for landing a plane. But a wet *sabkha,* those near low coastal areas at certain seasons, could be dangerous if a plane attempting to land should nose over and crash.

The caravan was well into the *sabkha* when it stopped for the night. Saddles and packs were taken from the camels, and the animals tethered. Tents made of goat skins were set up, and Sa'id Al'amman, one of the North Yemen Royalists and a member of the Sons of the Falcon, prepared supper over a charcoal fire.

Over a meal of unleavened bread, white cheese, and the indispensable bitter coffee sweetened with brown sugar, Camellion and the others discussed plans.

Colonel Bin Maktum gave an opinion. "We shouldn't have any trouble when we cross into South Yemen. No one is actually sure where the border is and the *Shurtat al-Badiya* is very inefficient. Besides, since we are Arabs and of the faith, the law of *Sharis,* of hospitality, must be applied. The desert police will have to let us enter. Not even al Bin Shaabi dares to interfere with *Sharis,* though he'd like to."

"He would be a fool if he even tried," Khumayyis ibn Rimthan growled. "Not only would his people not stand for it and consider him a heretic, but his economy would suffer. Within the last few years, he's let the coffee crop deteriorate. In many areas coffee has been replaced by *qat.*"

"The reason on Shaabi's part is realistic," Muhammad al-Auf commented. "Most of the coffee crop was exported. *Qat,* being a narcotic, can be sold close to home, almost anywhere in the Arab world.

"I see no reason to be concerned about a search," offered Ali Haddi, who was another Royalist, but not a member of the Sons of the Falcon. "The merchandise will prove that we are only simple merchants."

Thin- and small-faced, Haddi looked around for someone to reinforce his opinion. He got just the opposite from Marlon Clayton, who sat cross-legged like the other men. Of medium height and build, Clayton was thirty-six years old and had a fine face molded over strong bone, eyes set

31

wide apart, a firm, strong nose, and a generous mouth. Educated at Yale, he was also an expert with firearms, knives, explosives, and in the art of the deal-out-death-with-bare-hands—*And he loves the darkness. That alone makes me give him an A-1 score!*

The Death Merchant broke a piece of bread in half and was about to speak when Clayton said, "What bothers me is that we're carrying only British Lee Enfields and small arms under our robes. If we get trapped . . . we might as well be naked."

"You know why we must carry only old rifles," Camellion reminded Clayton. "Because that's all desert Arabs have. There's no place where we could hide even SMGS as small as an Ingram. The best we can do is Berettas and Brownings strapped to our thighs, under our robes." He glanced at Ahmed Shukairy and Rashid al-Khaima, both men sitting across from him in the circle. "Let's hope to Allah that the Sons of the Falcon unit in Aden can give us all the help we need."

"This is one fine time to hope!" Clayton said with pseudo-derision. "We're on our way and will be in Aden in several days. The time to have 'hoped' was back in Riyadh." Drinking coffee and eating dates, the CIA man winked at Camellion.

"The radio signal was sent to Nuri Boustani," said Ahmed Shukairy. Only twenty-four years old, he was dark and slim, as befits all desert people. He showed dirty teeth in a grin of reassurance. "He returned the signal, indicating that he is expecting us. We cannot know more until we make contact with him in Aden."

"If only we could have used frequency hopping," commented Clayton.

In the dim, flickering light cast by the fire in the center of the circle, the Death Merchant could see shadows drifting across Clayton's face. He could see also the expression in the Company man's eyes.

Clayton considers these camel riders a bunch of ill-trained, ill-equipped goons. Lacking equipment—yes. Barbarians, no. It is only that their culture and mores are different from ours in the West—and how can he expect Yemeni rebels to have sophisticated radio equipment?

In spite of his pragmatism about all cultures, Camellion was forced to admit that he felt vaguely uncomfortable.

Except for himself and Clayton, all the men were Arabs. *No! Seven are Semites! Only six are Arabs. The seventh is an Israeli!*

Rashid al-Khaima spoke while he loudly chewed white cheese. "When the crow is your guide, he can lead you only to a corpse." Seeing the Death Merchant's sharp stare stab at him, al-Khaima tacked on an explanation of what could have been an insult. "By that I mean, *Sahib* Gardner, we are on a mission that can lead only to death, perhaps our own deaths. Surely, we are as sick in the mind as you are. Why else would we be here on our way to Aden?"

"Very true," mused Camellion. "It is also the truth that our eyes are of little use when the mind is blind. We knew what our chances were before we came, knew that we might not even get the opportunity to kill Colonel Shaabi once we're in Aden. The idea is to try. If we can't kill Shaabi we get out and link up with the *Ibn'u Alib Saqr* in the Jabal Mahrat."

Shadows danced in silence across the face of Sa'id Al'amman as his ebony eyes bored into Camellion.

"Into the Jabal Mahrat! To do what?" he demanded roughly. "To sit there in misery with our brothers who are short of food, who have no heavy weapons, and who never knew when Colonel al Bin Shaabi might make another strike against them?"

"I am told that more supplies will be dropped shortly into the Jabal Mahrat," declared Camellion. "The drops will involve part of Plan-B. We shall discuss Plan-B. once we reach the Jabal Mahrat. Even should we succeed in terminating Colonel al Bin Shaabi, we may still have to head for the Jabal. Major Jahiz might close the border.

Sa'id Al'amman, as well as Ali Haddi and Khumayyle ibn Rimthan, gave Camellion a searching scrutiny.

"An airdrop!" scoffed Sa'id Al'amman. He reached for his water pipe. "From the Saudis? How can you believe their promises? It is because the Saudis have not kept their word that our brothers in the Jabal Mahrat are in such dire need. They feel that even Allah has deserted them."

"Al-dunyah bug'ah,"[2] Khumayyis ibn Rimthan commented sadly in Arabic.

2. "The world is spotted," meaning it is filled with good and bad, with success and failure.

Muhammad al Auf turned to Colonel Bin Maktum whose face was twisting in anger. Al Auf said accusingly, "Is Sa'id not speaking the truth, Sahib Bin Maktum? As a member of the General Security Directorate of *al-Mamlaka al'Arabiya as-Sa'udiya*,[3] you should have some knowledge why your government is no longer supplying the Sons of the Falcon in the Jabal with food, weapons and other essentials?"

Ahmed Shukairy sneered. "I still find it an extraordinary blessing of the Prophet that the Saudis even sent the helicopters for us."

"I am only a member of my government's security service," Bin Maktum said stiffly in defense. "I do not sit in on the meetings of the higher councils. I do know that my nation cannot risk a war with South Yemen at this particular time, not when we don't know what those damned Israelis might do. As Arabs, you know as well as I that the expansionistic policy of the Jews is a threat to the whole world. They proved their Hitler mentality to all of humanity by their sneak attack on *al Jumhouriya al 'Iraqia*."[4]

"Yes, there is truth in your words," agreed Sa'id Al'amman, exhaling smoke drawn in through the water pipe. He looked knowingly at Colonel Maktum. "It is understandable why your government does not want an open conflict with the Marxists in South Yemen. A two-front war would wreck your country."

"A war on two fronts?" Khumayyis ibn Rimthan blinked in confusion.

"The Jews could attack through the Sinai," explained Sa'id Al'amman. "The facts are clear. The Saudis could not even prevent Israeli war planes from flying over the Nafud,[5] even with all the technology the Americans have given you."

Colonel Maktum responded instantly. "The Israelis flew so low over the Nafud we couldn't detect them by radar," he said truculently. "That could happen in any sparsely populated nation."

3. The Arabic name of Saudi Arabia.
4. Iraq.
5. Technically, the An-Nafūd, the second largest body of sand in Arabia. In the southeast part of the peninsula, the An-Nafud has an area of 26,000 square miles.

"We can also thank the Americans for the plight of our brothers in the Jabal Mahrat," offered Ahmed Shukairy. "If the Americans call thee reaper, one would do well to whet his scythe." As Shukairy spoke, he looked at Marlon Clayton, as if expecting a reply from the Company man.

The Death Merchant, wise in the turns and twists of the Arab mind, knew that the cruel-eyed Shukairy was baiting Clayton—*I hope Clayton doesn't walk into the trap. Damn him, he had better not!*

Clayton didn't. "When the lion withdraws, the hyenas will play—so said the Prophet Muhammad." Clayton spoke in English for the benefit of the Death Merchant. "Should the United States withdraw its support of Israel, the Soviet hyenas would eventually feast on the fat of the entire Middle East. Is that what you would have, *Sahib* Shukairy? Would you have the philosophy of ungodliness, of Shaitan, try to replace the Koran?"

"Of course not!" was all a frustrated Ahmed Shukairy could say. He then countered with, "But who is to say that the Americans did not assist the Israelis in building nuclear weapons—and you cannot deny that those filthy Jews have nuclear weapons, weapons of hell. They pound their war drums day and night and pray to their Hebrew god to help them in their desires. Those Jews have sick minds and are throwing stones into the wells from which they drink."

Ali Haddi, getting to his feet, nodded gravely. "The Americans—clever they are. They have the Saudis tied to them with the strongest chain of all—Saudi investments in their nation."

"I haven't any knowledge of Israeli nuclear weapons nor of Saudi investments in the U.S.," Marlon Clayton said levelly. He, too, got to his feet, commenting, "It's getting chilly. I'm going to get a *kasha-bir*." Turning, he headed toward one of the low tents for the woolen garment.

Ahmed Shukairy glanced anxiously at the Death Merchant. "Surely, *Sahib* Gardner, as an American you must have an opinion?"

Hunched down, staring at the embers of the dying fire, Camellion did not turn his head—*I have lots of opinions, but you don't want to hear them, stupid!*

"The Prophet Muhammad also said that the tongue of

the wise is in the heart," he growled, "while the heart of the fool is in his mouth. I believe the Prophet was a wise man. I keep my opinions to myself, Sahib Shukairy."

Bin Maktum's voice was smooth, "Sahib Shukairy, one cannot argue with the wisdom of the Prophet."

Shukairy, knowing he had been defeated, wisely retreated into a fortress of silence.

Camellion continued to stare at the glowing charcoal, convinced that there could never be peace between the Israelis and the Arabs. Of course the Israelis had bombed Iraq's nuclear reactor. The strike had only been self-defense in advance. *Iraq won't even acknowledge the existence of Israel and is determined to wipe every Israeli from the face of the earth! Yet we're supposed to believe that the Iraqis were not going to build an A-bomb to use against Israel! Camel crap!*

Another certainty was that the desert Arab had not changed in nature over the slow flow of the centuries. There were still rapacious, predatory and avaricious, born freebooters, contemptuous of all outsiders and intolerant of restraint.

Ironic! Arabic, which had evolved as a dialect of nomad herdsmen in the desert, had been flexible enough to translate every subtle shade of Greek philosophy and art and pass it back to the West. At the height of its glory the Muslim civilization had been profoundly influenced by Greek thought: yet the Arabs had not been merely imitative, but had made their own great contribution to the world in history, physics, mathematics, philosophy, astronomy, chemistry, and medicine. Today 130,000,000 people spoke Arabic. A seventh part of the human race were Muslims.

Decay had set in. The Arab civilization had fallen apart. Even with the new riches in oil, many of the Arabs were trapped between the old and the new. The United Arab Emirates (on the eastern side of the Arabian peninsula, on the Persian Gulf and on the Gulf of Oman) is a good example.

In Dubai, one of the larger towns, the *shaikhs* at one time had had a contest to see who could own the tallest building in town. The last that Camellion had heard, the winner was the *shaikh* holding the mortgage on the thirty-nine-story Hilton Hotel sitting on the edge of town.

The Death Merchant smiled when he thought of *Shaikh* Mana bin Khalifa al-Maktoum, who was building a 70 million dollar sports complex, one that would include a fifteen thousand seat soccer stadium with artificial turf, a private clubhouse, a sports-medicine center, a pool and tennis and squash courts.

Poor old *Shaikh* al-Maktoum had never stopped to think who would use the vast sports complex!

Poor? All the *shaikhs* had money to burn. Literally, if they wanted to do so. It's estimated that the *shaikhs* and/or the Saudis are making money at the rate of almost $300.00 per minute—all from oil. *The paradox is that their people don't have the background—cultural or educational—to make use of the money. They can't run banks, airports, desalination plants or anything else that is modern.*

Everything was brand new in the United Arab Emirates, a loose federation of seven shaikhdoms that had not even existed until 1971. Now the federation was racing into the twenty-first century by attempting to skip the last two.

It was difficult to believe that only twenty years ago Dubai had no paved roads and no electricity, that water was sold from tin cans carried by donkeys, and that there wasn't a building more than two stories high!

Frightening! Even hideous! The Death Merchant knew that change would come, a very sudden, unexpected change that would plunge not only the Arab culture but the entire world back into the Dark Ages. Educated Arabs already sensed the slight breeze, an ominous soft-blowing wind that, before the end of the century, would change into a hurricane of destruction. Camellion then recalled a remark that Shaikh Qasin Ibn I'nqudi had made: *"My father rode a camel. When I was a boy, I rode around in a motor car. My son has three airplanes. I fear that my grandson will have to go back to a camel. . . ."*

Watching the glowing charcoal was relaxing. It was the NOW that mattered, the completion of the operation that, as yet, had not really begun. Electricity flowed through the neurons and dendrites and axons of Camellion's cerebral cortex. He was positive, absolutely certain: Of all the hidden perils, the Israeli agent was the most dangerous.

Webb swears there isn't any room for doubt. He's posi-

tive that one of the seven is an Israeli and a member of Mossad!

Camellion didn't like mysteries. *But I've got one!*

Not even Colonel Bin Maktum, as a member of Saudi intelligence, and Marlon Clayton, the CIA man, knew about the Mossad agent.

Certainly not Maktum. He's one of the suspects.

It was because of the deadly Mossad agent that the Saudis had suddenly changed their previous very cautious position in dealing with South Yemen and were doing all they could to help topple Colonel Qahtan al Bin Shaabi. Neither the CIA nor Saudi intelligence had planned it that way. A chain of circumstances had evolved that now made it possible for the Saudis and the Company to trap the Mossad agent.

Webb had told the Death Merchant: "We know he's one of the seven who will be going with you and Clayton. "It's up to you and we don't care how you do it. Find out who he is and . . . kill him."

Why? Camellion had wanted to know.

"For now, it's better that you don't know," Webb had said. "Once the job is done and you get back to Riyadh— if you do succeed and do return!—then you'll be told."

Another thought. *What evil lurks in the hearts of men? Only the Shadow knows. . . . And I don't expect to see him running around on this desert. Damn! What an unholy mess!*

The Death Merchant couldn't help himself. He suddenly laughed aloud, deep laughter that caused the other men, including Marlon Clayton, returning from the tent with a kashbir, to regard him with some slight alarm.

"*Sahib* Gardner, you were thinking of something amusing?" asked Sa'id Al'amman in a curious voice.

The Death Merchant turned and smiled at Al'amman.

"Yes—'The Shadow'!"

☐ FOUR ☐

Doubt and dread went along with the small caravan, increasing steadily. Countering these negative aspects was the desire to reach Aden, to make contact with Nuri Boustani and his small group of *Ibn'u Alib Saqr,* and to make final plans that would be half completed upon the death of Colonel al Bin Shaabi. The second part of the operation would be successful only after they had escaped from Aden and were either in the Jabal Mahrat or had returned to Saudi Arabia.

There was the constant monotony, broken only when one slept, a tedious sameness that, according to Marlon Clayton, ". . . is like going across the United States on a slow-moving freight train—riding inside a boxcar!"

A day, a night, and another half-day from the border of South Yemen, the caravan left the Empty Quarter and entered the lower highlands of the Jabal al Khdar. The sands became more rocky and there was vegetation of sorts, along with yellow-flowering tribulus, heliotrope, and a species of sedge.

Rashid al-Khaima warned: "We should meet the *Shurtat al-Badiya* by tomorrow, perhaps sooner if Colonel al Bin Shaabi has increased security."

The nine men and their two strings of camels traveled across the windswept uplands, over passes, through small but narrow gorges, under precipices and past massive escarpments. In the late afternoon they reached the Tuwaiq in'Atarit, a well that some of the ancients had named after one of the mountain peaks to the West.

Another caravan was already at the well, one made up of at least a hundred camels and forty men of the BeniBu Hassan, a well-to-do but warlike tribe that lived around Jaalan, in Oman, and followed the Ibadi sect of Islam. The BeniBu Hassan had the reputation of honoring their word and of being utterly merciless toward their enemies, the Awazim, who lived in eastern Saudi Arabia, and the Wa'Riin of the United Arab Emirates.

The BeniBu Hassan were no more than a mile away and had already seen Camellion and his group. All the Death Merchant and his men could do was advance. To remain stationary or to go in another direction would be to show fear.

"The BeniBu Hassan despise cowards," Marlon Clayton explained. "All we can do is ride right up to the well and pretend we don't give a damn."

"Their rifles don't appear to be any more modern than ours," observed Camellion, his eyes on the men of the Hassan, who were dressed in black striped *gallabiyas* and headwear of black checked *kaffiyehs* bound with bands of black knotted ropes.

Ahmed Shukairy said in a relaxed voice, "We don't have to worry about them. The BeniBu Hassan are a proud people. They consider themselves far superior to us 'lowly Bedu.' They only take booty in war. To harm us, to rob us, would be to dishonor themselves. All they can do is conform to the law of *Sharis*, welcome us to the well and ask us to pitch camp next to theirs."

"Just the same, we'll keep our pistols ready and post two men on guard when we retire," Camellion said firmly.

"Yes, guards we must have during sleeping," Shukairy replied. "While the BeniBu Hassan will respect us for our bravery, they would lose all respect and think we were fools if we did not post guards." Shukairy, who was posing as the head of the caravan, added very quickly, "do not forget, *Sahib* Gardner. Allah has cursed you. He has taken your speech and placed devils in your mind."

"Don't concern yourself, my Arab friend. I'll be the perfect dummy," an amused Death Merchant said, tucking a 9mm Hi-Power Browning auto-pistol into a pouch fastened to the decorated leather drawstring holding up his baggy trousers.

"You had better be," Shukairy warned. "Your life depends on it. One mistake and all of us will die. The BeniBu Hassan hate liars worse than they do cowards."

As though they owned the entire Arabian peninsula, the Death Merchant and his men rode up to the large group of BeniBu Hassan, who watched them steadily and impassively. They were tall men, their features broad but finely shaped; all were clean-shaven.

It was not difficult to spot their leader. His *gallabiya* was of better cut, his very large silver dagger, in its broad, curved scabbard, richly decorated with gold inlay.

Shukairy raised his right hand and looked down at the man, saying, *"Salaam alaikum"*—"Peace be on you."

"Alaikum as salaam," the leader replied in a firm, rather cold voice. He introduced himslf as Falih ibn Majudid, the eldest son of *Shaikh* Al bu Majudid, and—just as Shukairy had predicted—invited them to dismount, saying, "You are welcome. Allah has been good to us this day. He has brought us guests for the meal of the evening. Spread your tents next to ours and break bread with us."

Shukairy and the others dismounted, and Shukairy introduced the men, each of whom responded with a bow and *"Salaam alikum."* All except the Death Merchant who just stood there, his mouth slack, his head hanging to the left.

Shukairy waved a hand toward Camellion. "As you can see, my poor brother Yeho has been cursed by Allah for the sins of our father's father. "He is my curse and my shame."

"Al hamd u lillah" ("Praise be to Allah"), Falih ibn Majudid said solemnly. "Wise men do not try to understand his justice or his mercy."

The packs were removed from the camels. The animals were given water, fed, and tethered for the night. Three Nubian servants of the BeniBu Hassan laid out circular mats of rushes, and when the meal was ready to be served, Falih ibn Majudid invited Shukairy and the other eight to sit within his circle and to partake of the trays heaped with rice, dishes of vegetable stew, five roast chickens, dates, bowls of buttermilk, and jugs of sherbet.

As they ate, Falih ibn Majudid explained that he and his men were returning from Aden, where they had exchanged pearls from the Gulf of Oman for *qat* and bolts of cloth. His tone of voice was also a question, a hint that he was inquiring about their own business.

"We poor Bedu are also going to Aden," Ahmed

41

Shukairy said. "Nothing of value do we have, nothing except *narghilas* and knife blades, brass boxes and other inexpensive items. Cursed by those infidels from across the great sea. They take our grazing land in their greed for the black oil, and we grow poorer and poorer. . . ."

Muhammad al Auf asked in a soft voice, "Tell me, *Sahib* Falih ibn Majudid, has Allah blessed the Yemeni with a government more responsive to his divine will?"

"One lie in the Sultan's head will keep out fifty truths," Falih ibn Majudid said. "There are only lies in the head of Colonel Qahtan al Bin Shaabi, and Allah shall surely turn his face from him and the evil men who surround him."

As Falih ibn Majudid spoke, Camellion (who found it difficult to eat while pretending to be a near-idiot) saw that the son of *Shaikh* Al bu Majudid had a powerful virile face, clean-shaven except for a close-clipped mustache. He had dark bushy eyebrows that nearly met over a prominent fleshy nose.

The BeniBu Hassan chieftain warned the small group to be careful in Aden, that it was rumored that government spies were even in the various *suqs*, or markets. "It is said that some of them pose as beggars, others as sellers of produce."

Falih ibn Majudid then went on to say that he doubted if he would ever make another journey to South Yemen. "The Yemeni talk of war, and there is the stench of death in the air."

The Death Merchant and his group prepared to leave the next morning after sunrise, after a breakfast of buttermilk and sticky dates.

They packed the camels and gave them a drink. Several refused to touch the bitter-tasting water, so the men held their heads and poured it down their throats. They filled the waterskins and plugged the tiny dribbling holes. At length, they mounted the camels and started on the next leg of their journey. By midmorning they found a little parched herbage on the flank of a small clearing and let the camels graze for an hour. All around were whale-backed massifs rising above plains of white powdery gypsum. The area was bleak and cheerless, but by the middle of the afternoon they had left the uplands and, with vegetation all around them, could see fields of wheat and barley in the distance. A profusion of flowers: red and white anemones on the lower slopes, covering whole hillsides with carpets of color; and among them red ranunculus like poppies, yellow marigolds, gladioli, dark blue squills, and irises.

After being in the Empty Quarter and the highlands of the Jabal al Khdar, the outskirts of South Yemen looked like a paradise—green, peopled, prosperous.

By late afternoon, they had passed some unveiled women leading donkeys and square watch towers with whitewashed tops—a foretaste of Yemeni architecture.

They stopped to rest on a plain carpeted with thin grass and rocks. Camellion and four of the men consulted the map while the rest of the men kept a close watch on their surroundings.

Colonel Bin Maktum tapped an "X" on the map, which was marked in Arabic, then pointed to a mountain in the distance. "That's it, the Jabal as-Sudah, the Black Mountain. Even if it is bluish-gray!"

The Death Merchant got to his feet and straightened his *gandoura*. "We're right on course. In another four days we should be in Aden. We'll be one day late, but still on schedule."

"A day late?" Rashid al-Khaima's cruel eyes turned in alarm to the Death Merchant. "We will meet Nuri Boustanti on the afternoon of the fourth day. How can we keep the schedule we planned then?"

"It is a bit confusing, Gardner," intoned Clayton, picking at the right corner of his mouth with the tip of a little finger.

Camellion clarified his previous statement. "A day late as far as al Bin Shaabi and Major Jahiz are concerned. I'm basing that on the assumption that Shaabi and Jahiz expect an assassination attempt on the Victory Day parade. We won't be in Aden until the day after the celebration."

"Don't count on it," Clayton advised. "Shaabi and Jahiz are a couple of sick cookies."

Ahmed Shukairy, continuing to sit on his heels and toy with his *su'kok*, the short stick used to prod a camel, looked up disagreeably at the Death Merchant. "I am thinking of Sahib ibn Majudid's warning about government spies. We will have to be on guard every moment. How are we to know that Colonel al Bin Shaabi and Major Jahiz haven't somehow managed to place spies within Nuri Boustani's group."

"There's no way we can know," Rashid al-Khaima said crossly. "We are in the hands of Allah."

"That's all-or-nothing thinking, Ahmed," Marlon Clayton said with sarcasm. "And it goes for you, too, Rashid. Allah wills that we help ourselves."

"One cannot ignore one's feelings," shrugged Shukairy.

"Feelings aren't facts," Camellion said. "Nothing we feel counts, except to mirror our thinking. Our moods and feelings don't govern our thoughts. It's what we think and how we think that generates our moods."

Colonel Bin Maktum smiled slightly. "Like you Americans say—'Think positive.'"

At that moment, Ali Haddi, thirty feet away, yelled, "Look! Coming down the road!"

Camellion and the other men turned and saw four jeeps filled with *Shurtat al-Badiya* coming down the road.

"Our troubles begin. Our day will end in sorrow," Ahmed Shukairy said guardedly.

Camellion glanced at the North Yemeni Royalist. Every line of Shukairy's dark face showed fear of the unknown.

"Now would seem to be the time," Camellion said, his voice now softer.

Marlon Clayton blinked rapidly. "To do what?"

"Think positively."

There were sixteen of the *Shurtat al-Badiya*. They parked the jeeps by the side of the road, jumped out and came toward the small group, four of the brown-clad desert police remaining by the side of the jeeps, Soviet PPS submachine guns in their hands.

The lead cop, a short, chunky man with an enormous black mustache, shouted, "Round up your camels. We must search the packs. Who is the leader here?"

Helpless under the muzzles of the machine guns, Camellion and his people watched as the desert police carefully searched each pack, first placing each skin-pack on the ground, then removing its contents. The police then examined their old Enfield rifles, Captain Salah DaMuq grinning at the ancient long guns.

DaMuq looked at Ahmed Shukairy, who had identified himself as the leader of the caravan. "Tell me," demanded Captain DaMuq, "are you and the rest of this desert scum

44

going to try to reach Aden in time for our Victory Day celebration?"

Feigning ignorance, Ahmed Shukairy gave DaMuq an idiotic look.

"What is this 'Victory Day'? I do not understand such things."

The Death Merchant, playing his demented role to perfection, giggled loudly.

Captain DaMuq guffawed, nudged one of the policemen next to him and looked again at Shukairy. "He is as stupid as his brother. These Bedu—all stupid trash."

"That is true," the other desert cop answered laconically. "Allah made the Bedu from sands that were filthy. These fools are harmless."

Captain DaMuq glared ferociously at Shukairy. "Proceed but be very careful and don't break any of our laws," he said. His voice rang with authority. "Our nation is neat and orderly and we will not tolerate lawbreakers. Understand you stupid Bedu?"

Giving DaMuq a fearful look, Shukairy nodded his head so hard and rapidly that Camellion marveled that his head didn't snap off his neck and fall to the ground. Camellion couldn't understand a word of what the police and Shukairy were saying, but he knew from the intonations and expressions that he and his group were not in any immediate danger. From the laughter, he guessed that DaMuq had openly insulted them—*Wouldn't it be the joke of the month if Shukairy turned out to be the Mossad agent? It's possible. Any good agent of any intelligence service is a master actor.*

"Oh yes . . . yes, yes, Sahib, I understand," Shukairy said quickly to Captain DaMuq. "We all understand."

"I am not your friend, you stupid man," Captain DaMuq said drily and handed Shukairy a blue slip of paper. He gave Shukairy and the rest of the group a final visual inspection, then he and the other police turned, hurried back to the jeeps and drove off.

Clayton, watching the jeeps departing down the road, growled, "I'd like to get that son of a bitch in any dark alley on any night."

Ahmed Shukairy waved the blue entry pass in front of Camellion and grinned. "No more problems with the police—not with this."

45

"What kind of name did he call us?" Camellion asked Clayton.

Colonel Bin Maktum answered. "He said we were Bedu trash. His name was Salah DaMuq. He was a captain. He considers us harmless Bedouins, capable of only petty thievery."

"We can't get too fouled up," Camellion said with a tiny laugh. "We don't have a computer."

"Those low sons of Satan!" Rashid al-Khaima, his hands on his hips, stared at the open skin packs on the ground. "It will take several hours to repack and strap the packs on the camels. And it's too-late in the day to start." He looked from Camellion and Clayton to Bin Maktum. "We can spend the night on this spot."

The Death Merchant nodded. "Yes, you're right. "We'll repack but not put the packs on the beasts. The poor animals can use the extra rest." He started toward the opened packs on the ground, saying to Colonel Bin Maktum, "If we could only read the future for the next ten days or so, I'd feel a lot better."

"Dream on, my American friend." There was amusement in Bin Maktum's deep voice. "We knew our chances for success were less than slim before we even started for the Empty Quarter. The truth is that we are going to have to work on a whole series of assumptions, worthy of a theologian, to even get within shooting distance of Colonel Bin Shaabi."

"First we get to Aden and make contact," Camellion said. "I only hope we don't end up buried in that stinking city. . . ."

Four days passed. The caravan was on schedule. They knew they were only four miles from Aden when they saw the twin watchtowers, a hundred feet tall, built of clay and with projecting rings of slate—from top to bottom—to protect the walls against erosion by rain. The two towers had not been used in forty years.

The Death Merchant and his small band, now mingling with a stream of traffic pouring into the city—people of the various Arab tribes riding camels, horses, donkeys; or leading packed camels, horses, or donkeys—saw their first Yemeni houses on the northeast side of the city, fortresslike houses built of multicolored stone or brightly painted adobe mud brick, some three stories high. Some houses had tiny windows and crenelated roofs, others layered rows of stone slate jutting out to protect the walls against the seasonal rains.

This was the old spice route and this river of traffic would enter the Crater, the old commercial quarter of Aden. There were three other quarters—at-Tawāhī, the business section, Ma'alah, the native harbor area, and at-Wanani, a small residential section for the wealthy and the influential. There was an oddity about Aden. Although Aden was almost 3,000 years old, unlike other Arab Muslim towns (or medinas) it had never been walled.

Camellion and his group were quick to notice that, once they had entered the Crater, the brown-uniformed *al-Yemen i'Qrali,* the militia that acted as the city's police, was much in evidence. The *i'Qrali* was a branch of the *al-Yemen Bayyi'l'ali,* the South Yemeni Bureau of Internal Security. The desert police were also attached to the Bayyi'l'ali which was patterned after the Soviet Union's KGB and was bossed by Major Abdul Jahiz, Colonel al-Bin Shaabi's brother-in-law.

Three of the militiamen were directing traffic, an unnecessary job since the people with animals knew the way to the Crater's camp area, especially Muhammad al-Auf and Sa'id al'amman. Both Royalists had lived for years in Yemen and knew the city the way Camellion knew the Big Thicket of Texas, USA.

There were hundreds of travelers spread out along the stone-paved route, men and women from the various Middle East and African tribes—not all of them Semites as were the Arabs. There were the Hamitic Beja from the northern Sudan, with their copper-red to deep-brown skin; the tall Beraber with their colorful clothes and pretty unveiled women, the arms of the females loaded down with copper and brass bracelets; people of the Zeer, Yafelman, Zemmun, and other tribes who spoke the Berber language. And many, many Arabs; the Djerba, the Filala, the Kabyle, the Shammar, etc.

There were even a large group of the mysterious Tuareg, the "Men of the Blue Veil," whom the Arabs regarded with a mingling of fear, hatred, and respect. The Tuareg, or *Tawarek* ("God Forsaken") as the Arabs called them,

47

were an enigma in more ways than one. Very tall—some of the men were almost seven feet—the Tuareg did not have any clear origin. One theory had it that they resulted from the mating of Crusaders from Europe and Arab women—as good a theory as any. Another oddity is that while the Tuareg women never veiled themselves, the Tuareg men swathed their heads and faces and necks in a fifteen-foot veil as protection against the sun, sand, and wind. Furthermore, complex rules governed adjustment of the veil before male strangers.

At the gigantic *hur'jaa,* or campsite, Camellion's group unpacked the camels and tethered each animal to a long rope. Methodically, they set up the goathair tents and took the merchandise inside as protection against thieves. These were tasks in which "Yeho Shukairy" did not have to help. He couldn't. He didn't have the sense. He was a half-wit. Yet the role he was playing—a must since he couldn't speak Arabic—was difficult because he had to continue the role. Try acting like an idiot for only an hour! To do it constantly, even while eating, takes an enormous amount of will.

In case a Bureau of Internal Security spy was watching, Ahmed Shukairy led his "half-witted" brother into one of the tents, where Rashid al-Khaima and Colonel Bin Maktum were anxiously waiting, sitting on rugs.

"Only half of us can go into the Crater," Rashid al-Khaima said, his strangely accented voice coming out in a nervous whisper. "The rest of us must remain here to protect our merchandise."

"So who gives a damn?" remarked Camellion, feeling like teasing. "Let them steal the junk!"

"Oh, Almighty God!" exclaimed al-Khaima in indignation.

"This is not any time for humor, *Sahib* Gardner," admonished Shukairy, shaking a finger at Camellion. "We would be breaking custom. Goods are never left unattended."

The Death Merchant became serious. "You're right, Ahmed. We can't go against custom. Four of us will go into the Crater. The other five will remain at camp. Just one question: what arrangement will we make when we sell our merchandise?"

"That is not a problem," Rashid al-Khaima said

quickly. "Two men will remain with the camels. The remainder of us will carry the packs and go into the *suq*. That is the custom."

Added Ahmed Shukairy, "We will have to schedule the selling of our products with whatever plans we make toward killing that devil Shaabi."

"And that depends on the help that Nuri Boustani and his people can give us," interjected Colonel Bin Maktum.

An hour later the four were in the Quarter. Some of the buildings, made of brick or stone and plastered over with adobe, were very tall, some as high as nine stories, all of them painted in various colors and decorated with various designs. As many as six to eight people often lived in two rooms of these equivalents of Arabic slum tenements. Under the sheer walls of the buildings, the streets made one feel that he was moving through the bottom of a well.

Camellion and the other three took their time moving through the streets, for no one hurried—*It's not the damned custom*. The four even felt halfway safe. In their *gandouras*, they were only four more Arabs among hundreds. . . .

"See the dark narrow alleyways," Shukairy whispered to Camellion. "It would not be wise for us to take a shortcut through one of them, not even during the daylight hours."

The Crater was a traditional Muslim medina with its poor people, ancient houses, mosques, covered markets and buildings constructed around hidden courtyards, its streets a confused maze laid out in no particular pattern.

Finally they came to 'Unya-ift street and its *suq*, a quarter of a mile of covered market, the street itself too narrow and crowded for the jeeps of the militiamen. But the police were there, walking in pairs, watching everyone who was moving along the shops and stalls on either side of the street and, in some instances, in the center of 'Unya-ift. There were stalls and small shops offering everything from cloth and skins to religious charms to ward off evil spirits and to promote good health. Here in the 'Unya-ift *suq*, one could buy grain, jewelry—from junk trinkets to the expensive kind—ropes, knives, swords, axes, all kinds of dried fruit and vegetables; dried meat, skin or metal water containers, and the various kinds of Arabic clothing. There were shops that sold local crafts, or a wide variety of foodstuffs—cheeses, dates, fifty kinds of nuts, different types of bread, live goats or chickens, and dried gazelle meat. And just as there were a variety of commodities in the *suq*, there was a multiplicity of people of all Middle Eastern and North African cultures, haggling with the sellers.

It was an hour before Rashid al-Khaima—the only man who knew their contact by sight—saw Nuri Boustani. In a baggy white shirt, baggy red pants with vertical yellow stripes, the slightly bearded Boustani was a vendor of *tamarhindi*, a drink made from dates. The traditional brass urn, polished to a high gloss, was strapped to his back.

"Come, we will buy a drink of *tamarhindi*," said al-Khaima, quickening his pace.

Not a sign of recognition passed between Boustani and al-Khaima as Boustani took four small plastic glasses from the holder on the front of his wide belt and filled them from the spigot at the end of the pipe that led from the urn past his side and to the front of his body. Gaunt-faced, his brow plowed and furrowed, Boustani was in his forties and looked ravaged and wan, like a man battered by the sullen Fates.

He spoke in a low voice while he filled the glasses and handed them to al-Khaima and his three companions, all grinning, giving the impression that he and al-Khaima were making small talk. Al-Khaima put some coins in Boustani's hand and in a low voice replied in Arabic.

After a few minutes, Boustani went on his way, hawking his *tamarhindi*. Rashid al-Khaima and his three companions moved slowly in the same direction, sipping their almost cool *tamarhindi*, their eyes watching passersby.

"What did he say?" asked Camellion, speaking while holding the glass to his mouth. The *tamarhindi* tasted terrible—*like rotten nuts dipped in oil.*

"He said that we are to keep him in sight," whispered al-Khaima. "The sun is low in the heavens. Sahib Nuri will stop his lowly work and go to his house in another hour. We are to follow him."

"We're going to have the meeting in his house," Bin Maktum tacked on quickly, acting as if he expected Camellion to protest.

The Death Merchant didn't. He didn't like the arrangement and would have preferred to choose his own time and meeting place—*But thrashing around in the water isn't going to get us across the lake.*

The Death Merchant and the other three men with him weren't the only people on the narrow street shrouded in twilight shadows—the street lights (oil lanterns hanging from the front of the buildings) still had to be lighted. Yemenis were also on their way home, some with their wives or daughters, some of the women so heavily veiled[1] that one could only see their eyes.

The Death Merchant and his three helpers stayed a hundred feet behind Nuri Boustani who was deliberately walking at a slow pace, wanting to make sure they would not lose sight of him. Finally he stopped at the door of a two-story adobe brick house whose front was painted orange and whose single window frame, to the right was painted black.

Boustani paused before the door, unharnessed the brass urn from his back, glanced to the left, in the direction of Camellion and his group, then took a key from his pants pocket, unlocked the door, picked up the urn, opened the door and entered.

With Rashid al-Khaima whispering that Nuri Boustani was to be envied—"his father was a *haji*"[2]—they approached the narrow, brass-studded door, Camellion getting the feeling he was moving inside a pressure cooker that was about to explode. Colonel Bin Maktum, who was closest to the door, reached out and gently lifted a large iron ring and tapped it four times against its iron plate.

Nuri Boustani immediately opened the door and whispered—this time in English—"Come in. Hurry!"

Boustani opened the door wide and the four stepped into a large room lighted by a single oil-burning brass lamp suspended from the high ceiling by a brass chain. On the stone floor were large red cushions, scattered around a

---

1. It is not in the Koran that women must wear a veil; it is not religious law. Women wear veils over their faces because doing so is part of Arab culture and/or mores.
2. One who has made the pilgrimage to Mecca.

low stone table on which rested a charcoal brazier. A pot of coffee rested on the grill of the brazier. Close by, on a wooden table were cups, spoons, and bowls filled with brown sugar and goat's milk.

Camellion knew that he and the others had entered the majlis, the formal sitting room in which the women of the household were not permitted, except to wait on father, husband, brother or son, or guests. Camellion was quick to notice that the walls and ceiling were painted in stripes of blue, red, white and green. Anywhere else such a riot of clashing colors would have been unnerving. But not to a Yemeni, who found such a combination not only cheerful but restful.

Motioning for the four to sit down, Boustani peered closely at Camellion, Bin Maktum and Ahmed Shukairy. In particular did he visually inspect the Death Merchant who was no longer playing the role of a retarded person and was wondering why Boustani had spoken English—*If he thinks we are Arabs!* Was it possible that Boustani suspected that he was not an Arab. Not only possible, but probable, Camellion concluded.

Camellion sat down on a cushion between Bin Maktum and Ahmed Shukairy. He knew why Rashid had not introduced him and the two other men to Boustani as was the Arab custom. This was not a social gathering. It was business of the most dangerous kind, and security had to be maintained.

"Friend Nuri, can we talk here in safety?" inquired al-Khaima in his strangely accented English.

"The walls are thick, friend Rashid," replied Boustani, who was pouring coffee, "and the rest of my family can be trusted. They are in another part of the house." He began to spoon brown sugar into the cups. "But how is it possible for me to have assurance that I can trust the men who have accompanied you. I have noticed that the one whose mind has been cursed by Allah no longer seems to have a hundred *jinns* dancing on his head."

Boustani turned and, without looking at Camellion, handed a cup of the sweetened coffee to Rashid al-Khaima who promptly replied in a low voice. "He is an American. He does not speak our language. For that reason he is playing the part of a man whose speech and mind have been taken by Allah. His true face, the coloring of his eyes

52

and hair, betray one who is not from our land. He is disguised."

Finished with the second cup, Boustani turned and handed it to Colonel Bin Maktum. "An American! From the nation that protects our enemies, the Jews. This is most unusual in the eyes of Allah, friend Rashid."

The Death Merchant felt it was time for him to speak. "The government of the United States does protect Israel. My government wants peace in the Middle East. Yet my government and the Sons of the Falcon have a common enemy, Colonel Qahtan al Bin Shaabi. For that reason, I have come to your land that is feeling the cruel heel of those who hate Allah and hate the god of the Jews and the god of the *nasrani*, those who believe in Jesus Christ, whom the Koran honors as a great prophet."

Silently, Boustani turned and handed cups to Camellion and to Ahmed Shukairy, his face calm as glass and not revealing his hidden thoughts.

"The American can be trusted, friend Nuri," Rashid said in a gentle, almost gingerly voice. "He has suffered the same hardships on the Sea of Sand as I and my other two companions. With us he has come, placing his own life in the gravest of danger and in the merciful hands of Allah."

Colonel Bin Maktum spoke up in a straightforward manner. "I am the son of Nasir al-Maktum, of the tribe of the Anazah, from the northwest Najd. Am I not also from a nation that many Yeminis, living under both the South and the North Yemen governments, consider an enemy? I am here because we Saudis also hate Colonel Shaabi, who moves according to the will of Shaitan."

A thin smile slid across Boustani's bloodless lips. "*Salaam alaikum.* You are welcome in my poor house, son of Nasir al-Maktum."

"*Alaikum alaikum, Sahib Boustanti,*" replied Bin Maktum in a grave tone.

Boustani's eyes fixed themselves on Camellion. "*Salaam alaikum,* American. You are most welcome in my humble home. Your nation is vast and very powerful and you are but one of its inhabitants. I realize that you do not make decisions of state."

"*Alaikum alaikum, Sahib* Boustani," Camellion returned politely. "I am grateful for your hospitality. It has been

53

written by the Prophet that where the mind inclines, the feet will lead."

The Death Merchant could sense that his response pleased Boustani whose eyes now revealed a new warmth, a new acceptance Camellion did not confuse with total trust. It was the nature of the Arab to be secretive and to view an outsider, especially an infidel—and from the West to boot!—with silent suspicion. Nonetheless, the Arab was like the American Indian. Once he was your friend and knew he could trust you, he was then your friend for life. He would even die for you.

Until the discovery of oil, the Arab world remained an uncoveted backwater of the world. Basically, the various tribal societies remain the same, beneath all the regional variations; basically they are similar and consistent, the medium characterized by a balance uniting desert and oasis in a single world of agriculturalists, nomadic pastoralists—who alone can use the desert—and people whose existence falls between these two extremes, combining elments of both. This balance is one of as stark contrasts in human experience as in scenery. The nomad wakes to endure the sun. The oasis agriculturalist wakes to toil and earn his bread in his plantation's shade. The nomad's environment is one of heat, glare, and shortage—total exposure and the physical emptiness of desert existence—alleviated by space, movement, and freedom from the disease inherent in shapeless aridity continually sterilized by the sun. The nomad Arab and the Arab of the oasis mistrust each other. The agriculturalist is better fed, has more money and is better housed. But he is bound to the oasis, unlike the nomad, for whom the epitome of immobility is that of the summer camps when large numbers of people must remain in one place for months in crowded, dirty, and miserable conditions. In contrast, to the oasis dweller, immobility means ease, release, sociability and relaxation in the shade after the day's labor.

Slowly, Boustani stirred his coffee, his eyes holding the Death Merchant prisoner in their intense gaze.

"American, how can I and the group of Ibn'u alib Saqr in Aden help you and the Saudis?"

The Death Merchant had to know the answer; he would not rest until he did. "Sahib Boustani, you do speak very good English. I must apologize to you. I am in your house and accepting your hospitality and I do not speak Arabic."

Rashid al-Khaima and Ahmed Shukairy's eyes twinkled, and Camellion knew that they knew why he had complimented Boustani on his English. Camellion was also aware that if Boustani suspected his purpose, the man would not be insulted. He would accept the Death Merchant's suspicion as normal and respect him for it.

Boustani favored Camellion with a slight smile. "When the British were here and Aden was a Protectorate, I was boy and worked for a British importer," Boustani said patiently. "That is how I learned to speak English. Ah, American, your mind is filled with the question of why I spoke English when I opened the door. Is that not so?"

There was a time to lie and a time to tell the truth.

Now was the time for truth.

"Yes, Sahib Boustani. I was wondering why you said, 'Come in' in English. I was afraid that my disguise was imperfect."

Rashid al-Khaima, sitting next to Boustani, appeared delighted. "It is most simple," he explained to Camellion. "There are Yemenis in Aden who speak English, but that language is frowned on here in South Yemen. Poor Nuri has no one to talk to in English. He was practicing on me."

Boustani leaned sideways on the large cushion and half reclined. Bracing himself with an elbow, he swallowed half a cup of coffee, then carefully put the cup down in front of him.

"Rashid, we 'Sons' in Aden assumed you were either dead or in the Yemen Republic," he said. "We did not consider the possibility that you would seek the help of the Saudis and the Americans."

Al-Khaima looked up from his cup. "I didn't. They sought my aid through President-General Zarikid.

Boustani's eyes widened slightly in surprise. "You are a member of the Republic's intelligence," he declared.

"That is so. I am a member of the Yemi-I'shu'fi."

Ahmed Shukairy intruded with a bluntness that was typical of the man. "Sahib Boustani, our mission is to kill Colonel Shaabi. We need the help of your group to do it."

Boustani stared for a moment at the flinty-eyed

Shukairy, his expression scornful. He sat up then and his lined face became severe, his mouth slightly open.

"All of you are on a fool's mission," he whispered hoarsely. He thrust his head forward, his thin face giving the appearance of an animated skull. He said to al-Khaima, "Rashid, you, old friend, are part of such madness?"

"It is not madness to kill a monster," al-Khaima said, his face as wolfish as his voice. "We do not hesitate to step on the spider and the snake. Colonel Shaabi is even lower."

"We are not speaking of killing him," Boustani said angrily. "We are discussing the attempt. All of you are wearing veils upon veils and are blinded to reality. None of us could get close enough to Shaabi to kill him. He's guarded constantly, at his home, at Government House, on the road. We have heard that he and Major Jahiz have all sorts of modern devices, imported from Europe, to detect and trap intruders." He shook his head from side to side and spoke firmly. "We cannot help in any way. Our group numbers less than a hundred men, and the Koran forbids suicide."

"We are not on a suicide mission," Camellion said with whiplash emphasis. "Our objective is to kill Shaabi, then all of us get out of the country in one piece."

"Your goal is not possible, American," insisted Boustani. "To attempt to kill Colonel Shaabi must be viewed as self-death—suicide."

For reasons of psychological strategy, Camellion withdrew. "I do respect your opinion," he said tactfully. "However, I must tell you that I disagree with you."

"What weapons do you have?" There was urgency and a lack of composure in Boustani's low voice. "It is impossible for your group to have smuggled automatic weapons and grenades into the country."

"We have only pistols," Camellion was forced to admit. "We haven't grenades or any other kind of explosives."

Rashid al-Khaima looked seriously at the Death Merchant. "Nuri does speak with the sense of a wise man," he intoned in a practical way. "We knew in advance we could not do the job without the help of Nuri and the *Ibn'u alib Saqr*. Sell our goods tomorrow and return home. That is all we can do."

56

Ahmed Shukairy nodded vigorously and finished his coffee.

Bin Maktum said thoughtfully, "Rashid is right. What else can we do?"

"I am sorry that we cannot assist you." A note of apology had trickled into Boustani's voice, which was just above a whisper. "But you are asking that which is not possible." He spread his hands once more in a gesture of helplessness. "As I have explained, even when Colonel al-Bin Shaabi appears in public, he is extremely well guarded. A good example will be when he takes an aircraft from Aden Airport the day after tomorrow. Any number of precautions will be taken by Major Jahiz and his *al-Yemen Bayyi'l'ali* agents. There will be great numbers of them at the airport."

A wave of excitement flowed through the Death Merchant.

"Shaabi will be at the airport," he said. "Is this information public?" He acted and spoke in casual manner. "How did you receive this information?"

Nuri Boustani drew back slightly. "The information was not made public, but I cannot tell you how I know. Understand, American. It is a matter of security."

"You are positive?"

"I am certain. Colonel al-Bin Shaabi will be—" Boustani paused and stared in alarm at the Death Merchant. "NO! Do not even think such thoughts. We will not help you try to kill Shaabi at the airport. Such an attempt would be insanity."

"It would be as spreading roses before swine!" moaned Ahmed Shukairy.

"Listen to him, *Sahib* Gardner," Rashid al-Khaima implored Camellion. "I tell you, Allah does not care for the cries and the ambitions of dogs."

The Death Merchant reassured al-Khaima and Boustani. He looked at Boustani and smiled. "Yes, it would be insanity. I asked because I was curious. I did not mean to inquire about your security."

"I am glad to hear you speak with sense." Relief spread over the face of Boustani. "Only on the orders of Ali Sa'galli, the chief of the *Ibn'u alib Saqr*, would I help in any plan you might devise. Life is a gift of Allah. It should not be throwed away."

"No, no, Nuri!" al-Khaima said quickly. "One should say *'thrown'* away."

Nuri Boustani thought for a moment. "Very well. *'Thrown'* away." He made a tch-tch-tching sound. "It is doubtful if we in Aden shall ever see Ali Sa'galli and any of the others ever again. They are isolated in the Jabal Mahrat." There was fury in his gaze as he fixed hard eyes on Colonel Bin Maktum. "Ali Sa'galli and his men are almost totally without supplies because the word of the Saudis is like the promise of the night rubbed with butter. The butter melts when the light of day shines on it."

Colonel Bin Maktum shifted uncomfortably; however, his voice was firm with assurance. "By now that promise has been honored. Unless something went wrong, supplies were dropped to Ali Sa'galli yesterday."

Boustani's face brightened. "Rashid, he speaks the truth?"

"Yes, as it was told to him in Riyadh," responded al-Khaima. "*Sahib* Maktum is a brother in spirit. I would trust him with the veil of my wife[8]."

Hope appeared in Boustani's eyes, but his words were a warning. "Be very cautious when you depart from the city, until you are free of this land. It is possible that Colonel Shaabi has guessed that an attempt will be made on his life."

"Do you have any evidence?" asked Camellion, encompassing them all with his quiet, rational voice.

"There is a rumor," replied Boustani, "that anyone leaving the city on the old spice route is being questioned and their packs carefully searched. This is most unusual. The police only search at the border or just past the border when one enters the country. I advise extreme caution until you are free of this land."

"There couldn't have been any breach of security," Bin Maktum's tone was not commendatory. "It is only coincidence that Colonel Shaabi has guessed that someone will try to kill him."

Coincidence? The Death Merchant had doubts. Under ordinary circumstances, he would have agreed with Colonel Bin Maktum. The bug in the brew was that Mak-

---

3. A very common Arab expression, the same as the American expression, "I would trust him with my life."

tum was not aware that an Israeli agent was in their midst—unless he is the agent! The fact that Maktum was in the Saudi security directorate didn't free him from suspicion, not as far as Camellion was concerned. He had trapped too many double—and even triple—agents to be surprised at anything in the intelligence/espionage game. And it was a game, the deadliest in the world.

Another mystery was why the Mossad agent had to be terminated. Whatever the reason it had to be extremely vital and fall within the Company's *sensitive compartmented information*[4] category. Or the Saudis, as concerned as they were about a two-front war, would not have revived the air-drop into the Jabal Mahrat.

Camellion didn't show it, but his mind was racing, putting together a plan.

Success means that the 4th of July will be early this year.

☐ FIVE ☐

At nine o'clock the next morning, Muhammed al Auf, Ali Haddi, Sa'id Al'amman and Khumayyis ibn Rimthan trudged out of the *hur'jaa,* all four weighed down with packs. They were on their way into the Quarter to barter the knife blades, tobacco pouches and other merchandise. No sooner had they departed from the campsite than the Death Merchant dropped the bombshell. He told the four men with him that he had devised a plan to kill Colonel Qahtan al Bin Shaabi—"We'll hit him at the Aden Airport!"

Sitting in a circle under a goathair canopy held up by six poles in front of the tents, the men stared accusingly at him, making him feel like a Catholic who has just told his

---

4. One of the higher classifications—a notch above TOP SECRET.

parish priest that he was going to be married to a Baptist by a Justice of the Peace!

"Rahmat Ullah!" ("Allah's Mercy!") exclaimed Ahmed Shukairy, breaking the short silence. "You are trying to commit suicide and are determined to make us commit self-murder with you." His furious gaze stabbed at Camellion. "We will never reach the airport. If we do—with the help of *Ullahi*—we won't be able to get within shooting range of that demon Shaabi."

Colonel Bin Maktum regarded the Death Merchant with narrowed eyes.

"Why didn't you tell us last night at Boustani's house?" he asked in a cultured voice, his British accent making him seem out of place and time as he sat there, cross-legged, in his dirty *gandoura*. "I presume this plan of yours is not the child of some sudden inspiration on your part?"

Rashid al-Khaima shook his head, sadness in his eyes. "Today we are fire. Tomorrow we will be ashes," he complained bitterly, staring at the ground as if transfixed.

"Gardner, I think Ahmed has a valid point." Marlon Clayton tossed his cigarette into the still warm ashes of the breakfast fire. "And we can't pull off the job with only pistols—no way. I for one don't intend to try."

Rashid al-Khaima and Ahmed Shukairy looked in dismay at Clayton. How could Clayton refuse to follow Gardner? They couldn't fathom such disloyalty. They couldn't because, as Arabs, they could not conceive of any man breaking his word after he had given it. The answer came quickly to the two Yeminites: Clayton was from the corrupt West and was an infidel.

Bin Maktum made small circles in the dirt with the tip of a *su'kok*.

"Let's not make hasty decisions," he said, looking up and then across at Clayton. "Let's hear Gardner's plan."

The Death Merchant gave them the broad details, his voice driving, his words rapid and low, and, much later in the day, when the other four returned from the Quarter, he laid out the plan for them.

The four, who had gotten only thirty-one pounds of *qat* for the merchandise and were calling the traders in the *'Unya-ift suq* "diseased thieves" and the "offspring of ugly harlots," suddenly forgot all about the *suq*. When the

60

Death Merchant was finished outlining the scheme, Muhammad al Auf was the first to comment.

"The plan could work," he muttered. "At the point you mentioned, it's only six kilometers to the airport." Then a mournful looked fell over his face. "But nine uniforms—"

"Without bullet holes!" interposed Ahmed Shukairy angrily. "Nine uniforms without bullet holes. I say to you, Muhammad, you and Gardner have more hope and faith than a Jew! We'll all be killed!"

"When we cut across the country to go to the airport, what are we going to do with the camels?" asked Ali Haddi, the displeasure deepening on his face. "We can't leave the beasts standing there. Someone might become suspicious."

"We might not need more than two militia uniforms," Camellion said cheerfully. He mopped sweat from his brow, remembering the information that Nuri Bousanti had given them while they had eaten supper in his house. Was the information accurate? Camellion was gambling that it was.

"Boustani said that armored cars are parked at the east and west sides of the airport," Camellion said. "That's the 'top' and the 'bottom' of the field. We can grab one of those armored cars and be across the field before anyone realizes what is happening. What we'll have to watch is the timing."

"What are we going to do with the camels?" repeated Ali Haddi, his eyes never leaving the Death Merchant.

Camellion sighed. "The camels will not be a problem. Colonel Shaabi isn't due to take off until 02.30 hours—two-thirty in the morning. We have to camp for the night. It will be business as usual. We'll tether the camels, set up the tents, build a fire and have the evening meal. When the time comes, we'll move out. Anyone passing won't bother to investigate; everything will look normal."

The Death Merchant looked from face to face, seeking hope but finding only resistance. Intuitively, he knew the eight men would go with him to the Aden Airport. The Arabs would have to; their honor demanded it—*And so will Clayton. He'll not have a choice in the matter.*

"I'm not concerned about getting to the airport," Bin Maktum said, glancing at Shukairy and al-Khaima. "I should think that some of you Yemenis know the region between the watch towers and the airport. You—Rashid. You grew up in Aden."

"I am familiar with the area," admitted al-Khaima glumly. "At that hour of the night we'll not meet anyone, and there are enough trees and rocks for cover."

"I have a question," spoke up Khumayyis ibn Rimthan, who had a stubble of a beard, a thick mustache and was almost bald. "How do we get inside the fence of wire with pairs of militiamen patrolling on the outside and the inside?"

More gloom came from Clayton who forcefully reminded the Death Merchant that nine men were four too many to ride in even a large Russian armored car. "What are the four left over supposed to do—walk or fly?"

Camellion shrugged and stared right back at Clayton. "I suppose we'll have to grab two armored deals or maybe three," Camellion said curtly. "Don't worry about the fence. I have that figured out. Two or three of us will go over the fence and grab a car, after we take care of any guards. Then we'll take out a section of the fence by ramming it with the car." He grinned with all the enthusiasm of a Syrian wine merchant. "I admit, there's an element of risk in the operation."

This new announcement brought more looks of disgust from the men. Seemingly, Colonel Bin Maktum was the exception. Then again, he was an expert at masking his true feelings.

For a short time, silence was a palpable presence in the circle. Then Khumayyis ibn Rimthan pulled a ragged breath and said in a voice only slightly above a whisper, "*Sahib* Gardner, you have built this plan around what you presume to be fact, that Colonel Shaabi is going to take off tomorrow morning and fly to Libya. Most skeptical am I. There isn't any evidence that al Bin Shaabi and that crazy Muammar Kaddafi even know each other."

"Kaddafi is an oddball, but he's far from being psychotic," Camellion said. "He is more dangerous than a woman bent on revenge."

"Rimthan's right, Gardner," snapped Clayton, who wasn't giving an inch. "Why we can't even be sure that Nuri Boustani was telling us the truth. How—"

"Nuri is my friend!" Rashid al-Khaima said angrily,

glaring at Clayton. "I would trust him with the veil of my wife! You are implying that he is a traitor."

A look of sudden alarm swept over Clayton's face. To insult a good friend of an Arab was to insult the Arab!

Clayton didn't try to cover up his faux pas, nor apologize for his breach of Arab social etiquette. "I said we can't be sure that Boustani was telling us the truth, and I meant it. He may be your friend, but he is an unknown quality as far as facts are concerned."

The Death Merchant said quickly (*All we need is for al-Khaima to blow his stack and pull that knife of his! Clayton would break both his arms!*), "*Sahib* al-Khaima, it is possible that the source of Boustani's information has been deceived, that he or she was deliberately fed false information. Major Jahiz is no fool. He could be playing a waiting game."

"They both speak words of wisdom, Rashid," murmured Sa'id Al'amman, who always looked as if he were about to pick a fight with someone. "Everything we are doing to do is based on the assumption that the devil Shaabi will be at the airfield!"

"Why then are we taking such risks?" Ali Haddi said as innocently as a child. "To do what we are going to do makes us like dry reeds seeking the company of fire."

"We're doing it because it's a chance, the only chance we have," the Death Merchant said, struggling to control his temper and disliking himself for almost letting his anger get the better of him. Facts were just that—facts. Al'amman was right. The entire strike was based on a lot of premises that could be as valid as—the theory of reincarnation!

Another flaw was that if Colonel Shaabi didn't take off from Aden Airport the next morning, it was unlikely that any plane would be ready to take off. But . . . there was an answer to that little problem.

"I would still like to know how even two or three of us are going to get inside the fence." Khumayyis ibn Rimthan, determined to get an answer, stared at Camellion.

Camellion snorted and his lips puckered in anger. "Damnit, man! There's nine of us. If you can't figure how seven can get two over the damned fence—and it's not topped with barbed wire—you'll have to wait until we get there to find out."

"The pyramid method," Muhammade al Auf said, as if speaking to himself. "Two climb over seven, or three over six."

"Gardner, are you sure you can pilot a Russian plane?" Colonel Bin Maktum said, staring blandly at Camellion. "All the lettering on the instruments panel will be in the Russian language."

"I speak ten languages and read five," Camellion said. "Russian is one of the five. Now ask me who will fly the plane if I catch a slug, damnit!"

Strangely enough, while the other men stared at the Death Merchant, Ahmed Shukairy laughed. "I was going to ask how we're supposed to know when Shaabi is at the airport."

"And the airplane he will be using to fly to Libya!" from Sa'id Al'amman. "Nuri Boustani said there are any number of aircraft on the field."

"The plane that Shaabi will take will be either a transport or a large passenger job," said Camellion. "We know that Colonel Shaabi is well protected, When we see his limo drive up to a large plane, we'll know. That's where the timing comes in—to arrive on the spot and blow up Shabbi[1] without wrecking the damned plane."

"But we'll have to destroy the several dozen fighter craft at the airfield," Marlon Clayton said, studying his hands. He looked up, his eyes half closed against the glare of the sun. For a moment, Camellion could have sworn that Clayton almost smiled. "But count me in," Clayton said. "I don't intend to hitchhike across the Sea of Sand. . . ."

1. Pronounced SHA-AH-BEE.

☐ SIX ☐

There was nothing unusual about the small caravan leaving several hours before sunset. Bedouins and other nomadics were notorious for disliking crowded conditions of city life. It was *ja'kuli*, custom, for a caravan, especially a small one, to leave Aden before darkness and camp outside the city. That way, caravans could get an early start the next morning and not be bothered with a lot of traffic.

Five other caravans left the campsites at the same time that the Death Merchant and his group departed, the camels walking lazily and snorting in protest with their burdens of men, tents, and poles. No one even bothered to look back at Aden.

The west was streaked with brilliant red and orange by the time the Death Merchant and his men passed the two unused watch towers. The tawny plain blending with a lot of green, halfway blended with the dusky sky. The rainy season was almost upon the peninsula and clouds moved slowly across the heavens.

Camellion's caravan proceeded to an area that Ali Haddi remembered and maintained would be a good spot to set up the tents. Another caravan had beat them to the place. They proceeded another mile to the northeast, Ahmed Shukairy complaining all the way, muttering how Allah had turned his face from them. Already bad luck had reared its head. Another mile to the northeast meant an additional mile to the airport.

They set up the goathair tents in a rocky region that was thick with patches of *gobba* grass and several popular trees. A fire was started. Colonel Bin Maktum and Khumayyis ibn Rimthan prepared supper—baked wheat cakes, fresh mutton, boiled vegetables and dates, washed down with fresh goat's milk.

"Gardner, what time are we going to leave?" asked Bin

Maktum toward the end of the meal. "I suggest we leave as soon as it's dark. That will give us time to study the airfield for an hour or so."

"An excellent idea," Camellion said. "I was planning to do it that way." He glanced at the sullen faces of the silent men eating what might very well be the last meal of their lives. "If Colonel Shaabi doesn't show up, we can always return to the camels and be on our way. Personally though, I prefer to fly."

Ahmed Shukairy's eyebrows ascended. "If no one has stolen our camels and tents during our absence. We are being foolish. We are as fools counting the days of the month that do not belong to us."

Ali Haddi broke off a piece of wheat cake. "We are going to have to go seven kilometers on foot," he said forlornly, "and there will be a full moon. Evil is always at its best during a full moon. Let us pray to Allah that the clouds remain thick."

Muhammad al Auf stuffed dates into his mouth and spoke while eating.

"Madness this is. I am convinced of it. We are in a paradise in which sick hogs feed."

The Death Merchant didn't make any comment. After all, the best reply to the babbling of fools was silence. But you sure couldn't break a bronc without putting a halter on him.

Dressed in black *gallabiyas* bought in Aden, they left the camp immediately after dark, Rashid al-Khaima taking the point, leading the way, each man carrying his Lee Enfield rifle. If they were discovered by the al-Yemen i'Qrali, the Enfields, compared to the automatic weapons of the militiamen, would be as useless as ice cubes in Antarctica; however, the rifles did give one a feeling of security, and, as Sa'id Al'amman had wryly remarked, "They will make good clubs."

At times they could see the rising full moon, an enormous ball of faded red low in the east. At other times there was almost total darkness as strato-cumulus clouds crept over the face of Earth's satellite. With al-Khaima checking the compass occasionally, they moved in a southwesterly direction. They could have saved a lot of precious time if they could have approached the east end of Aden Airport. They couldn't. The large hangars were on the east end. The north side was also lighted, and so was the south side. Their only choice was the "bottom" of the field, the west end.

Rashid al-Khaima proved that he was very familiar with the region by leading the Death Merchant & Co. on a fast pace that took them across small open spaces—when clouds covered the moon—and through brush and tiny arroyos. At one point they had to climb a rather long slope whose uneven surface was covered with oak and deodar trees. Another time they had to stop, listen, and check when they heard sheep in the distance. Investigation revealed a shepherd and his flock bedded down for the night. They crept by the sheep, sixty meters to the north of the flock. With weapons ready and good sense absent—unquote Khumayyis ibn Rimthan—they hurried toward their destination, wrapped in darkness and feeling the hot *shamāl* blowing from the north.

They made better time than the Death Merchant expected. Soaked with sweat, they turned at the proper time and moved straight west. An hour and fifteen minutes later, reaching their destination, they found themselves 125 feet from the chain link fence at the west end of the airfield. Time: 24.30 hours, one half hour after midnight.

Lying flat behind blackberry bushes and underneath some chenar trees, the trees of the Yemen desert, they surveyed what lay ahead. In the moonlight they could see two Soviet armored cars, one to the left, one to the right, a 400 foot horizontal space between the two cars.

"Those armored cars don't look very impressive to me," said Marlon Clayton. "And they're not very big."

"It's a *Boyevaya Machine Desantnaya*, or BMD for short," Camellion whispered. "It's really an armored scout car."

"But it's got a turret cannon; that's what counts," said Clayton. "How many does it carry?"

"Five. Six can squeeze in without any difficulty."

Whenever the moon was free of the clouds, Camellion and his men could see fairly well. But, lying down as they were, they couldn't see the hangars and the aircraft parked at the east end of the field, 5,000 feet away. At that distance they couldn't have seen clearly if they had been on top of a watch tower. What they needed was binoculars. They didn't have any. They had only the small Eye.

To the left, a hundred feet inside the fence, was a rectangular shaped building, a large shed of corrugated iron. This building was used to store paint and the motorized striping machine that marked the side of the four 5,000-foot long runways with white paint.

Camellion was quick to notice that he and the others were right smack in the middle of luck insofar as the runways' lights were concerned. Only the first 4,000 feet were lighted; that left a full 1,000 feet in darkness—*Which explains why the BMDs and the guards are at this end of the field. Damn poor security.*

Camellion wondered if the guards might be Cuban. Intelligence estimated that there were two hundred to three hundred of Castro's crackpots in Yemen, under a Major Luis Pisario who took his orders from the Russians.

"I don't see any guards," whispered Marlon Clayton, who lay next to the Death Merchant, directly to his right.

"I don't see God either," retorted the Death Merchant. "That doesn't mean he's not there, or here. What we're going to do is wait. Pass the word. We're going to wait until we see guards on both the inside and the outside of the fence. They have to be on some kind of schedule."

He reached underneath his *gallabiya* and pulled The Eye free of its long leather holster. The device was a tube seven inches long and a half inch in diameter. Camellion unscrewed the two ends of the tube, or eyepieces, and, using his thumbnail, pried the smaller, or inner, tube up an inch, then extended it to its full four inches. "The Eye" was a small but powerful night telescope, and although it could not even be compared to a night vision scope, it was still ten times more powerful than unaided vision.

Rashid al-Khaima wriggled his way around to Camellion and whispered vehemently as Camellion began to scan the area through The Eye.

"*Sahib* Gardner, are we going to lie here and do nothing? No guards are about. Let's cross the fence and take cover in the darkness behind the shed. From there we can plan our next move—a dash to the two armored cars."

"My impetuous friend, take a look to the left," said Camellion and handed The Eye to al-Khaima. "You have to adjust the smaller tube by pushing it in and out." Then he chuckled. "It's better to endure the flatulencies of the camel than the prayers of the fishes. This means it's better to stay put awhile and live than to rush in and maybe die."

There were times when Camellion would like to have hit Rashid al-Khaima; there were those other times that he found the member of the North Yemen intelligence service amusing. Either way, al-Khaima was an "excess" man. Everything he did was in excess, even eating. Either he wanted to retreat at full speed or else toss all caution to the sand and attack with all the daring of a Kamikaze. Ahmed Shukairy had the same recremental traits. To a certain extent, so did the other Arabs, except Bin Maktum, who had been educated in the West. If anything, Bin Maktum was too cautious.

Rashid al-Khaima cursed in Arabic, then said bitterly in English, "May Allah curse the memory of their fathers." He had found the two guards. They were walking side by side outside the fence, both wearing dark brown shirts and pants and field boots. Peaked garrison caps were on their heads. Soviet AKS-74 assault rifles were slung on leather straps over their shoulders.

"They are not Yemenis," al-Khaima said, his voice filled with hatred. "They are infidels from the West."

"They're Cubans," Camellion said. "Russians wouldn't be doing guard duty."

The two Cubans, one smoking a cigarette, moved on slowly to the south. Soon they had vanished in the darkness. Camellion looked at his wristwatch, then accepted The Eye which al-Khaima returned to him.

It was another five minutes before they saw the two guards inside the fence. Two more of Castro's chili-peppers walking from the south to the north. They, too, were carrying AKS-74s.

Another twenty-five minutes turtle-crawled by.

"Damnit, Gardner, let's do something!" Clayton urged impatiently. He turned and looked at Camellion who was peering through The Eye. "Damnit to hell, it's right at one o'clock."

"I said—we wait!" Camellion said, his voice pure ice. "Oh-ho! There's two more of Fidel's freaks coming from the north, outside the fence. Apparantly they patrol every half-hour outside the fence, with the 'inside' guards coming five minutes behind them."

"We can't be all that certain," Clayton said. This time his tone was amiable.

"I say we cross the fence," growled al-Khaima, his voice low and strained.

"We're going to—as soon as we see the two inside guards," Camellion said. "I expect we'll see them in five minutes."

He was wrong. It was seven minutes before two Cubans, inside the fence, put in an appearance, sauntering from south to north. Soon the two had disappeared in the darkness.

"We're moving in. Pass the word," Camellion said to Clayton. "Let's do it fast and tell them to stay as low as possible."

As a unit, the nine men got up and raced across the clearing. A large cloud had just begun to cross the face of the moon, and they desperately hoped that they could complete the cross-over before the cloud passed.

Ali Haddi got down on his hands and kness. Facing Haddi and parallel to him, Sa'id Al'amman took a position on his hands and knees, bracing himself against the ground with the heels of his hands.

"Are you ready?" whispered Muhammad al Auf, staring down at the two men.

"I am," said Haddi.

"Yes—hurry," Al'amman whispered.

Slowly, but with precise movements, al Auf climbed on top of Sa'id Al'amman, carefully lowered himself and moved into a shaky position that placed his knees on the broad part of Al'amman's back and his hands on the middle part of Ali Haddi's back.

"I'm ready," al Auf said.

Rashid al-Khaima, who had removed his sandals, first used Sa'id Al'amman's lower back as a "step," then climbed onto the back of Muhammad al Auf and very carefully stood up and faced the south, his body half twisted. The four-men pyramid tottered slightly, but the four men held on from sheer desperation, the faces of Ali Haddi and Sa'id Al'amman showing the severe strain from the effort.

The Death Merchant went first, Bin Maktum and Clayton helping him to the back of al Auf. Very steadily, Camellion, facing the fence, bent his knees, then sprang for it like some big cat. Rashid al-Khaima, balancing himself with his right arm, put his left hand under Camellion's left foot as the Death Merchant's fingers hooked themselves through the openings in the chain-link wire at the top of the fence. Rashid pushed upward on Camellion's foot with all his might, the effort giving Camellion the extra time and leverage he needed to pull himself up another two feet and swing his right let over the top of the fence. He didn't have to concern himself with the sharp ends of the wire poking into his body since there was a thick one-half-inch in diameter wire attached to the vertical ends and running horizontally across the top of the fence. In an instant, Camellion had swung himself over the fence. For a moment, he braced himself with both hands on the top wire, then, bending his legs slightly, pushed himself from the top of the fence and dropped to the ground, rolling over easily on his left shoulder as he landed.

Colonel Bin Maktum was next to crawl up on the human pyramid. In another ninety seconds he was over the top and beside the Death Merchant, breathing heavily.

It was then Marlon Clayton's turn.

Camellion had chosen Bin Maktum and Clayton because they not only had a lot of savvy in killing but because they were familiar with tanks, armored cars and heavy weapons. The Death Merchant had also chosen Ahmed Shukairy as one of the first inside the fence. The sullen and mercurial Shukairy was deadly with a knife and could slice the backbone of a scorpion in half at fifty feet.

But Shukairy's crossing the fence was not to be. He was about to put his right foot into the hand of Khumayyis ibn Rimthan and crawl up on al Auf's back when Ali Haddi muttered, "We must stop. No longer can I maintain this tortuous position. Remove yourself, friend Rashid."

Carefully, Rashid al-Khaima jumped to the ground, muttering, "Haste comes from Satan. Wise slowness comes from God."

The Death Merchant, barely able to see the faces of al-Khaima and the other men outside the chain-link fence, knew there wasn't time to re-form the pyramid. *There's time, but they won't be in the mood. I'll have to make do with Clayton and Maktum.*

71

"Rashid, you and the others know what to do and how to do it," Camellion said in a low voice. "Don't miss. Make sure! Be positive before you strike."

"Mad'iya lah as Ullahi!" ("May Allah protect you.") Rashid whispered, after which he and the other on the opposite side of the fence raced back to their former positions.

The wind was still hot and there was the fragrance of blue gentians in the night air. Camellion, Bin Maktum, and Marlon Clayton, keeping low, hurried to the rear of the paint storage shed to their left. Reaching the rear of the building, they lay down, Camellion and Maktum facing the north, Clayton the south. The Death Merchant slipped a hand under his *gallabiya* and pulled a 9-millimeter Hi-Power Browning from the holster strapped to his thigh. From a holster strapped to his left calf, he pulled three "Little Brothers," three needle-nosed ice picks, the top end of each blade firmly imbedded in a iron-pipe handle filled with lead. Clayton pulled a 9mm Sile-Benelli B76 self-loading auto pistol from underneath his black robe while Bin Maktum lay with a 9mm Walther P-38 in his left hand.

Ten minutes . . . six hundred "standing-still" seconds . . . dragged by. The last of the cloud drifted across the face of the moon and there was suddenly soft moonlight in the area. However, the soft yellow light did not touch the Death Merchant and his two men, all three of whom were on the west side of the paint storage shed. They might as well have been invisible.

Two hundred feet to the left was the first Soviet BMD armored car, or, to be technical, "air-portable fire support vehicle," resting in such a position as to place it fifty to sixty feet in front of the shed—if one had cared to stretch a horizontal line from shed to car. Two hundred feet to the right of the shed and seventy-five feet to its front was the second BMD, its low silhouette a dim shadow in the moonlight.

Two men were leaning against the front of the vehicle, smoking.

"Where are the three other Cubans?" asked Clayton in a whisper. "In this heat, they can't be inside. Or could they?"

"Sure they could, but it isn't likely," Camellion replied

in a voice so low that Clayton hardly heard him. "On a monotonous guard job like this, two men per car is sufficient. Now be quiet. Voices carry. Even whispers can be pushed along by a breeze."

He thought of the Israeli Mossad agent. Who could he be? One thing was certain at this point. Whoever the agent was, he would not interfere with the attempt to terminate Colonel Qahtan al Bin Shaabi. If anyone hated the Israelis, it was Bin Shaabi. Another plus in the Death Merchant's favor was that the Mossad agent—even if the Israelis had not wanted Shaabi dead—could not interfere with either the attempt against Colonel Shaabi or the escape by air from Aden airport—*Unless he wants to commit suicide by cutting his own throat!*

The Death Merchant pulled The Eye from his pocket, extended the tube and began to scan the area to the north, outside of the fence. Seconds merged into minutes. At length he saw them: two Cubans walking eight to ten feet from the fence, two unsuspecting Cubans, spotting them a minute or so before Rashid al-Khaima and the other men saw them.

Bin Maktum, who had not yet seen the Cubans, whispered, "What is your American expression about the water never becoming hot in a pot being observed?"

"A watched pot never boils," chuckled Clayton.

"Both of you be quiet," Camellion hissed disdainfully. "I've spotted them."

The two Cubban *soldados* walked lazily toward the south. One man carried his AKS-74 in his right hand. The other man had his Soviet assault rifle slung over his right shoulder, his right hand on the sling strap.

Presently, the two Cubans reached a position that made them even with the rear of the shed. Then they were past the shed. Three minutes more and they were a hundred feet past the point where Rashid al-Khaima and the other Arabs were waiting behind the blackberry bushes.

Watching through The Eye, the Death Merchant saw three shadowy forms rise up from behind the bushes and noiselessly move at an angle toward the Cubans whose length of life had suddenly decreased to zero.

One of the Cubans might have heard a foot bend or break a twig or come down too hard on a rock. Or it could have been that strange kind of instinct that touches off a warning. Whatever it was, the Cuban started to turn around, to check the area behind him. The other Cuban paused.

Too late! Ali Haddi, Rashid al-Khaima, and Sa'id Al'amman were only forty to fifty feet away. Just as the Cuban turned, the three Arabs threw their *kisels,* the curved, flat-bladed daggers that all Arabs carried in their belts across their stomachs.

The Cuban who had turned around was the recipient of two of the *kisels.* One buried itself in his stomach. The second caught him in the left side of the chest, streaking in with the blade flatways, so that the sharp steel slid easily between his ribs.

The other Cuban stopped and jerked violently, a knife blade buried deeply between his shoulder blades. The assault rifle slipped from his numb hand, his body jerking first one way and then another. In that horrible moment he realized that he and Raul were under attack and did his best to shout a warning. He didn't have the strength; the shock was too great. Only a choking gurgle came out of his mouth, his scream drowning in the pool of blood rising up in his throat. With a great roaring in his ears, he found the world spinning around him, spinning faster and faster; and, catching a brief glimpse of Raul, who was already dead and on the ground, found himself falling. No sooner had he lost consciousness and struck the ground than Rashid al-Khaima and the other men were dragging him and the other dead *Cubano* to the bushes, Ali Haddi carrying the assault rifle that Raul Sastine had dropped.

"To use a trite American expression, it went off like clockwork," whispered the Death Merchant to Bin Maktum and Marlon Clayton, both of whom had seen the swift and efficient termination of the Cubans.

"En general, fue un buen trabajo," ("All in all, it was a good piece of work") Clayton said in idiomatic Spanish used by American Latinos. "We had better do as well when our turn comes."

"I will," Camellion said. "Now shut up."

The forward section of a cloud began to cross the face of the white-yellow moon. The Death Merchant waited, counting off the seconds . . . 1001, 1002, 1003. . . . He now had only one major concern: that the two guards walking inside the fence may have spotted the action out-

74

side the fence. If they had seen anything unusual, they wouldn't start shouting and firing, not if they had common sense. They would ease quietly to one of the BMDs and use its radio to sound a warning and to call for reinforcements.

Two minutes passed, then three, then four. Camellion, who had shifted his body, peered to the south through The Eye. Five minutes. Six minutes. Bingo! He barely saw the outline of the two men.

Right on schedule. Coming to their own execution!

He watched the two Cubans until they were even with the shed. Càrefully he put down The Eye, picked up two of the "Little Brothers," stood up and waited until the two Cubans had walked around fifteen feet to the north. NOW! He drew back his right arm and, holding the ice pick by the end of its handle, threw it.

Time: half the blink of an eye. The tip of the ice pick was only inches from Andres Dorticós's back as Camellion "border-crossed" the "Little Brother" in his left hand to his right hand, drew back his right arm and again threw a weighted instrument of death.

There were times when Camellion did miss an inch or two. This time he didn't. This time the thin blade of the ice pick struck exactly where he had wanted it to strike— in the back of Emilo Yañes's neck. The Blade, pushed onward by the momentum of the lead handle, bored all the way through his throat, tearing through his Adam's apple and pushing itself out the front of his throat.

Both Dorticós and Yañes jerked like rag dolls, Dorticós spinning around a second after the second "Little Brother" buried itself between his shoulder blades. Blood trickling out of Dorticós's mouth, blood spurting from Yañes's mouth. The two men crumpled in a heap, their peaked caps falling off when their heads struck the hard, dry earth.

"Work quickly but silently," Camellion whispered, emphasizing "silently." "Keep in mind that there are armored cars only several hundred feet to each side of us."

They hurried to the dead Cubans, Colònel Bin Maktum picking up the two caps and the Russian A-Rs. The Death Merchant, after pulling the two "Little Brothers" from the dead men and wiping the bloody blades on the pants of the corpses, began dragging the dead Emilo Yañes by his

75

wrists. Clayton, his back to Andres Dorticós, pulled the dead man across the ground by his feet, holding the booted legs of the corpse against his sides.

Reaching the back of the shed, Camellion and his two helpers went to work. While Camellion unbuckled the Sam Browne belts and the holstered 9mm Berettas, Bin Maktum pulled off boots. Next came the brown shirts and the brown pants.

"Damn it, the front of the shirts are soggy with blood," Clayton said in disgust.

"Into each life some rain must fall—or blood in this case," replied Camellion. "Anyhow, why worry? Their clothing is too small to fit you. Bin and I will have to do the job. You'll have to wait here."

Within another ten minutes, the Death Merchant and Bin Maktum had undressed and put on the clothing of the two dead Cubans, the wetness of the blood, on the front of the shirts, hot and soggy against their chests. Camellion wasn't concerned about the blood. Maroon on dark brown would not be noticeable—*And by the time they do notice, it will be too late. . . .*

Camellion finished buckling the Sam Browne belt and straightened his cap. Colonel Bin Maktum finished checking the Beretta, shoved the auto-pistol into its holster, secured the flap and picked up the AKS-74 assault rifle.

"Ready?" Camellion asked Bin Maktum and picked up his own A-R.

"Which car first, the right or the left?" whispered Bin Maktum.

"The one to our right, to the north. Just act natural. We'll walk right up to it."

"Watch out for oversized hail," chided Marlon Clayton, "and things that go bump in the night."

"Yeah, and the galloping gowumpases are bad this time of year," Camellion said with a straight face.

As bold as new brass, the Death Merchant and Bin Maktum left the rear of the storage shed and began walking north.

Camellion knew. He could sense the bony bastard grinning and gliding along with them—the Cosmic Lord of Death!

This night he had better be on our side. . . .

☐ SEVEN ☐

First there was the dim, shadowy outline of the Soviet BMD air-portable fire support vehicle. Gradually, as Camellion and Colonel Bin Maktum ambled closer to the vehicle, they could see the three rubber tires on the right side of the armored car and discern individual features of the gray-painted vehicle. The turret, with its 50mm smooth bore cannon, was pointed east and the turret hatch was open and thrown back. They could also see part of the barrel of a PKMT machine gun protruding from the front of the hull below the turret housing.

Walking side by side, swinging their automatic rifles easily in their right hands, the Death Merchant and Colonel Bin Maktum could smell tobacco smoke and hear two or three men talking in low tones, Camellion catching an occasional word in Spanish.

Camellion and Maktum knew they would have to strike with lightning speed before the Cubans got a good look at their faces, although there was the possibility that the Cubans by the armored car were not acquainted with the guards walking-the-fence.

Camellion leaned close to Maktum and whispered, "Let me do the talking. When I say 'Go' in English—do it."

Closing in on the car, Camellion said in Cuban-type Spanish, loud enough for the Cubans by the BMD to hear, *"Anoche cogi un jalco en compañía de varios amigos[1]."*

The idea was to find out the position of the Cubans, and it worked. Smoking a cigar, a man stepped from the front of the vehicle. Another man was behind him.

"Anything wrong?" the first man asked. A large man with broad shoulders, he had a full guerrilleros beard and carried a holstered Beretta.

1. "Last night I got drunk with several friends."

77

"What are you men doing here?" the second man asked in a puzzled tone.

Only a few feet more! Close enough to let them have it!

The two Cubans did not even have the time to become suspicious. Instead of answering, the Death Merchant said GO in a low voice to Bin Maktum, then burst into action with all the suddenness of a hidden hand grenade exploding. A high leap, his right leg shooting outward and upward in a TNT *Mawashi Geri* roundhouse kick, the automatic rifle in his right hand coming up simultaneously and with equal speed.

Bartolomé Predes and Orlando de Rivera were not the only ones surprised. So was Colonel Bin Maktum. Because of Camellion's incredible speed, the Saudi intelligence agent didn't even have a chance to go into action.

The muzzle of the AKS-74 A-R stabbed into Orlando de Rivera's throat, just below his chin, the hard steel of the barrel going three inches into the flesh. The Cuban was as good as dead. With the top of his Adam's apple crushed, he couldn't even scream. All he could do was shriek within himself at the intense pain and at the horror of the situation in which he found himself. Helpless, he found the ground rushing up to meet him and heard the roaring of the velvet blackness bombarding his brain.

Bartolomé Predes wasn't much better off. The heel of the Death Merchant's right foot had fractured Predes's breast bone and slammed him into a state of shock. Before he could even let out a groan, Camellion's right arm moved to the right and the barrel of the assault rifle crashed against Predes's right temple—the sound similar to a large twig being snapped.

Camellion didn't waste time watching the Cuban fall. With an amazed Bin Maktum watching him, he leaped onto the front of the vehicle and was stepping onto the turret decking when Rafael Forcade, who had just completed the hourly radio report, began easing himself up through the turret.

Although Forcade's capless head and neck and shoulders were outside the turret, the Death Merchant realized instantly that he didn't have the time to clobber the Castro creep with the automatic rifle. At the moment, he was balancing himself with his right arm and could not possibly swing the A-R in time. The Cuban would see the weapon

78

coming down at him and drop back down ínto the interior of the vehicle. By the time Camellion could lean down into the turret and put a Beretta bullet, or an A-R slug, into the man, the Cuban would have switched on the radio and yelled for help.

Forcade—he looked like he had more hair than head!—paused, his hands on the rim of the turret, and looked up in confusion at Camellion who, speaking Spanish with a Cuban flavor, said in a relaxed voice, "We need your help. We think José broke his leg."

"José?" began Forcade. "Who is—" The Cuban paused, fear on his face when he saw Camellion's left foot streaking toward him. He didn't have time to duck. The sole of Camellion's foot crashed into his face, the grand-slam breaking his nose and knocking out five of his upper front teeth. Forcade gave a kind of gurgling squawk and dropped back down into the interior of the armored car, his action, purely involuntary, due to shock and weakness.

Double damn! Camellion didn't dare shove the A-R into the turret and fire. In the quietness of the night, the shot would ring out—hollowly from within the car—and warn the other Cubans in the BMDs.

He took the only course open to him, confident that for a fifth of a minute the Cuban would be helpless, his mind in limbo from shock and from the effort of reorganizing his startled thoughts. Camellion threw the automatic rifle to the ground, made a leap and dropped down through the turret, putting his arms in front of him to protect his head and face. His left foot made contact with the center top of the Cuban's right thigh; his right foot landed on the seat of the machine gunner.

The interior of the Soviet BMD was lighted only by a pale green glow from the instrument panel, but the slight light was sufficient for the Death Merchant to see that a now terrified Forcade was trying to tug his Beretta pistol from its holster with his right hand and switch on the radio with his left—and doing a poor job of both. He was still dazed from pain and his mouth and nose were dripping blood and gore.

Having dropped all the way into the armored car, Camellion turned and grabbed Forcade's right wrist with his left hand and, using a right handed knife-edge chop, knocked the man's hand away from the radio. A lightning quick one-two-three Shito-Ryu karate four-finger spear stab into the Cuban's solar plexus and it was all over for Rafael Forcade. He gasped loudly and sagged unconscious.

"Gardner?" Bin Maktum had crawled onto the top of the armored car and was peering down into the turret, his Beretta drawn. "Are you all right?"

"Yeah, just ducky," Camellion said. "Stay where you are, and in a minute you can pull this Caribbean crackpot out of here."

Camellion pulled the Beretta pistol from the Cuban's holster and shoved the weapon into his own belt. One expert rip with the broad, sharp blade of his *kisel* and the chest strap of the man's Sam Browne belt was slit. Camellion shoved the *kisel* into its holster, underneath his shirt, and unbuckled the main belt from around Forcade's waist, after which he pulled off the flap-style holster, shoved the end of the belt through the buckle, dropped the leather over the Cuban's head, tightened the loop around his throat and shoved the end of the belt through the turret opening.

"Pull him up," he whispered to Bin Maktum who, leaning down, was able to reach the end of the belt with both hands.

"Not bad," congratulated Bin Maktum. "We pull him up and hang him all at the same time. Cold blooded but effective."

"I didn't train for the priesthood," Camellion said drily. "PULL!"

Between Bin Maktum's pulling and Camellion's pushing upward, they managed to get the corpse out of the car. Bin Maktum rolled the corpse to the ground and jumped off the car. The Death Merchant first took a pair of binoculars and its case, hanging from inside the car, then hoisted himself through the turret and stood up on the car, he and Bin Maktum fully aware of the giant risk they were taking. At any moment, one of the other armored cars might come rolling up, or, if the other Cubans had heard a strange noise, one of them might switch on a spotlight, which each car had mounted to a brace on the turret body.

Luck! Taking out the binoculars and peering closely at them, Camellion saw that the instrument was 20 × 50 power, the lens amber coated for night viewing. He raised

80

the binoculars to his eyes, his fingers working the focus knob. He turned and looked to the right. *Well, 'pon my soul!* There sat another Russian BMD, slightly over three hundred feet away. The three crew members were sitting on the ground, leaning against the front of the vehicle.

The Death Merchant turned to the left. There in the distance was another armored car, but its crew was nowhere in sight.

Camellion stared toward the east, carefully adjusting the binoculars for full range focus. There were the hangars, the entire area of the forward section of the Aden Airport lit up as bright as high noon. In front of the first three hangars—to his left—he could see a dozen Soviet fighter jets. *I can't make out the type. They're too far away.*

His heart gave an extra beat when he saw the twin-engined transport plane being towed from the middle hangar by a tractor, being pulled toward the center runway where a fuel tank-truck was waiting. The airplane appeared to be an AN-26, but he couldn't be sure.

He jumped from the car to the ground and said to Colonel Bin Maktum, who handed him an AKS-74 A-R, "They're getting the airplane ready for Shaabi. I'm almost positive."

The Saudi agent appeared puzzled. "On what do you base your opinion, my American friend?"

"Experience—damn it!" cracked Camellion. "Someone is going somewhere in that plane or they wouldn't be preparing it. Come on. We'll whack out the Cubans in the next car to the north. The crew is sitting in front of the car."

They repeated their previous performance. They shouldered their automatic rifles and walked right up to the armored car. One Cuban was getting to his feet and a second man was greeting them as Camellion and Colonel Bin Shaabi jammed two of the men viciously in the chest with the barrels of the AKS-74s and the Death Merchant broke the face bones of the third man with a deadly karate snap kick. The three Cubans toppled. Ten seconds more and all three were dead, Camellion having broken their necks with deadly *Uchi Mawashi* stamp kicks.

Bin Maktum, pulling a 9mm Beretta from a dead man's

flap-holster, said with deliberate calmness, "Now all we have to do is smash over a section of the fence. Is that the idea?"

The Death Merchant shoved another Beretta pistol into his waist, already heavy with another Beretta auto-loader. "Can you drive one of these babies, Sahib Maktum?"

"Yes, but I can't muffle the noise from the engine," Maktum said seriously. "Nor can you. The other Cubans will surely hear us—certainly the noise from two cars."

"It can't be helped," Camellion said tightly. "We'll have picked up Clayton and have knocked over a piece of the fence before the other Cubans get wise. Let's get aboard. I'll drive."

They climbed into the armored car through the turret, Camellion settling down in the driver's seat, Bin Maktum taking the machine gunner's seat. The Death Merchant scanned the controls that were similar to those of an ordinary automobile. The exception was that the armored car had more shifts, had independent drive to all six wheels and had an armored body similar in style to earlier Soviet armored half-trucks. Based on a Zil 8 × 8 truck chassis, the BMD rode on double-suspension units and had a 40 GAZ-40 six-in-line water cooled gasoline engine. A unique feature of the vehicle was the means by which the driver could vary the tire pressure to suit the surface of the terrain.

The Death Merchant pressed the ignition button and the engine rumbled into life, the sound only slightly louder than that of an automobile, which meant that, because of the quietness, the sound was four times more than it should have been.

The inside of the car was hot and smelled of metal, leather, and stale tobacco smoke. Camellion didn't bother to use the driver's periscope. Wanting all the view possible, all the forward vision he could get, he cranked open the steel armor plate over the 15″ × 7″ opening in front of the driver, then shifted to forward and fed gas to the engine. The Soviet BMD rolled forward.

"American, how are we going to know when al Bin Shaabi arrives?" There was a honed awareness about Bin Maktum who gave the Death Merchant a perplexing look. "How can we possibly synchronize our attack with his arrival?"

Speeding up the vehicle, Camellion began to turn the vehicle to the south. "Friend Maktum, you know the answer," he scoffed. "But you hate to admit it, the same as I do."

"A hit or miss proposition," Colonel Bin Maktum stated.

"Exactly. We have about forty fifty-millimeter shells. All we can do is hope that Shaabi puts in an appearance. If we get lucky, we might be able to blow him into the next world. If we can't, we'll either have to get airborne in that transport or we'll never see dawn. And don't give me a line about the will of Allah. I get enough of that from the others."

Colonel Bin Maktum's rather good-looking face broke into a mischievous grin. "What do you think I am—a superstitious Arab?"

In spite of the gravity of the situation, the Death Merchant found himself laughing. Colonel Bin Maktum was indeed an Arab, but he was not superstitious. Nor was he a devout Muslim. He couldn't be. He was too educated— *And when education moved in, superstition dissolves into nothingness.*

"I'll let you out by the other car, the first one we took," Camellion said, slowing down when he saw the outline of the vehicle through the open window. "Drive over to the shed and pick up Clayton. Yell out his name, just to be on the safe side."

"He does seem—what is your American expression? " 'Elated over the trigger?' "

" 'Trigger happy.' Clayton's not trigger happy, not in the sense that you mean. It's just that he wants to play it double-safe. It can't be done, not on an operation of this nature—and take an A-R with you."

Camellion braked the car, Bin Maktum hoisted himself through the turret, jumped to ground and hurried to the other armored six-wheeled vehicle which resembled a British Boarhound; however, a *Boyevaya Machine Desantnaya* was only half the size of a Boarhound.

The Death Merchant started up and headed for the section of fence directly to the rear of the paint shed, executing a wide half circle before he stopped twenty-five feet in front of the fence.

Question: Should he attempt to push over the section of fence or shoud he slam into it?

Answer: Each thirty-foot section of chain-link was firmly attached to steel poles set in concrete. *I'll never be able to get the traction on this hard ground. I'll have to smash into the fence—and damn the noise!*

Camellion revved up the engine, switched on the rear periscope, put the vehicle in reverse and pushed down on the gas pedal. The square rear of the metal box on six wheels headed for the middle of the section of the fence that the Death Merchant had chosen. First, the rear bumper—a solid chunk of metal—tore through the wire, ripping the steel strands as though they were spider webs. And with a sound *that they must have heard all the way to Aden!* The sloping rear glacis plate followed the bumper, widening the already large rent in the ripped wire. The Death Merchant had slammed into the fence at forty mph and almost half of the BMD had shot through the fence.

Camellion slammed on the brake, shifted gears and stepped on the gas. The armored car moved forward. Camellion stopped, shifted to neutral and looked into the rear periscope. The armored car had not torn the section of fence from the supporting posts. It had ripped an enormous hole in the wire, large enough to drive a small car through. He saw something else that gave him a good feeling. The men who had been behind the bushes had gotten up and were running toward the fence.

Looking through the driver's window, he saw the other BMD backing up at a fast rate of speed. Evidently, Bin Maktum was going to pull alongside him. The Death Merchant found himself thinking of the Saudi agent with a new respect. Maktum could drive like a vet from the Indy 500!

While Camellion was pulling himself up through the turret opening, Rashid al-Khaima and the other Arabs came through the rip in the chainlink fence. The Death Merchant stood up on the small turret platform, so that half of his body protruded from the top of the BMD. The other Soviet vehicle was parked only six feet away and Colonel Bin Maktum was standing in the turret.

"A nice job of driving," Camellion congratulated him

and motioned for the other men to climb aboard the two armored cars.

"*Sahib* Clayton did the driving," Colonel Maktum said. "He insisted. He seemed to be positive of his ability and I saw no reason to argue with him like some music hall wag."

Camellion smiled. Bin Maktum was one helluva Arab. He not only spoke with a British accent but now and then used British expressions.

Muhammad al Auf, Ahmed Shukairy and Ali Haddi rode in the Death Merchant's BMD; and when al Auf growled that he was familiar with armored cars—he had driven one when he had fought with the Royalist forces of General Ibn Zarikid—Camellion told him to drive. "I'd rather handle the cannon."

"I will fire the machine gun," Ahmed Shukairy said firmly. "I also fought with General Zarakid." His husky voice dripped with poisonous hatred. "I only hope I get to kill some of those Cuban devils and the South Yemeni sons of diseased sows."

Marlon Clayton was behind the wheel of the second armored car. Bin Maktum was at the cannon, Rashid al-Khaima at the PKMT machine gun. Ali Haddi was down at the bottom of the turret well, his back against the front of the first-aid locker.

Camellion's armored vehicle was the most crowded, somewhat like a large sardine can with Sa'id Al'amman and Khumayyis ibn Rimthan hemmed in at the rear of the turret compartment. But there was still ample room for Camellion, al Auf, and Ahmed Shukairy to do what they had to do.

The Death Merchant stood up on top of the turret rim and had a final look through the binoculars at the east end of the airport. The Soviet transport plane was exactly where he figured it would be at the end of the center runway. The refueling tank truck had pulled away and the props on the two engines were slowly turning over.

Bingo! It was Christmas and his birthday all rolled into one! Camellion also saw—far to his left—a long red car that looked like a Buick. The car was preceded by two motorcycles and a BMD and followed by a Soviet BTR-60, or armored personnel carrier, and another BMD.

Camellion lowered the binoculars and called over to Bin

Maktum who was watching him from the turret of the other BMD. "I think Colonel Shaabi is about to arrive at the airport. He's in a car with armor in front and in back of him, about a mile south of the north side entrance."

"It has to be Shaabi," Maktum agreed. "No one else in South Yemen travels with all that protection. What is your plan?"

"Tell Clayton to head straight for the hangars and to park fifty feet directly in front of the transport. It's sitting just right for a takeoff and we can't have it moved. I'll try to get Shaabi with—"

Camellion paused and jerked his head to the right. Four hundred feet away a spotlight had been switched on and was moving back and forth. At any moment the white beam would find the two armored cars and the ripped fence. Far to the left, Camellion could hear engines and see lights pointed toward the east, lights mounted on the front of the BMDs which had yet to turn to the right. Camellion's face reflected concern—*the Cubans are aware that something is amiss.*

"Get going," he said to Colonel Bin Maktum. "We'll take care of them and catch up with you—and tell Clayton to turn on the radio. Tell him I'll contact him in German. I don't want either the Cubans or the Yemenis to know what we're saying."

Nodding, Colonel Maktum disappeared into the turret and closed the hatch. Camellion stepped down from the turret platform but left the hatch open. He settled down in the gunner's seat, in back of Shukairy and, listening to Clayton pulling ahead in the other BMD, said to the three other men, "The Cubans are coming to investigate. We can knock out two of the cars before their crews realize what's going on."

"Ah, American, do not forget that they, too, can fire at us," al Auf said worriedly.

"Sure they can. What we have going for us is that they don't suspect the real truth. I intend to blow hell out of them before they get the chance to fire at us."

Camellion began to work the turret pedals, swinging the cannon to the right. He was forced to admit that the Soviet equipment was of excellent quality. Not only was the 50mm cannon simple in operation, the weapon was stabilized both in elevation and azimuth by means of gryoscopic equipment. That is, it maintained the angle and bearing set by the gunner, regardless of the maneuvering of the armored car.

Camellion picked up a 50mm APCR (Armor Piercing Composite Rigid) shell, shoved it into the cannon, closed and locked the breech, switched on the electric Venkitev sight and pressed his face to the large rectangular rubber cup, his left hand slowly turning the elevation wheel of the smooth bore gun.

"Sahib al Auf, turn on the radio," Camellion ordered. "After I fire the first shell, head for the airport and don't spare the horses."

"Horses?" al Auf's voice floated up to him. "We do not have horses. I do not understand."

"Head for the airport at full speed!"

Within three more seconds, Camellion saw the BMD coming at him from the right, the front of the armed vehicle presenting a narrow silhouette. The two headlights, mounted on the front glacis plate, didn't make aiming any easier, the bright glare almost blotting out the vehicle.

Voices poured out of the radio, the words in Cuban-type Spanish.

One man was saying, "One of our vehicles is headed toward the east. Has there been a change in orders?"

Came the reply, evidently from the commander of another BMD, "I don't know. I haven't received any change of orders. As far as I know, we are to stay in position by the fence. I'm moving to the south to investigate the noise I heard."

Another voice came in, the tone strident. "This is Captain Macuriges. Move your vehicles back into positions by the fence. I'm going to check with one of our other cars. If its crew doesn't know what's the source of the sound, I'll radio Comrade Tarasov at the command post. Wait! Wait!"

You won't wait long, damn you! Camellion moved the smooth bore cannon another few inches, centering the red dot in the ring sight on the foot-high glacis plate sloping in the turret deck.

Captain Macuriges's voice again. This time he was very excited.

"There's a large tear in the fence. A big rip. Someone

87

has entered from the outside. We can see the hole clearly in the light."

The Death Merchant knew that Captain Macuriges was in the approaching BMD that now was only 100 feet away. He knew because the spotlight raking the fence was mounted on the turret of that armored car.

"*¡Madre Dios!*" Macuriges yelled from the radio. "The car in front of us! Its cannon—"

The Death Merchant pulled the trigger underneath the handle of the breech, the BMD jumping back slightly as the 50mm cannon fired with a loud *BBBLLLAAMMMMM*, its muzzle flashing a foot-long tongue of fire.

God Himself couldn't have improved on the Death Merchant's aim. The armor-piercing shell bored through the 20mm armor just below the turret and exploded with another crashing roar, the blast killing Captain Sotero Macuriges and the other two crewmen instantly and ripping the vehicle apart. There was a fleeting flash of red, a ball of smoke and, while parts of the turret shot upward, the sides and front plates shot outward, much of the hot, twisted meal decorated with huge chunks of bloody flesh. If it had not been for the imperfection of the human eye, the same deficiency that makes "motion pictures" possible, Camellion would have seen two heads—Captain Macuriges's and Roberto Figueras's—rocketing toward the dark sky.

Immediately, Muhammad al Auf shifted gears and pressed down on the gas pedal. The armored car leaped forward, its speed increasing. Camellion began swinging the turret to the left, to line up the gunsight on another enemy BMD, then yelled down at Ahmed Shukairy to turn up the volume of the radio when he heard Clayton's voice speaking in German, coming out of the set. As the machine gunner, it was also Shukairy's job to handle the transceiver.

Once Ahmed had turned up the volume, Camellion had no trouble hearing what the CIA man was saying. "*Ich*—I can see Colonel Shaabi's car. It just pulled into the airport and is moving fast. I guess they heard the explosions. You want us to open fire on the son of a bitch?"

What a dumb question! Unable to use the mike attached to the radio, Camellion yelled down to Shukairy, "Tell him in English to open fire on Colonel Shaabi's car, but have him caution Bin Maktum about even coming close to the transport. That plane is our only transportation out of this hell hole."

"It shall be done, *Sahib* Gardner," Shakairy yelled back.

Furiously, the Death Merchant worked the pedals that moved the turret, one side of his mind cursing the Russians for not equipping the armored car with a modern electric mechanism to move the turret. It wasn't that the Soviet engineers didn't know how. It was the Soviet military mind which always took the pessimistic view. Why equip a BMD with an electric mechanism subject to failure at perhaps a crucial time? Safer to do the job manually.

Just as Camellion was about to grab in his sight one of the armored jobs to the left, Muhammad al Auf increased speed, the BMD leaping ahead at a top speed of 50 MPH. *Damnit!* The Death Merchant again moved the turret and the smooth bore weapon—*I'm only inches from centering in on the critter!*

BBLAMMMMMMMMMM! A tenth of a second later another terrific *BLAAAMMM!* During that infinitesimal shave of a second, the Death Merchant, his face pressed to the face cup of the sight, saw the muzzle flash flame from the cannon that had fired. The smooth-bore was on the same enemy BMD at which he was aiming.

The shell, falling short, had exploded only ten feet to the left of Camellion's vehicle, the terrific concussion a solid wave of noise that smashed at the Death Merchant and the three men with him in the armored car, the tenth-of-a-second torture comparable to a grenade exploding in the center's of one's brain.

The vehicle rocked on its torsion bar springs, and there was a loud ping-ping-ping sound from steel fragments raining against the left side of the speeding vehicle. Fortunately, none of the hot pieces fell through the open hatch of the turret.

"Ru'i Ullahi a'I rahmat t'sauq!" Ali Haddi yelled frantically.

You dumb sand crab! Allah's not going to have mercy and save you! But I'll try! Possessed of a deadly calm, Camellion moved the cannon. That's it! Center the right side. A bit more azimuth to correct the arc. A slight turn of the wheel. There! On target. *Do it!*

Camellion pulled the large trigger.

BBBLLLLLAAAMMMMMMM! The BMD jerked and shuddered. The smooth bore roared like a vengeful dragon and the APCR shell was on its way. Another flash of red, followed by a crashing detonation. The enemy armored car dissolved with all the speed and destruction of a large tin can blown apart by a stick of dynamite, the hot, twisted metal—now junk—flying in every direction possible, along with the torn apart bodies of the Cuban crewmen.

Camellion began to swing the turret and to search for another enemy BMD on his left flank.

It was not the best of days for Colonel Qahtan al Bin Shaabi and Major Abdul Jahiz, neither of whom had expected any trouble at Aden Airport. The first explosion, far to the west, had taken both men by surprise. Even so, during the following moments of astonishment, they still did not consider the possibility that the airport was being atacked. It was unthinkable. Who would dare attack Aden Airport? In the old days when the Yemen had been under control of Great Britain, the airport had been a commercial facility. The civil war had changed all of that. Now only Russian and East German aircraft landed at Aden Airport, which had been turned into a base for the South Yemen air force.

The explosions of the second and the third shell convinced Colonel Shaabi and Major Jahiz that the airport was under attack and that they were probably the prime targets.

Major Jahiz said bitterly to Colonel Shaabi, "And you were the one who insisted that an attempt on your life would be made at your home. *Haqui!* We were both outsmarted."

Hunched down in the rear seat, to the left, Colonel Shaabi shook his head vehemently and ordered the driver to speed up; then he said to Major Jahiz, "You're jumping to conclusions, Abdul. The attack is only coincidence with our being here. With the security we have, only our most trusted people knew when I would arrive at the airport. How could those stupid swine be after me? Why they're at the other end of the airport."

Jahiz hesitated, an indecisive expression on his cruel face.

"Perhaps you are correct, perhaps not. My fears will only be quieted when you are on the airplane and on your way to Libya." He leaned closer to Shaabi and lowered his voice to a whisper, "We must have a nuclear weapon. That madman Kaddafi has more than enough money to pay for a nuclear bomb."

Jahiz and Shaabi both glanced warily to the right, toward the west end of the airport, concern manifesting itself in their eyes.

"How could rebels have taken over some of our armor?" demanded Jahiz sullenly. "Somehow, they overpowered the crews. I tell you, something is very wrong."

"More speed, you fool!" Colonel al Bin Shaabi spit out at the driver, keeping his voice low to hide his apprehension. "I must board that plane."

It was imperative that Colonel Shaabi become airborne for more reasons than one. Not only was he to have a meeting with "Brother Colonel" Muammar Kaddafi, the mystic and madman boss of Libya, but how would it look to Kaddafi if rebel forces prevented Shaabi from taking off—right in his own back yard?

The big Buick had raced into the airport and was a hundred feet past the main gate when an enormous *BLAMMMMMM* crashed against the automobile. An APCR shell had exploded only fifteen feet to the right, the concussion making the vehicle rock and, seemingly, crushing the heads of the four men in an invisible vise of sound waves. Colonel Shaabi and Major Jahiz were tossed from one side to the other, both men cursing furiously in Arabic. Yaslai Q'id'll, the driver, fought the wheel as Djar Jaz, the bodyguard on the right in the front seat, was thrown against him.

"Goddamn them! They're firing at us!" yelled Shaabi in rage, his mouth twisting with hatred. "I'll have them slowly skinned alive for their pathetic attempt against me. I swear it."

The sinister Major Jahiz let Shaabi have a condescending look. There wasn't anything "pathetic" about a shell that had almost blown them off the face of the earth.

A man who never placed pride and prestige above common sense, Major Jahiz swung to Colonel Shaabi. "Order

Q'id'll to turn into the first hangar and drive to the rear," he said aggressively. "We will never be able to get to the plane. If they can't hit the car with a shell, they will try for the plane. It's so big a target they won't be able to miss."

"They are trying to kill us," acknowledged Shaabi.

"Tell him to turn," Jahiz said in a louder, more desperate voice. "Our lives are at stake. Our enemies are bearing deadly gifts that are coming closer."

"You're right," admitted Colonel Shaabi, surrendering. He leaned forward and barked at Yaslai Q'id'll, "Turn into the first hangar and go to the rear. Radio the other two armored cars and the carrier and tell them to intercept the camel dung firing at us. Instruct—"

Another thunderous explosion snipped off his words. But again Bin Maktum had missed the speeding red Buick. However, the shell had done plenty of damage, exploding between the rear of the BTR-60 armored troop carrier and the front of the last BMD in the column, the concussion slamming against the two vehicles and raining red-hot shrapnel against the front of the armored car and the back of the personnel carrier. The thirty terrified Yemeni soldiers in the BTR-60 were not harmed. They were protected by armor plate. Faris al Jesim and Atarit Idiz'q, in the driver's compartment of the armored car, were not. The armor plates over the windows had been raised and sharp, hot shrapnel shot through the two openings. Faris al Jesim let out a high piercing scream of agony when jagged bits of metal turned his face into bloody jelly, blinding him in the process. Idiz'q shrieked, bits and pieces of sharp shrapnel shredding his face, exposing the upper jawbone on both sides. His face dripping blood, he put up his hands and fell back. Pasi K'ovqui, the commander in the turret, was helpless and also in agony from shrapnel that had peppered his left lower leg, three of the chunks of iron embedded in the bone.

Out of control, the BMD swerved sharply to the left and actually increased speed. Faris al Jesim had passed out from pain and shock, had slumped over the wheel, and his foot was pressed down heavily on the gas pedal. The armored car tore forward.

Mechanics, technicians, and members of the i'Qrali could hardly believe their eyes when they saw the BMD roaring toward them. Frantically, they jumped to one side to give the mechanical monster a closer path. At the same time that the armored car crashed into the section of the hangar wall, just left of the wide entrance, slamming into it with the loud sound of tearing metal, Yaslai Q'id'll turned sharply to the left and speeded the red Buick into the hangar—just in time! Thirty feet behind the Buick another 50mm shell exploded, showering the area with hot metal, as well as the front of personnel carrier now turning to the right, the driver having recieved his instruction from Yaslai Q'id'll. The two men on motorcycles weren't about to commit suicide by attacking a couple of armored cars. They, too, swung to the left and started toward the entrance of the second hangar. The first BMD in line and the BTR-60 personnel carrier headed for the two armored cars that were closing in on the front of the airport.

Another series of shell explosions, one right after the other. The gunner in the BMD that had been with Colonel Shaabi's column had swung his cannon very quickly. But he fired too quickly at the first enemy car driven by Marlon Clayton, who had closed the front windows in the driver's compartment by lowering the armor plate and was driving by looking through the wide-angle periscope. The shell roared off thirty feet behind Clayton's vehicle, leaving a small crater in the asphalt. A fraction of a second later, Bin Maktum, in Clayton's armored car, fired, and the Death Merchant pulled the trigger of the 50mm cannon in the turret of the vehicle that Muhammad al Auf was driving. This time Bin Maktum didn't miss. His shell hit the other BMD dead center in the driver's compartment. A giant *BLAMMMMMMMM!* A flash of fire and another explosion that turned the Yemeni BMD into ten thousand pieces of ripped apart junk. The massive turret, now in three twisted sections, rocketed sixty feet into the air, came down, bounced hard, came down again and rolled into one of the Mikoyan-Gurevich MiG 23S fighter planes parked one hundred feet in front of the first hangar, shaking the jet plane when it hit the tail assembly.

In the meanwhile, the Death Merchant's uncanny aim paid off, his shell exploding the last armored car that had been parked by the west side fence.

The Death Merchant's small force closed in, Camellion methodically sighting in on the personnel carrier. He knew

his was a small command, and it was a dark one . . . a
dark command of pure destruction.

Now Belial can take over. . . .

☐ EIGHT ☐

Having the advantage very often means the difference between life and death, and the Death Merchant and his
force of eight did have the upper hand. For how long was
anyone's guess. Almost! Camellion's analysis was conclu-
sive: the Yemenis had been caught unprepared. But they
wouldn't remain disorganized indefinitely. He and his
people would have to get on board the transport before the
enemy did some quick addition and came up with the correct answer, with the realization that escape in the airplane
took precedence over killing the colonel. Once the enemy
got wise, they'd fire on the aircraft—*blow it apart before
we could even get aboard.*

Camellion laughed softly. *All Allah would say, "If the
mother-in-law is quarrelsome, divorce the daughter." As
Camellion would say, "If the enemy has the firepower to
blow up the airplane, get rid of the firepower."*

Through the periscope, above the faceplate of the cannon sight, he saw that Marlon Clayton, ahead of his own
vehicle by 150 feet, was cutting his BMD sharply to the
right, in preparation to parking a hundred feet in front of
the Soviet airplane that had been readied for a takeoff.
Camellion was close enough by now to see that the plane
was an Antonov-26, a craft that had two Ivchenko
A1-24A single-shaft turbo-props and had been designated
"Coke" by NATO. One of the world's most numerous
transports, the AN 24 was primarily a civil craft and was
used extensively in Communist countries; and it wasn't a
fast plane, having a typical cruising speed of 430 KM/H
(or 267MPH). *But it's more than enough to get us to the
mountains—but only if the Saudis have made the air drop!*

Camellion yelled down at Muhammad al Auf, "Cut over to the left. We're going to take out those jet fighters." He barked orders at Ahmed Shukairy, who was directly below him, hunched over the machine gun, "Ahmed, when we get close enough rake the hangars."

Mechanics and other workers were trying desperately to shove the Mig 23S fighter jets back into the hangars, pushing against their wings and tail assemblies. It was an absolute must that these sleek fighters be destroyed. Once Camellion and his people were in the air, a single Mig 23 would be able to being them down with either cannon fire or air-to-air missiles.

Ahmed Shukairy opened fire with the PKMT machine gun while the Death Merchant was bringing the 50mm cannon to bear on one of the jet fighters. A hail of 7.62 rimmed type 54R projectiles spit from the muzzle of the PKMT at a velocity of 2,755 feet per second. *Zip-zip-zip-zip.* Thirteen men died instantly, knocked over by the steel-cored spitzer-shaped projectiles. *Clang-clang-clang, clang.* Big slugs hit two jet fighters and an instant line of holes appeared in the fuselages. The clear bubble covering of one jet, pushed back from over the cockpit, fell apart from the impact of projectiles. Other bullets found the instrument panel of another plane and dials were turned into junk. More projectiles found the fuel tanks and the fighter exploded. One moment it was an airplane. The next instant there was a huge *WHOOMMMM*, a giant ball of red-orange fire, then a lot of black smoke and parts of aircraft flying all over the place.

The Death Merchant pulled the trigger. The cannon roared, the 50-millimeter shell exploding between the port side of one jet and the starboard side of another, the big blast crumpling the ends of the stubby wings.

Camellion yanked open the breech, saw the automatic extracter pull out the hot shell casing and heard the casing clang loudly when it hit the metal floor of the turret well.

He yelled down at al Auf as he turned and spun the wheel control of the turret hatch, "Drive north. We'll rake the planes, then turn around, go south and we'll work over the hangars and the control tower."

Marlon Clayton's vehicle had reached its destination, Clayton jerking to a stop about a 150 feet in front of the twin engined Antonov-26. In such a position, its front facing the south, the armored car's cannon and machine gun could fire either south, or, if the turret was turned, west or north. Toward the west—why bother? The Death Merchant was taking care of the northern salient. Bin Maktum decided to concentrate on the blue and gold Control Tower, on the roof of which Yemeni militiamen and members of the *Bayyi'l'ali* the South Yemen Bureau of Intelligence, were struggling to get a twin-barrelled 23mm automatic ZU-23 AA gun into operation. But the gun's purpose was to fire at aircraft overhead, not at armored vehicles on the ground. There was simply no way the frantic Yemenis could depress the barrels to get the necessary trajectory. There wasn't any way the HEI armor-piercing shells could reach the BMD.

From inside the tower, the Yemenis opened fire with a DShK-38 heavy machine gun, a cloud of 12.7mm projectiles striking the front and the top of the BMD Clayton was driving, scores of ricochets screaming. It was like being in a dark green house during a hail storm, with a dozen Banshees wailing a weird warning of approaching death. Death came. . . .

BLAMMMMMMMM! Colonel Bin Maktum's shell bored into the northwest corner of the north side of the Control Tower. Another monstrous *BLAAMMM,* a flash of fire and eighty percent of the control tower flew outward into the hot *shamāl*. And mangled bodies soared and tumbled with the ripped wreckage.

Like a large broken toy, the AA gun toppled downward, hit the ground, bounced and rolled over on its mounting. Where the tower had been there wasn't anything but foundation, burning debris and a lot of black smoke crawling up to the sky and the screams and cries of the wounded.

Turning the turret, Colonel Bin Maktum snapped orders in Arabic at Rashid al-Khaima, "You can fire at the last hangar. There's plenty of room. There's no danger of hitting the airplane."

"Yes, I can see clearly," al-Khaima said happily. "See what they are trying to do? They think they're going to set up heavy machine guns and they're wheeling out a large mortar. I'll put a stop to that nonsense."

As happy as a drunken hillbilly with a credit card, Rashid al-Khaima began firing. . . .

Colonel Qahtan al Bin Shaabi's red buick had reached the end of the long hangar and he and Major Jahiz and the two other men had taken refuge in a prefabricated double-walled office toward the northeast corner of the building. Reports kept pouring in to Captain Ibri l'Nurtoki, the commander of the airport, on a walkie-talkie. The news was all bad. Those Russian fighter jets that hadn't been exploded were burning. The Control Tower had been destroyed and thirty-four men killed. Militiamen had attempted to set up two heavy machine guns and a large Soviet 24 Omm mortar. The 24Omm was one of the largest in the world. Mounted on two large wheels, the weapon looked more like a cannon that a "stovepipe," and it did have awesome power, firing a 100kg bomb, three rounds per minute to a maximum range of 8km.

The militiamen had not succeeded with either the mortar or the machine guns. Rashid al-Khaima had killed every man around the weapons.

Beside himself with rage and frustration, Colonel al Bin Shaabi almost shouted at Major Abdul Jamiz who was equally as thwarted and helpless. "Do something, Abdul!" snarled Shaabi, who was crouched under a table with Jamiz and Captain l'Nurtoki. He glared at Major Jamiz. "How is this going to look to the Soviet advisers and to Kaddafi?"

Sweat rolling down his face into his beard, Major Jamiz turned his cruel eyes to Captain l'Nurtoki who looked like a man about to have a heart attack. "Haven't you any tanks available?" demanded Jamiz. "I thought half a dozen T-72 tanks were stationed here?"

"Sir, they were," replied l'Nurtoki in a quivering voice, but they were taken to the city for the Victory Day parade, on Colonel Shaabi's orders. The tanks have not yet been brought back to the airport."

Major Jamiz looked accusingly at Colonel Shaabi who was turning purple in the face. Before either man could speak, there was a gigantic blast in front of the 200-foot long hangar and a sea of fire poured thirty feet through the wide front entrance.

Well . . . kiss my transmission! The Death Merchant grinned like a hungry wolf that had just spotted a fat calf. It had been a long shot but his shell had hit the target, had hit the fuel tank truck. Ten thousand gallons of jet fuel had exploded into a vast ocean of flame, giving Camellion the impression that a tremendous dam holding back the Lake of Hell had burst. As though alive, the fire spread, tendrils of fire creeping and flowing across the asphalt, eating, burning in all directions.

Marlon Clayton raced the BMD ahead of the fire, the three tires on the left side of the car rolling through the forward streams of the fire.

The Death Merchant yelled at al Auf, "We'll rake the hangars, then go to the port side of the airplane." Then he half turned and shouted to Ali Haddi, "Use your automatic rifles; fire through one of the side ports."

Below Camellion, Ahmed Shukairy shouted up at the Merchant of quick and violent death, *"Sahib* Gardner, we must hurry! We cannot continue to fool them indefinitely about the plane."

"We're in the hands of Allah!" Camellion replied with bitter sarcasm. He shoved a shell into the open mouth of the breech, closed and locked the breech, sighted in on the second hanger and pulled the trigger. The big blast, sounding like thunder tossed to earth by a vindictive god, destroyed three tractors used to pull aircraft out of and into the hangar, killed nine militiamen and sent fifty other men scurrying from the rear of the hangar. Five of Ali Haddi's AKS-74 projectiles killed three of the fleeing men.

The Death Merchant managed to get off four more 50mm shells, one of them blowing apart the Soviet 240 millimeter mortar, by the time al Auf had driven past the front of the last hangar and was executing a sharp turn that would take the armored vehicle to the left side of the Antonov-26 short-haul transport.

Most of the hangars were burning in the front, the flames crackling, the thick black smoke stinking of wood, paint, metal, fabric, plastic, rubber, and roasting flesh. At times the smoke was so thick, depending on the capriciousness of the shamal, that Muhammad al Auf and Marlon Clayton could hardly see where they were going. But the last run had been made and now it was time for the final thrust.

Camellion leaned down and said in a loud voice to Ahmed Shukairy, "Get on the radio and tell Clayton to be prepared to move when we give him the word. Tell him for now to remain parked where he is in front of the plane. The crew might still be on board. I'll have to get inside the craft and see. Have you got all that, Ahmed?"

"Yes, I understand completely," Shukairy replied and reached for the mike.

The Death Merchant yelled again at al Auf, "Park us close to the door on the port side. Get within six feet of the door. I'll jump from the top of the car."

An expert driver, it took al Auf only a few minutes to take the armored car to the left side of the Soviet transport plane and to park it in the position desired by Camellion. No sooner had al Auf stopped the car than Camellion began checking two 9mm Beretta auto-pistols and Shukairy turned around in the machine gunner's seat and stared up at him.

"*Sahib* Gardner, I conveyed your instructions to Rashid," Shukairy reported. "Rashid said to inform you that men are on the airplane. He and Clayton saw several faces behind the glass of the cockpit."

"Damnit. I suspected as much," Camellion said, his expression becoming fierce. "OK. Ahmed, you cover me with an A-R. Let's pop open the hatch and have a look."

Camellion spun the hatch-cover wheel, watching as the round hatch swung back and opened the turret to the smoky night. He said to Ali Haddi, "Ali, once I leave the turret, you stand up with Ahmed and keep a lookout. If you shoot at anyone, make damn sure that one of your slugs doesn't strike the plane."

Feeling that he had just booked passage on the Titanic, he stuck his head through the hatch. The port side door of the AN-26 was only a short seven feet away, its bottom a foot higher than the top of the turret of the armored car. Curved inward to fit into the metal fuselage of the craft, the door was closed.

And probably locked from the inside!

Camellion dropped back into the turret, shoved the two Beretta pistols in his waistband and asked Ali Haddi to hand him one of the automatic rifles lying flat on the floor of the turret well. "A spare magazine, too. I'll have to blow away the metal from the lock."

99

Ali Haddi muttered something in Arabic (all Camellion could make out was *Ullahi*—Allah). Camellion accepted the AKS A-R from Haddi, thrust himself up through the hatch opening, brought up the automatic rifle and again looked at the closed door of the Soviet aircraft. Then he looked at the small windows set forward from the door. Had he seen a face at once of the windows?

No doubt they're waiting for me. Time's a'wastin'! Do it!

He brought up the AKS, pushed off the safety, switched the firing lever to full automatic, aimed at the section of the door around the square inset in which the handle was set and pulled the trigger. The whang of the sharp-nosed projectiles, cutting through the aluminum around the hatch, was lost in the roaring of the AKS.

The projectiles having shot away the inside latch, the door automatically swung open. The impact of the projectiles, in shooting away the latch, had forced the door open a few inches. The weight of the door, tilted at an upward angle, due to the incline of the plane, did the rest. The door hung back on its hinges.

Ahmed Shukairy rubbed his chin fiercely and stared at the Death Merchant. "Ah, *Sahib* Gardner, how are you going to get inside the airplane? They will be waiting for you."

Pulling the Beretta pistols from his waistband, Camellion did some rapid, hard thinking. The cables to the rudder and the tail flaps were in the bottom of the fuselage. If the windows were shot out on the port side, the slugs would either break the windows on the starboard side or else bore through the starboard fuselage.

"Ahmed, how good a shot are you?" Camellion asked.

"I am very good." The rest of the Royalist rebel's answer surprised the Death Merchant. "Ali Haddi is better."

Admiring Shurkairy's answer, Camellion looked down. "*Sahib* Haddi. When I get on top of the car, you cover me. When I tell you to, shoot out the windows on this side. Think you can do it without wounding the plane?"

The Arab's eyes glittered slyly. "I know I can, *Sahib* Gardner."

"Okay. Come on up."

It was a tight squeeze, but Ali Haddi managed to step onto the turret platform and stand up tall through the

100

opening and cover the plane as the Death Merchant pulled himself up through the open hatch and scrambled to the top of the armored vehicle. He pulled both Beretta auto-pistols and the single word popped out of his mouth—"Shoot!"

Ali Haddi's SKA-74 snarled, the 5.45mm projectiles smashing through the glass of the windows, the slugs zipping through the interior of the craft and hitting some of the other windows on the starboard side.

The Death Merchant, his left foot pushing against the outer rim of the turret, leaped from the armored car through the open door of the Soviet transport, twisting his body in such a way that he would land facing the port side of the plane. If any of the crew were waiting, his only hope was that Ali Haddi's terrific firing would keep them down and give him the edge.

The Russian pilot, the copilot, and the engineer, who also functioned as the radioman and navigator, had left the cockpit and had crept to the cargo hold, which had been fitted with half a dozen plush seats on each side and a refrigerator to keep tea, milk, and other nonalcoholic drinks cold. Toward the rear of the plane were benches, on both port and starboard, bolted to the wall. These benches were for Colonel Shaabi's private bodyguard.

Vladimir Popski, the pilot, was crouched between two of the seats on the starboard side, a Stechkin machine pistol in his ham of a right hand. Oleg Paseyreo, the copilot, and Alutin Kikrov, the engineer, were between seats on the port side. Like Popski, both were veterans of the Soviet air force, had been attached to the GRU for three years, and were armed with Vitmorkin 16-shot machine pistols.

Camellion had calculated correctly: the three Russians had not expected an automatic rifle to start firing through the windows on the port side. Fearing for their lives, all the three could do was to stay down and hope for the best. They didn't know it, but they might as well have been whistling past the graveyard of their dreams. They were doomed to die without even hearing their own screams.

I should have the inside of my head examined! A Beretta auto-pistol in each hand, the Death Merchant headed for the carpet, his body jerked inward to keep the impact from his tailbone and landed on the fleshy part of his buttocks, his eyes darting from side to side, analyzing the view of the interior. *Good! No one is on the benches. Either they're down between the seats or still in the cockpit. If they're in the cockpit, we're all as good as dead. I'll never be able to snuff them without wrecking the instrument panel.*

He scooted on his butt to the rear of the last seat on the starboard side and, wishing that he had a couple of .44 AMPS, began pumping 9mm Parabellum projectiles around the end of the red velvet covering. *Bring 'em out! Make 'em return the fire. Find out their positions!*

None of the Russians had seen Camellion's body rocket through the port side doorway of the plane. Now, hearing his two Berettas cracking, they knew that either one or two of the enemy, whom they presumed to be Yementi Royalist rebels, was inside the plane.

During that very very short space of time, Alutin Kikrov was the first of the three to make a fatal mistake. There was a 2.41 second lag-time on the part of Al Haddi who had stopped firing and was again swinging the A-R to the left, his intention to again slam slugs through the now shot-out windows.

Kikrov reared up only a few inches at the precise moment that Haddi started firing. Very quickly the Russian ducked back down when he heard the roaring of the automatic rifle. He was a shave of a second too late. A single 5.56mm projectile struck him several inches above the right ear with an audible thud. Kikrov's peaked cap jumped six inches and so did the top of his skull, some of the hair and bone fragments and brain matter splattering over the side of Oleg Paseyreo, the copilot, who let out a strangled cry of disgust and alarm and, for a moment, forgot all about Camellion in the rear of the AN-26 transport. Reflexively, Paseyreo, who was closest to the aisle between the seats, jerked back from the dead Kikrov who was falling toward him. In doing so, Paseyreo exposed part of his back and left side. Camellion had him! Two of the Death Merchant's 9mm Parabellum slugs caught him. One bullet struck him in the left hip and came to rest in his colon. The second slug shot between his ribs and dug a bloody tunnel through his lungs before it struck a rib on his right side, deflected downward and

102

came to a halt in the upper portion of his liver. Rapidly dying, Paseyreo fell unconscious in the aisle.

Camellion, who had reloaded the Beretta in his left hand, resorted to an old trick, one that sometimes worked but never backfired.

He said in a loud voice, "YOU CHARGE UP THE LEFT WITH THE UZI! I'LL TAKE THE LEFT, RASHID, USE GRENADES!"

The frantic Vladimir Popski—no longer thinking clearly—leaned around the end of the seat and fired off a stream of slugs from his Stechkin machine pistol. The slugs buried themselves in the bulkhead door to the small storage compartment in the rear of the airplane—all except one. It went all the way through and struck a part of the fin structure of the tail assembly.

The Death Merchant, who had reared up from behind the last seat on the starboard side, fired seven rounds into the back of the seat protecting Popski. Three slugs ripped through the red velvet and the padding, hit springs and were stopped. Two bullets zinged all the way through and missed Popski. They slammed into the rear of the back seat in front of him. Two other jacketed hollow point projectiles sliced through the seat and these two caught Popski. One broke his left clavicle. The second bullet struck him high in the right arm and broke the humerus bone. The Russian let out a loud cry of pain, shock, and terror; a signal to the Death Merchant that he had won. Camellion dropped flat to the carpet and fired underneath the seats with the Beretta in his right hand, all three of his slugs popping Popski who had fallen to the floor. A bullet in the lower left side of Popski's neck! A slug in the hip! A third bullet in the Russian's left outer thigh! Popski was finished, his life's blood spurting from his neck and strangling the scream gurgling up in his throat.

Hearing gunfire far to starboard and return AKS fire from the armored car parked to port, Camellion shoved full magazines into the Berettas, got up from the floor and moved up the aisle toward the cockpit. Once he saw that there were only three crewmen and that they were frigid cold cuts, he raced for the cockpit, opened the door and looked in. The compartment was empty.

He turned, started for the rear of the plane and, almost slipping in a pool of blood soaking into the rug of the aisle, reached the side of the open port door. The firing had stopped, but Camellion believed in being cautious. Ali Haddi might have a nervous trigger finger—*"Elated over the trigger!" as Bin Maktum would say!*

He shouted, "Ali, don't fire. It's *Sahib* Gardner. Answer me."

"I hear you," came the reply.

The Death Merchant leaned around the open doorway. "Tell Shukairy to get on the radio and order Clayton to move the car to the port side. Then all of you get into the plane; jump from the top of the closet car."

Ali Haddi looked puzzled, like a man who had just discovered his legs had been cut off below the knees.

"But, *Sahib* Gardner," Haddi said, "this vehicle must also be moved. The tail of the airplane will catch on it."

"I'll rudder around it," Camellion said, an urgent note in his voice which was very suddenly harsh and ruthless. "Hurry up and do what I told you. We've got to get out of here. MOVE, MAN!"

Ali Haddi blinked in confusion and dropped down into the turret. The Death Merchant ran back to the cockpit, settled down in the pilot's seat and glanced over the instrument panel, any number of side thoughts skipping around in his mind—*The USSR spends $600 million a year on terrorism, directly or indirectly. USA—California—ironic! California has executed one criminal in 20 years, but the criminals have executed 30,000 victims during that same period. No wonder we have crime! Can I fly this pile of Russian nuts and bolts? I have to! Damn! REMEMBER! You have to!*

He made a pretakeoff check. Flight controls! He tested them; they did have free and easy movement. Fuel selector valve for both engines. Elevator trim wheel—set for takeoff. He noticed the wheel set in the panel, beneath his right hand, had a small white line on it. He positioned the dials to read TAKEOFF (in Russian). The ignition switches! *Turn them on. Now the throttle.* The black knob in the center of the panel. *Damnit, be careful of carb heat. Push the throttle forward until the tachometer reads 1700 rpm.*

The props of the airplane were now spinning, the craft shaking and shuddering like an animal on a leash. Camellion's hands moved over the instrument panel. Vacuum! Check it—4.6 to 5.4 inches. Magnetos: check. Turn the key to the left detent, then note the rpm drop by turning the key to BOTH. Use the same procedure with the right detent. *Uh-huh. The drop should not be more than 175 rpm with these turboprop jobs—I think! And watch the carb heat, stupid! The hell with the nav charts. I have to get us off the ground first.*

He glanced through the slanted glass of the cockpit. Marlon Clayton had moved the armored car and the long runway was clear.

Almost clear. . . . Five hundred feet in front of the airplane was the smoking wreckage of one of the BMDs, the burnt corpse of a Cuban draped over the rim of the turret, the man's blackened arms hanging downward.

It will take a triple miracle to get us out of this mess! I should have stayed at home and played chess. Uh-huh. And God bless the Martian navy! He did some more looking and checking. Primer: *Yeah, on three strokes.* Throttle open one-eighth of an inch. All switches on. Oil pressure okay. . . . He had already set the altimeter. Now do the DG, the directional gyro, and set it to the compass. . . . He was revving up the engines when he detected a man coming up behind him and heard a voice say, "They are coming aboard this plane, *Sahib* Gardner." Ahmed Shukairy sounded as nervous as a new bride about to slide into bed beside hubby. "Any special instructions?"

Marlon Clayton stuck his head through the compartment door, his red-rimmed eyes fixing themselves on the Death Merchant. "Are we ready to take off, Gardner? We'd better be! I think the Yemenis are wise. A group of them have been trying to rush us from the hangars, but we've cut them down so far. Now we're running out of ammo."

"We're running out of time as well," Camellion said with brutal honesty. He turned in the pilot's seat and looked up at the two men. "Ahmed, get back there and tell everyone to hang on and to keep firing from the windows—and watch that open door when we take off, or you fellows will be sucked right out. Get going! When all our people are inside, come back and let me know."

Shukairy turned and hurried back to the main part of the plane. The Death Merchant said to Clayton, "Park your butt in the copilot's seat. I'm going to need your help."

The CIA man's eyebrows lifted in alarm. "Me? I

105

thought you could fly this damned thing! I can't even fly a Piper Cub!"

The Death Merchant swung back toward the instrument panel, his stare stabbing at the tachometer. *Good! 2,600 rpm.*

"I can fly this baby," said Camellion almost angrily. "But we have an unusual situation here. I—"

"'An unusual situation!'" fumed Clayton. "That's the damndest understatement of the year!"

"I need you to shove in the throttle and to release the wheel brakes. I'll tell you when."

"First you'd better show me *how!*" Taking some unusually powerful puffs from the cigarette in the side of his mouth, Clayton entered the cockpit and sat down heavily in the copilots seat, a frozen expression on his face.

The Death Merchant had revved up the engines and pushed in the throttle as far as he dared. To push in the throttle more while the brakes were on, would case the plane to nose over. Visually, the Death Merchant made a last minute check on the instruments. He looked at the artificial horizon, or attitude indicator. Beneath the A/H was the DG, the directional gyro. To the left of the A/H was the airspeed indicator. The altimeter was to the right of the ASI. Next to the altimeter was the turn-and-bank indicator, then the VSI, or vertical speed indicator.

Camellion stared at several dozen more instruments. Everything was in order.

"I said that you had better show me how," Clayton said. He leaned sideways toward Camellion, then glanced from him to the control panel.

"This is the brake handle." Camellion patted a rectangular-shaped handle that was below the radio, set vertically so that its outer edge protruded outward from the panel. "When I tell you, wrap your hand inside the handle and pull it out all the way."

Ahmed Shukairy, who had rushed back to the cockpit and stuck his head through the door, interupted. "*Sahib* Gardner, all our men are in the plane."

"Very well. Get back to them, Ahmed," said Camellion. A great calmness, an inner ataraxy, had come over him. It was really very simple. Either they would succeed in taking off, or they would not. If they were successful and got airborne, there wouldn't be anything to worry about—for the moment. If they failed and crashed, then they'd go up in flames and smoke. There would be one big bang. Death would come so fast they wouldn't have time to know it, time to suffer—*In which case we'll all be stone cold dead and fried to ashes in South Yemen. Still nothing to worry about. After all, all men die. It's only a question of when. Yes . . . it's all relative. . . .*

The Death Merchant touched the throttle and looked at Clayton.

"This is the throttle. You push it in. I'll tell you when and how fast to do it."

"That's all there is to it?" Clayton sounded relieved. "Is there anything else?"

"This lever here," Camellion said. He put his hand on a six-inch long handle protruding from underneath the center of the instrument panel. "This retracts the landing gear. When I say pull it out, you pull it out."

"Let's get on with it," Clayton said nervously. "From the sound of the firing, our time is up."

Settling down in the seat, the Death Merchant gripped the control wheel with both hands and placed his feet firmly on the rudder pedals. Even above the roaring of the two Ivchenko turbojet engines, he and Clayton could hear the furious snarling of automatic weapons, both from inside and outside the Soviet transport plane.

Now! "Pull out the brake handle," the Death Merchant shouted. "Pull it out all the way."

Marlon Clayton did as directed. The aircraft moved forward. The Death Merchant pushed the control wheel forward to get the tail off the ground and jammed his foot down on the right rudder pedal, desperately hoping that his purely mental calculations were accurate and that the portside horizontal stabilizer would miss the armored car. He glanced at the ASI—*airspeed: 106 mph.*

One-thousand-and-one! One-thousand-and-one! Two seconds! That's it! We've missed the BMD. Or we'd have heard the big slam seconds ago!

Still holding the control wheel in the same position, he pushed down on the left rudder pedal and straightened out the airplane, now thinking of the wrecked armored car directly in front of the Soviet transport plane. The damned BMD appeared to be so close that he had the impression he could reach out and touch the blackened metal and the charred corpse draped over the turret rim.

"Push the throttle all the way in!" shouted the Death Merchant to Clayton, who instantly reached out and shoved in the knob.

The two turboshaft tirboprop engines screamed with unleashed power.

At that moment the lights on both sides of the long runway went out. Darkness! As though someone had dropped a black blanket down over the glass of the cockpit.

Well, fudge! Either the fire at the airport had damaged the power system or else the Yemeni dumbbells had finally gotten some smarts and had turned off the runway lights. Yet there was no stopping. *This is it! Success or failure! Life or death! The hell with it in spades. What is—IS! What will be, will be!*

The Death Merchant pulled back firmly on the control wheel, moving it and the column, to which the wheel was attached, toward him. The nose of the (Oleg K.) Antonov-26 lifted sharply, so steeply that Camellion and Clayton were pushed back against the seats.

"Pull out the landing gear lever!" yelled Camellion. "Now—all the way!"

Clayton's left hand shot out, and he pulled out the handle, all the while muttering, "Oh boy! Oh boy! Oh boy!"

The AN-26 climbed steeply into the early morning sky, the four large wheels of the landing gear slowly receding into the wheel-wells.

The wheels missed the burned out armored car by only a foot and six-point-four inches. . . .

☐ NINE ☐

Heaven was an Antonov-26 Soviet transport plane escaping into the black sky, climbing, climbing, gaining altitude with the swiftness of an attacking hawk—400 feet . . . 600 . . . 700 feet . . . 1,000 feet. At 1,350 feet altitude, the Death Merchant throttled back to relieve the strain on the turboprop engines, and he cut the rate of climb by a third. Nine minutes later he levelled off at 10,-500 feet and set the plane on a course that headed the airplane north by northeast, in the direction of the Jabal Mahrat, the mountain range that began 180 miles northeast of Aden.

The sweat of tension dripping from Marlon Clayton's face, he watched the Death Merchant adjust the aileron and wing flaps and the elevator trim-tabs, the CIA man marvelling at the calmness displayed by the man who called himself "Noah Gardner," at the gentleness of his hands on the controls—like a skilled horseman who knew his mount. By God! It was uncanny! Abnormal! Didn't Gardner have any nerves?

"Well, we made it! We're not dead!" Clayton found that his voice sounded weak and strained even to himself. "We're damned lucky, I tell you." He pulled a handkerchief from his left rear pocket and wiped his face.

"You'll never know how lucky," Camellion said, with a slightly bitter smile, his voice as cool as his movements. "I'm not sure, but I think we took off in a crosswind. I had to gamble that we had the power to grab the sky. We're still a long way from Safe City. You had better go back—"

Camellion paused and glanced around when he sensed that a man had just stepped through the narrow doorway into the cockpit. The man was Colonel Bin Maktum whose clothes smelled of smoke, sweat, and burnt cordite and whose face looked as though it were coated with soot.

Camellion glanced up at the Saudi Arabian intelligence agent.

"Are the men safe?" Camellion then turned back to the instrument panel, concerned about the turboprop engines. They sounded smooth enough—*but am I getting the correct revolutions per minute?* He looked at the tachometer. *Yeah, it looks okay.*

"Every man is still blessed with health," Bin Maktum said. "Every man but Khumayyis ibn Rimthan. While he was running from the armored car he was in the BMD parked close to the plane, he caught a bullet high in the leg. We managed to get him on board, but we haven't been able to stop the bleeding. Sa'id Al'amman is also hurt. He is not hurt seriously."

"Where did he catch a slug?" Camellion asked.

"He didn't. While you were roaring the engines, I and al-Khaima and Al'amman fastened the port door with several leather sling straps from the Soviet automatic rifles. Sa'id slipped and cut his left arm on a piece of jagged aluminum sticking out around the shot-off latch. The wound is not serious." Bin Maktum paused. "We must find out if the drop was made to Ali Sa'galli and his men in the Jabal Mahrat. If the drop wasn't made. . . ." He let his voice trail off . . . an implication of doom that dangled into nothingness.

"Gardner, you haven't turned on the navigation lights, have you?" Clayton's eyes widened and a startled look flashed over his face.

"No, and I'm not going to," Camellion said, somewhat amused. "We don't have to worry about another plane running into us, not over South Yemen."

Colonel Bin Maktum was very serious. "We must assume that fighter jets will follow us. They will come from the base at Wusadi, and the pilots will be Russian."

"We'll have a half-hour before they can even begin to catch up to us," Camellion explained. He switched on the radar located in the nose radome, relieved that the screen above the center of the instrument panel and the operation of the set were similar to a Hughes APG-63 R-S. "As soon as we contact the Company station in Riyadh, I'll take us down to five hundred feet until we reach the edge of the

110

mountains. The jets will never find us at that low level, and they won't be able to do much searching once we reach the mountains."

Clayton rolled his eyes. "I hope to God you know how to work that radar! I'd just as soon be shot as scattered all over a mountain."

"Not to worry," Camellion said with a lilt. "God protects drunks and fools and we're cold sober. We'll make it, provided the creek doesn't rise and the corn stays dry. On the other hand, you might not make it. You're the only one in your right mind!"

Bin Maktum looked startled. Clayton drew back in surprise. "How in hell do you figure that, Gardner." He felt that the Death Merchant was skirting on the edge of grim humor, but he wasn't sure.

"It's the left side of the brain that does the work if a person's right-handed. When a person is left-handed, it's the right side of the brain that does the work. You're left-handed, Clayton. Therefore, you're the only person aboard in his 'right' mind."

Clayton looked relieved. Bin Maktum smiled. Camellion checked the compass. The AN-26 was on course. He switched on the automatic pilot, checked its TACAN, then settled back, sighed, and studied the radio transmitter, a 720-channel set that had low, medium, high, and very high frequencies covering from 30 to 300 kHz, 300 to 3,000 kHz, and 3,000 to 30,000 kHz, respectively. The VHF band was from 30,000 to 300,000 kHz.

Camellion pushed his tongue along the inside of his lower lip. Well now. . . . The low, medium, and high frequencies were susceptible to interference from natural radiation, such as sunspots or thunderstorms. On the other side of the coin, Very High Frequencies were remarkably free from static interference. However, they had a different problem: shortness of range, especially when used between ground stations. The High Frequency waveband was fine for long distance, say from New York to London, or from Chicago to Moscow, but only when conditions were good and there wasn't too much radiation.

I don't want to contact Moscow—only Riyadh. It's not more than 800 miles to the northeast.

Choosing the Medium band, Camellion switched on the set and turned the dial to the prearranged set—2,469 kHz.

111

He then picked up the mike and began to speak in a strange language, an odd language that sounded as though each word had no more than two syllables.

Bin Maktum and Marlon Clayton didn't know that the Death Merchant was speaking the language of the American Mohawk Indian. However, they did have a good idea how the system of communication worked. "Gardner's" words would be picked up from the air, relayed to a computer in the CIA station in the American Embassy in Riyadh and "deciphered"—translated/transcribed into English. The computer would change the return message—from the radio operator—in English into the Mohawk language and send it to the radio, which would disperse it into the air waves. Should the Soviet station in Aden or anywhere else pick up the message, the Russians wouldn't be able to understand it.

Five times the Death Merchant repeated the message.

Several minutes passed before the reply came, the message lasting for one minute and forty-seven seconds. Three times the voice synthesizer of the computer repeated the message. At length, Camellion turned off the transmitter/receiver.

"Did the Saudis make the drop to Ali Sa'galli and his men, or didn't they?" demanded Clayton, unable to stand the suspense.

"Right on schedule." Camellion grinned at Clayton, then at Bin Maktum. "Ten tons of food, medicine, ammo, and arms."

He reached down and pulled a pad and ballpoint pen from a side pocket attached to the pilot's seat.

Marlon Clayton grinned and rubbed his hands together. "Good Now we don't have to fly the Empty Quarter and die of thirst waiting for choppers to find us."

"We can't make bricks without clay," Bin Maktum said steadily. "Was the special radio and the operator dropped to Sa'galli?"

The Death Merchant, writing on the pad, didn't look around as he spoke. "Yes, both the 'Black Box' and a Saudi agent trained to operate it. Furthermore, Ali Sa'galli and his people are expecting us. They know we're in a Soviet plane; we won't have any problems. All I have to do is use the navigation equipment to figure out these coordinates. Once we have that I'll know where to take this baby down. To coin an old phrase, we'll have it made in the shade."

"Or crash in the darkness if the jet fighters find us," Clayton said gloomily. He thrust out his left hand. "Give me the coordinates. I'm damned good at navigation. I learned it when I was in the U.S. Navy. I was still wet behind the ears." He jerked his head around toward the engineer-navigator table in the small section behind the copilot's chair. "Everything is there that I need. A CR series computer, a navigator's rule, the works." He accepted the slip of paper from Camellion. "It's a damned good thing we brought silk maps of the Mahrat Mountains with us or we'd be up stink creek."

His eyes on the A/H, the Death Merchant didn't speak. The silk maps of the Jabal Mahrat had been his idea. Each man carried a 24" x 13" silk map, folded into a 2" square that was taped to his leg in a moisture-proof container—another reason why the tiny force in leaving South Yemen could not have withstood a possible stark-naked search by the *al-Yemen i'Qrali*.

Camellion decided that there was something wrong with the A/H, the attitude indicator. When he had engaged the A-P, the craft had been flying level. Now there was a slight tilt to the left. Hardly noticeable. But it was there. *Why?*

Watching the A/H and trying to decide the cause of the slight tilt, he saw Clayton, from the corners of his eyes, get up from the copilots chair and move back to the tiny navigation table, then heard Colonel Bin Maktum, still in the doorway, say, "I don't suppose it would be possible to contact Ali Sa'galli and have the special operator beam us in to where his men are holed up in the mountains?"

"And it's also possible that the Soviet jets would pick up the same beam," declared Camellion. "We'd lead them straight to Sa'galli and his men."

Bin Maktum was clearly worried. "How can you be sure of getting us to the right position in the mountains, even after *Sahib* Clayton makes the proper computations? You must realize I am not familiar with navigation, except on land."

"We have a VOR and a ADF on this plane," Camellion explained patiently. "Once we pinpoint our destination, we'll tie in the Automatic Direction Finder and the Very High

Frequency Omnirange receiver to the Omega Navigation System. That system will keep us on the right heading."

"I thought you said we couldn't use a beam?" Bin Maktum was confused and his expression showed it.

"We can't—not a directional signal beam like you mean." The Death Merchant went on to explain that Omega was a network of eight transmitting stations located throughout the world[1] to provide worldwide signal coverage. These stations transmitted a phase stable 10kW signal in the Very Low Frequency (VLF) band; because of the low frequency, the signals were receivable to ranges of thousands of miles.

Clayton, who had taken out his silk map and was working with a CRS. computer, called out, "I'll have the location in another five minutes. The way it's beginning to shape up, Ali and his boys are deep within the mountains."

The Death Merchant glanced at the radar screen, then turned and looked at Bin Maktum. "Colonel, go on back to aft and tell the men to hang on. I'm going to switch off the automatic pilot and take us down to 700 feet."

"One more question." Bin Maktum spoke in the cautious English of one not using his native tongue. "How can you land in the darkness? I presume it will be daylight by the time we reach our destination?"

"You presume correctly." The Death Merchant turned off the automatic pilot, took the controls and pushed the wheel on its column downward, away from him. The Soviet plane began going down. "Better get to the other men and let them know what's going on."

Nodding, Colonel Bin Maktum nodded and left the doorway.

Marlon Clayton soon calculated that Ali Sa'galli and his band of Sons of the Falcon were waiting on a large plateau 3.6 km past the thirteen-thousand-foot pass of Shah jin A'inii.'

"The plateau has to be on west slope of Mount Tirich

1. The eight stations are located in Norway; Liberia; Hawaii and North Dakota, USA; Réunion; Argentina; Trinidad; and Japan. Each station transmits on four basic navigational frequencies: 10.2 kHz, 11.05 kHz, 11.3 kHz, and 13.6 kHz.

Mir, or our maps of the mountains are incorrect," Clayton said.

The Death Merchant looked down at the slip of paper Clayton had given him. The heading was printed clearly. Was it correct?

"You had better be damned sure about these coordinates," warned Camellion. "Once we put down, it's not likely we'll be able to take off again."

"Listen, Gardner. I know how to navigate, even if I don't fly," Clayton said angrily. "I said the plateau has to be on Tirich Mir. That's it. So tie in the VOR and the ADF with a signal from Liberia on the ON System. Or do your own damned navigating!"

"You got it, pal. . . . We'll use your figures."

Khumayyis ibn Rimthan had bled to death. The other men covered his face with a handkerchief and strapped the corpse horizontally to the bench on the starboard side, using several sling straps from Soviet assault rifles. No one put his thoughts into words; yet they were all very much aware that if Noah Gardner made a series of mistakes, they too would become statistics, their dead bodies torn apart when the AN-26 slammed into and exploded against a mountain.

They'd be just as dead if Colonel Shaabi's Soviet-made jet fighters got lucky and brought down the transport with either cannon fire or a missile.

Three times within an hour and a half they heard fighter planes streaking high overhead, almost 15,000 feet above the AN-26. The third time the jets shot above the plane, three of the Mig-23s picked up the fleeing craft on their radar and zoomed down after it. But a Mikoyan-Gurevich Mig-23 (or "Flogger"), travelling at almost 900 mph, is at a great disadvantage in attempting to attack a propeller-pulled airplane flying at an altitude of only 680 feet and at a speed of 320 mph. The Russian pilots didn't dare reduce speed too quickly: they could have a flame-out and crash.

The expected missiles didn't come. The Migs had taken off so fast that they had not been armed with air-to-air heat-seeking missiles. All the Russian pilots could do was streak down and fire GSh-23 twin-barrel cannons at the

AN-26, which the Death Merchant, his eyes on the radar screen, kept skidding from port to starboard and back again. The Migs had only split seconds in which to fire, and then they were gone. The 23mm projectiles hit only open air, although one struck the middle of the Pitot probe[2] protruding from the nose of the transport.

The Migs zoomed back and forth and more-or-less stayed with the Antonov-26 until the east became painted with streaks of red. By then the Soviet transport was over the lower foothills of the mighty Jabal Mahrat with its sawtooth ridges and twisting, white-capped peaks in the distance. Daylight opened over the region, a vast area that, from the air, appeared as wild and as alien as some uninhabited planet in another galaxy. Hills sped by below, some only covered with rocks, others green with holly-oak, walnut, and deodar trees; and if one looked closely, one could see large areas covered with flowers . . . pinkish-red *raqmahs* or cranesbill, the white and yellow *khubbayz,* or "little baker," violet-red Arnebia decumbens and 'i'suffar, the "yellow one."

There were criss-crossing gullies, weirdly-formed crevasses, treacherous gorges, and jumbles of sheer cliffs of many colors: amber, rust red, slate gray, orange-yellow, brown-black. There were still the lower reaches of the mountains, so there were very brief eye-catches of tiny farmsteads and postage-stamp-size fields heavy with maize. Now and then a stone white-roofed house surrounded by a short wall, with crawling patches of early morning fog dissolving slowly from the heat of the rising sun, flashed by.

All the South Yemen fighters turned and headed for home, all except one Mig-23 whose crazy-brave pilot veered off in a dive and sent his sleek machine of destruction screaming after the lumbering (by comparison) AN-26.

Staring through the overhead glass of the cockpit at the approaching enemy aircraft, Camellion muttered under his breath, "God Almighty! That Ivan is one determined son of a bitch."

He kept his eyes glued on the altimeter. "God helps

2. The Pitot tube, or probe feeds the oncoming air to the airspeed indicator, which, balancing this against "static" air, gives the plane's airspeed in miles per hour.

those who help themselves," he said, "and he's made a mistake—the pilot, not God. Although I don't like the way He's been operating!"

He shoved the control wheel and its column forward. The nose of the AN-26 dropped. Rapidly losing altitude, the Soviet transport headed down into a narrow valley. On either side were jagged, serrated peaks rising to thousands of feet, their sheer massiveness dwarfing into insignificance the rocks and the forest-covered floor below.

It wasn't the bed of the valley that concerned the Death Merchant, Clayton, and the men in the main section of the airplane. Their apprehension was generated by the monumental granite cliffs on each side of the AN-26, cliffs that, as the airplane lost altitude, seemed determined to crush the craft, beginning with the wingtips, making even the Death Merchant wish, in a vague sort of way, that he had gone into another line of work—*Like diving into a glass of water from a height of five hundred feet!*

His hands steady on the control wheel, Camellion stared through the cockpit glass, watching the dangerous area ahead.

The Russian hotshot, intent on destroying the AN-26, zoomed his Mig straight in, the blue and white jet streaking downward like a bolt of lightning. He had time to fire for only two seconds. *ZINGgggggg! Zip! Zip! Zip!* There were a series of extremely fast ricochets from inside and outside the aircraft, then a loud popping sound from inside the refrigerator of the AN-26. A 23mm projectile had torn through the roof of the airplane, stabbed into the refrigerator and broken a bottle of goat's milk.

SSSPLATTERRRRRRR! Another 23mm projectile came in at a sharp angle from the left, shattered part of the cockpit's overhead glass and zipped out through the windshield in front of the copilot's seat.

Clayton, five feet away in the navigator's seat, yelled and threw up an arm in front of his face.

The Death Merchant—his heart pounding hard within his chest; the cold wind whipping at his face—muttered, "This isn't turning out to be one of my better days. . . ."

Eight seconds later, the Russian pilot had the worst day of his life. The AN-26 was flying from west to east. The Mig-23 had screamed down from the northwest, had fired off a two-second burst, and then had streaked, less than a

117

hundred feet above the AN-26, toward the southeast. The pilot had then attempted to pull up and fly over the cliffs on the south side of the valley, 1,682 feet ahead of Camellion. He didn't have the time. The Mig, travelling at 783 mph, was moving too fast. The Mig slammed into the face of a cliff and exploded into a dirty ball of black whose center was a brilliant red tinged with yellow and orange. Scratch one Mig-23. The jet had become bits and pieces of junk raining down into the valley below.

Oh boy! Kiss my transmission! Camellion pulled back sharply on the wheel and the control column to avoid any of the debris that might be in the way. He kept the airplane moving upward, gaining latitude until he was at 2,400 feet and the cliffs were far below him, and the sky a wide highway of sunshine. Far in the distance were the truly giant mountains of the Mahrat range—Mt. Suritnijin, Mt. Kanukiu, Mt. Likabad, and the most important mountain of all: Tirich Mir.

"Next time remind me to stay home!" Clayton tried to sound cheerful as he pushed himself from the navigator's chair and turned unsteadily to leave the cockpit. "All this mess and we still struck out with Colonel Shaabi."

"What do you mean—struck out! We didn't even get up to bat," the Death Merchant said, his eyes glued to the attitude indicator. *Damnit! The tilt is worse.*

He continued to pull back on the wheel and the control column. He had to reach an altitude of 12,500 feet to land on the plateau.

"I'm going on back and check on the others," Clayton said and squeezed through the cockpit door, his feet crunching on glass shot from the top and front windshields.

Ignoring the cold wind blowing in through the windshield, Camellion checked the vital instruments. The oil pressure was okay. Altitude: 9,640 feet and going up. Turn and bank: *off!*—The needle indicated a list. The ADF was right on the mark, the needle on 21.6, the heading 130.50.22. The VOR signal was strong in the earplug.

The tilt to the left both worried and puzzled him. He turned the wheel slightly to the right and pushed down slightly on the right rudder pedal. No change.

Another problem was that he didn't have any way of knowing how fast the airplane was going. The airspeed in-

118

dicator was at a ridiculous 67 mph. Due to the Pilot tube's having been shot off, the ASI was useless. All he could do was guess at his speed, basing any assumption on the tach readings, on the rpm of the engines.

A very undependable method! I'm not that good of a pilot! I'm too inexperienced!

Camellion's thoughts were interrupted by Clayton who returned to the cockpit and reported that every man in the rear was unharmed—"But they don't like being faced with something they can't fight, something they don't have any control over."

"I don't either," the Death Merchant said, again looking at the attitude indicator.

From the expression on Camellion's face and the tone of his voice, Clayton detected instantly that all was not right with the aircraft. He didn't want to ask, afraid of the answer he would get. Yet he had to know.

"What's wrong, Gardner."

Camellion told him about the tilt, then explained that, because the attitude to the left could not be corrected— "I'll have difficulty in landing this baby."

"How far away are we from the plateau on Tirich Mir?" Clayton was more nervous than a cat stalking along on celophane. He shoved a clipboard against the jagged hole in the windshield in front of him.

"Getting closer all the time," Camellion said. "See that big mountain about—"

The aircraft began to shake violently, as if from an earthquake!

While Clayton's mouth flew open and his eyes grew larger, Camellion glanced at the oil pressure. The oil pressure of the port-wing engine was falling rapidly. The shudder increased. Camellion knew what was wrong.

"The propeller of the port engine is out of pitch," he announced. "I have to shut it down or the engine might shake itself right out of the nacelle. We can make it on one engine (*I hope!*) Don't worry!"

Clayton paled and bit his lower lip. The Death Merchant shut off the engine. The prop stopped revolving and the shuddering and violent shaking ceased.

Camellion checked the ADF and the VOR. Right on course. Obviously! There, ahead, was Tirich Mir, the mountain seemingly filling most of the bright eastern sky.

The Death Merchant ruddered to the right, to starboard, and pulled back on the control column, the controls responding sluggishly.

Where was the plateau?

"There isn't any place to set down," Clayton said, sounding very calm. Camellion banked sharply to starboard and started to take the transport plane around the south side of Tirich Mir. Clayton caught himself by grabbing an arm of the copilot's chair.

The seconds dragged into minutes, the minutes into 9.4 minutes. They had flown around the south side of the mountain, where snow glistened in the sun and where the rocks showed black, purple, pink, and brick-red; and were now approaching the east side, flying in a northwest direction.

They both saw it—a day-star flare exploding in all its white brilliance, 5,000 feet ahead. Then another flare went off, opening like a beautiful white orchid. A few seconds later, both men saw the Austin-D lamp blinking from far down on the east face of the mountain.

Understanding Morse Code, Camellion and Clayton read: LAND HERE. WE ARE AT THE END OF THE PLATEAU. IT IS 333-METERS-LONG AND WIDE ENOUGH. THERE ARE SOME ROCKS. THE GRASS IS SHORT.

The message continued to be repeated, the A-D lamp blinking like a tiny sun.

"Lower the landing gear," Camellion ordered Clayton. "We've found our landing strip." Now all I have to do is land. *Uh-huh. That's all. The odds are 50/50.* Moments later, the odds decreased by a factor of 48. The portside wheels would not lower. The green light remained dark. Camellion tapped the panel. The green light for the port wheels did not light up.

"Try again," the Death Merchant said. "Pull up the starboard wheels. Then lower them again. Maybe the port wheels will go down with them."

The port wheels didn't. The two wheels remained in their wells.

"Now what?" asked Clayton. "And I'm not the praying type."

The Death Merchant brushed a sleeve across his face to soak up sweat. "Go back and tell the men to hang on. I'm going to belly-skid her. There isn't any other way. You might as well stay back there. You'll be safer."

"You mean we're going to crash?"

"It's very possible."

Without another word, Clayton got up from the copilot's chair and left the cockpit. Camellion throttled down, shoved the control column forward and began the descent. *What a damned mess!* The craft was tilting to port, he didn't know his airspeed, and the wheels wouldn't go down. Rapidly the airplane lost altitude.

Individual features of Tirich Mir began to reveal themselves: steep cliffs, crooked gullies, tumbled masses of giant boulders, and long slides of scree, the dazzling pyramids of snow thinning out halfway down the mountain, the plateau itself much lower than the snowline.

Camellion finally saw the tableland, the flat area sticking out of the mountain like a tiny ledge that continued to grow larger and larger as the airplane closed in on its final resting place. Once it landed, it would never take off again.

Suddenly the uneven plateau was the size of a block in a small town. A few more moments and it was the size of a football field. Then even larger—the tops of trees below flashing by beneath the rapidly lowering Antonov transport.

At last, clear country. No trees. A rock here and there, but off to one side, not in front of the airplane.

Guessing at his airspeed, the Death Merchant cut the throttle and shut down the starboard engine when he guessed he was at an altitude of 200 feet. He pulled back on the control wheel column, to lift the nose and keep it even with the tail section. The length of the plane had to be horizontal as its weight carried it to the ground.

It took less than 30 seconds for the airplane to make contact with the ground . . . grass, weeds and plants brushing against the underside hull, twigs of bushes snapping off. The bottom of the plane struck the ground. The aircraft bounced ten feet up, came down again and stayed down and charged forward, small, sharp rocks on the surface ripping through the aluminum hull and slowing the plane's speed.

The Death Merchant gripped the control wheel with such force and kept his feet on the rudder pedals with such tension that his hands and ankles ached. What mattered was that the transport was slowing down rapidly.

We might even make it in one piece!

The belly-landing would have been eighty percent perfect if it hadn't been for the tilt to the left, which caused the tip of the left wing to be several feet lower than the tip of the right wing. There was a loud crashing sound when the forward edge of the left wing struck a fairly large rock, then snapping and popping noises as inner braces and spars were ripped loose. The torn half of the wing flew up into the air while the remainder of the aircraft was carried violently to the left. The fuselage began to skid, then spin, the tail section jumping to the east, the nose and cockpit section skewing toward the west. By the time the airplane came to a complete stop, the craft had turned completely around and the Death Merchant, in the cockpit, was staring toward the west.

The wind blowing into the cockpit was cold. Except for the eerie whistling of the wind the silence was overwhelming.

Camellion unbuckled his seat belt—*Pray as if everything depends on God and work as if everything depends on YOU!*

Sometimes it works. . . .

☐ TEN ☐

At about the same time that the Death Merchant was coming down for a landing on Mt. Tirich Mir, Colonel Qahtan al Bin Shaabi was fighting to control his temper, a lunatic fury that was actually interfering with his thought processes. His face smoke-smudged, his pearl-gray uniform grimy and stinking of burnt oil and other incinerated materials, Colonel Shaabi stood with an equally dirty Major Abdul Jahiz, a terrified (of Strongman Shaabi) Captain I'Nurtoki, and a dozen wild-eyed bodyguards. The men stood at the beginning of the center runway, surveying the smoking ruins. For all practical purposes, Aden Airport was no longer a functioning installation. All the hangars, except one, had been destroyed by fire. The hangar still standing was so badly damaged it would have to be torn down and rebult. Thirteen M-G Mig 23S fighter planes, worth more than $65 million, were now scattered all over the tarmac and were burn-blackened pieces of rubble.

Thirty-four men had been butchered. The control tower no longer existed. Only the radardome remained untouched. The final spit in the face was that the *Ibn'u alib Saqr* rebels had stolen Colonel Shaabi's personal airplane, a gift of the Soviet government.

Colonel Shaabi and the men with him stared at fire control personnel spraying foam on the fires still burning and ambulance and al-*Yemen i'Qrali* men loading the dead into vehicles. Still another severe blow to Colonel al Bin Shaabi's pride was the report from the air base at Wusadi that one of the fighter jets had crashed, and that the AN-26 had escaped.

"They will pay for this. General Zarikid and Ali Sa'galli—that stinking offal of a syphilitic sow—will pay in blood!" Colonel Shaabi said hoarsely. "We'll wipe out Sa'galli once and for all. Then we'll deal with that damned filth, Zarikid. As soon as possible, we'll search out Ali Sa'galli and his cursed assassins in the Jabal Mahrat and destroy them down to the last man."

Thinking that Shaabi sounded like a raging wolf with laryngitis, Major Jahiz's cruel face did not reveal the alarm and surprise he was feeling. He was used to Shaabi's wild and neutrotic ravings, but this time he realized that Shaabi meant what he said.

"The majority of our men are not skilled in mountain fighting," ventured Major Jahiz. "We have already made two assaults against the Sons of the Falcon and lost three hundred men."

Shaabi turned to Jahiz, who continued to stare straight ahead.

"Damn you! Don't you think I remember those defeats?" he said in a low, scornful voice. "We no longer have a choice. After what happened here this morning, we either have to destroy Ali Sa'galli or forever look like terrified children in the eyes of the Soviets. Anyhow, Sa'galli's position is different from six months ago. He has to be very low on arms and ammunition, and he can't have more than several hundred men."

"We had better use Rabadh Yahya Tabriz and his DASNI," suggested Jahiz. He turned then and looked at Colonel Shaabi, their gaze meeting and locking. "The question is, will Tabriz do it? Will he attack Sa'galli? His men aren't enthusiastic about riding in helicopters."

"He'll do it for a thousand automatic rifles and a hundred thousand rounds of ammunition," snapped Shaabi, his tone skidding on fury. "And don't you dare tell me how General Kasmanovisky and the rest of those Russian bastards will balk at giving us such an amount of arms for Tabriz. They don't have a choice. After all, it's they who have been insisting that we attack and wipe out Sa'galli."

Major Jahiz permitted himself a slight smile. "Suppose the Soviets call our bluff when you threaten to expel them from the country?"

The clever Shaabi proceeded to exhibit some of his keen insight that had enabled him to become the dictator of South Yemen. "General Kasmanovisky won't dare risk calling our bluff. Neither will his bosses in Moscow. The Soviet trash believe that we Arabs have more pride than sense. They would be afraid that if they said 'no,' we would have to expel every Russian to save face."

"It will be several weeks by the time the Soviets supply the arms and we get them to Rabadh Tabriz and his sadists. Jahiz wrinkled his nose in disgust as the wind blew the odor of burning rubber and plastic into his face.

"I know that." Colonel Shaabi suddenly seemed pleased with himself, with his decision to destroy the Sons of the Falcon. "Tomorrow, we'll make arrangements with the Russians and get word to Tabriz. We'll attack Ali Sa'galli the same day we turn the weapons over to Tabriz."

Jahiz thought for a moment. "First we have to find Sa'galli. The Jabal Mahrat is vast and dangerous."

"We'll find the son of a bitch. We'll use helicopters with the best heat-sensing equipment from East Germany," Shaabi rasped triumphantly. "No matter how long it takes, we'll find Sa'galli and his scum."

Major Jahiz didn't make a reply. A strange sense of

foreboding had crept over him. No! He was being uneasy without good cause. Colonel Shaabi had stated the problem, and a problem well stated was a problem already half solved.

☐ ELEVEN ☐

The Death Merchant sighed. *The easiest way to get into trouble is to be right at the wrong time. The easiest way to get out of trouble is to be right at the right time. I was right. We made it. How about that?*

He unbuckled his seat belt, looked intently at the instrument panel and sniffed the air. No smell of smoke. All the switches were off—*and I'm in one piece.*

In contrast, the Soviet transport was dead. The nose was crumpled. The port side wing had been ripped in the center, and with it had gone the turboprop engine. The starboard wing, while still attached to the fuselage, resembled a gigantic piece of aluminum foil, folded lengthwise, that had been powerfully squeezed by two monstrous hands. The starboard engine had been knocked upward, its prop pointing toward the sky.

Camellion glanced down at the partially demolished floor of the cockpit, pushed himself from the pilot's seat, made his way through the compartment door into the main section of the airplane and saw in one long glance that the seven other men had not been injured. All seven were on their feet, all seven looking at each other as if they were astonished to be alive.

"Gardner, you'll never get your pilot's license—not with the kind of half-ass landings you make!" joked Marlon Clayton. He leaned down and looked out a starboard window. "I don't see anyone out there. It's as empty as a graveyard."

"They're out there, waiting for us," Ahmed Shukairy said. "They are being cautious."

125

Rashid al-Khaima pushed fingers through his heavy black hair, his obsidian eyes appearing more truculent than usual. "We should leave our weapons inside the plane, at least until we have established our identity with Ali Sa'galli's men. Some of us are wearing the uniform of the enemy."

"Nonsense." Colonel Bin Maktum picked up a Russian assault rifle. The Center at Riyadh told Sa'galli about us or his people would not have signaled us."

"Rashid's correct," Camellion said in a direct voice. "We've come this far. Let's not push and shove our luck. We'll leave our automatic rifles in the plane. The men not in uniform can go out first—their hands above their heads—and call out to our hosts."

"*Sahib* Gardner is right," Ali Haddi said, his eyes sweeping the other men. "To take unnecessary risks would be foolish." He moved to the port side of the AN-26 and began unbuckling one of the leather sling straps holding the door.

The men in black *gallabiyas* were the first to move out the door onto the coarse grass. The Death Merchant and the men in Cuban uniforms followed, every man raising his hands above his head after he passed through the door and was outside of the plane. Very quickly they found Ali Sa'galli's men approaching from all four directions, all carrying a variety of assault rifles and submachine guns, many of the muzzles pointed directly at Camellion and his group of seven.

With a strong wind blowing against them, the Death Merchant and his group stopped twenty feet from the wrecked aircraft and waited for the closest group to reach them, nine rebels coming from the south.

Tall for an Arab, a gaunt-faced man, wearing a felt circular cap with a wide tubular rim and a kind of overcoat of oatmeal-colored homespun material, came forward, an FN automatic rifle cradled loosely in his arms. Camellion and his men were quick to notice that the man's finger was only a hair away from the trigger.

"*Salaam alaikum*," Ali Haddi said firmly. "I am Ali Haddi, a Royalist. Those in the uniform of the enemy are friends. It was necessary to obtain the uniforms in order for us to escape Aden Airport."

"*Alaikum as salaam*," replied the bony-faced man, staring at Ali Haddi. He continued in English, his eyes inspecting each man individually. "The message from the Saudi Arabian capital told us that you would be arriving on this high place in a stolen aircraft. The one who is called Noah Gardner. I am to ask him for a password that only he would know. It was given to him by radio from Riyadh."

His hands still above his head, the Death Merchant said, " 'The Falcon flies from the face of the sun and strikes with the swiftness of the thunderbolt.' "

"I am Yadollah I'Zoir." The man with the emaciated face smiled, showing broken *qat*-green-stained teeth. "Lower your hands. Have you any weapons?"

"They're in the airplane," Colonel Bin Maktum said, then introduced himself as a member of the Saudi Arabian General Security Directorate.

"One of our men is dead," Camellion said. "He should be buried."

I'Zoir motioned to several of the men with him. "Get the weapons from the inside of the plane." As several of the men hurried past the group and started for the port side door, I'Zoir replied to the Death Merchant. "We don't have the time to bury the body. We must wire the craft and leave as soon as possible. The body will be destroyed when the aircraft blows up."

"You're going to blow up the aircraft?" Ahmed Shukairy said with intense emotion. "But why—to hide it from Colonel Shaabi's searching jets?"

"We are going to wire the plane with a dozen grenades," I'Zoir said sternly. "When Colonel Shaabi's men locate the airplane, they will land and inspect the craft. When they open the door, they will be blown to bits."

"Sneaky but effective," Camellion said with a smile. He didn't believe he'd get an honest answer, nonetheless, he asked, "How far will we have to travel before we come to your base?"

"You will know after we get there, *Sahib* Gardner," I'Zoir said evenly. "The distance is far, yet close . . . depending on one's ability to travel through these rough mountains."

Camellion nodded, a twinkling of satisfaction in his eyes. A perfect answer, the answer he had expected.

By then, the other rebels, who had approached from the

east, the west, and the north had arrived and were eying Camellion and his group with a mixture of suspicion and curiosity. Like Yadollah I'Zoir and the men with him, the newcomers were dressed in goatskin great coats, high boots, and carried various kinds of weapons. One man carried a G3SG/1 SG (*Scharfschutzen Gewehr*) Heckler and Koch A-R, a very modern weapon. Other rebels were armed with Polish, East German, and Portuguese weapons, either assault rifles or submachine guns. One man even carried a Mark 1., 9mm Welgun, a relic from World War II.

The rebels who had gone inside the wrecked airplane came out carrying Soviet A-Rs, which they handed to Camellion and his men. Two other men from I'Zoir's group, one carrying a bag of grenades, hurried inside the plane. It took them only fifteen minutes to wire the grenades inside the craft and to attach the wire from the pins to the door, in such a manner that when the doors was opened, even as little as six inches, the pins would be pulled and the greandes explode in unison.

"We will go," announced I'Zoir. "But first, you men in sandals must wrap your feet in sheepskins. . . ."

Several of the men came forward with large squares of sheepskin and leather thongs.

The mountain tops, hidden in clouds, loomed majestically; the route taken by the men, often over accumulated detritus from the cliffs above, was extremely treacherous. At this height of almost 6,000 feet above sea level, the air was clean, fresh-smelling and cold. All Camellion and his men could do was tough it out until they reached the rebels base, where, according to Yadollah I'Zoir, they would be given clothes suitable to the climate of the Jabal Mahrat.

Carefully the men moved along crumbling tracks, often in single file, all of them feeling small in the vastness of the mammoth rocks. On all sides rose cliffs and screes, and through swathes of lowering clouds, sharp and white against a blue sky, Camellion & Co. could glimpse snow. Except for a dwarf juniper now and then, the landscape was bare of trees until, going lower, they entered a small valley and came to scattered groves of birch. On either side of the valley the ranges were cleft by gorges, down which misty blue water from melting snow surged among the boulders. In this tremendous country of great heights, Camellion felt the same sense of space and cleanness that he had known in the *Bahr as-Safi*, the Sea of Pure Sand. They moved slowly through the valley, past russet-colored bogs, patched with the dark green of bog-myrtle and laced with a network of ice-fringed rivulets. Within the valley were smaller mountains—gigantic hills actually—each scarred with tiny gullies and hollows filled with moss.

Toward the east end of the valley was a sheer granite cliff, 700 feet high, its face ribbed with ledges of various sizes. The entrance to Ali Sa'galli's headquarters was under an enormous hundred-foot long ledge that, running crookedly, horizontally, was only twenty feet from the floor of the valley and was partially hidden by masses of boulders and scree that had fallen over the years from the cliff above.

The entrace to the cave was so small that only two men could enter at a time and so low that they had to duck. But, after the party was met by half a dozen other rebels carrying oil lamps, the Death Merchant and his people saw that the cavern moved not only downward but gradually widened out.

Some fifteen minutes later, when they finally stood before Ali Sa'galli, they were several hundred feet below the floor of the valley and in an enormous "pocket" twice the size of an airplane hangar. Some portions of the roof were as high as 200 feet; other sections of the roof as low as fifty feet. In many places enormous stalactites hung threateningly. However, there were no stalagmites.

In areas free of stalactites, the rebels had pitched scores of goatskin and camelskin tents. There were numerous campfires, the Death Merchant noticing at once that the smoke was being sucked upward, meaning that within the gargantuan cavern there was an updraft, a wind entering from the valley floor and taking its exit somewhere far above the cliff and the ledges. *A flaw!* thought Camellion. Sensitive instruments used in detection could pick up the smoke with its cooking odors.

Once Camellion & Co. were face to face with Ali Sa'galli, the usual *Salaam alaikum* and *Alaikum as salaam(s)* were exchanged, after which Ali Sa'galli invited Camellion and his group into his tent. On the way to the tent, a large affair supported by numerous poles, the Death Merchant noticed many crates of arms and ammunition, of grenades, tinned food, medicine, clothing, and other equipment stored between many of the tents.

Inside the tent, furnished with only rugs and cushions, the proper amenities were first observed—tea served in small handleless cups, the men sitting on large cushions. Ali Sa'galli spoke quiet orders and men, dressed in sur-coats, leather boots, and fur-lined caps with ear-flaps, brought blankets for Camellion and his people to wrap around their shoulders, Sa'galli explaining that later they would be given clothing "suitable for this mountain climate."

Not all the members of the Sons of the Falcon were dressed alike. Many wore loose wide-bottomed trousers tucked into boots, with their jackets shoved under their cummerbunds. The clothes of most of the men were dyed with blues, greens, and browns of varying shades, woven with wide, light-colored stripes and patterns. Most of the men wore bandoliers, formidable daggers in their cummerbunds, and carried either revolvers or holstered auto-loaders.

Ali Sa'galli himself wore boots, khaki pants and shirt, and a felt jacket. He still bowed to custom, however, by wearing the traditional kaffiyeh. A compactly built man of some forty-five summers. He had a wedge-shaped face, thin lips that were pinched, and deep lines around his mouth and nose. While clean shaven, he had long wavy hair that was unbraided and fell about his shoulders.

Sa'galli's intelligent eyes fixed on the Death Merchant.

"*Sahib* Gardner, we have been told by this Saudi—" he indicated a man to his right—"that you would reveal a plan that will free us from the prison of these mountains and perhaps give us back our country being despoiled by that evil disciple of Shaitan, Qahtan al Bin Shaabi."

Camellion's silent gaze demanded an explanation from the other man, who was solidly built, had a strong jaw, and gave the appearance of quiet efficiency. Judging his age to be about thirty, Camellion noticed that the man's fingers were very long.

"I am Jajik bin Huwair of the Saudi intelligence serv-ice," the man said casually, a slightly imperious note in his voice. "I am the special radio operator that was dropped with the supplies. I was instructed by Shaikh Qasin Ibn I'nqudi to inform *Sadat*[1] Ali Sa'galli that you, *Sahib Gardner, would give him the details of Operation Camelback.*"

The Death Merchant pretended not to notice Bin Maktum and Marlon Clayton turning to him in surprise. Rashid al-Khaima, al Auf, and the other men almost glared at him, as much as to say, *Why didn't you tell us about Operation Camelback—whatever it might be?*

"Did Shaikh I'nqudi give you any other orders, *Sahib* Huwair?" Camellion broke off a piece of sweetened lavosh—flat round bread made since Biblical times—and dipped part of it into the cup of hot tea.

"I was told to follow your orders. Should you have been killed in Aden, my instructions were to follow the orders of Colonel Bin Maktum. Should both of you have been killed, I was to radio Riyadh for further orders." He paused and smiled. "Allah was kind. Both of you survived."

Bin Maktum, glancing reflectively from Camellion to Majik bin Huwair, interjected very rapidly, "The airdrop must have been made close to this location. Those crates we saw outside couldn't have been carried very far, not over this kind of terrain."

"There should also be a crate marked 'CFX-C1000,'" Camellion said. Breaking off a piece of lavosh, Camellion looked at bin Nuwair.

"Yes, there is such a case," Nuwair admitted.

"Special equipment?" Ahmed Shukairy turned calculatingly to the Death Merchant, his slim body as taut as a skin stretched over a drum.

Ali Sa'galli saved the Death Merchant the trouble of answering.

"The helicopters delivered the material a few miles from this cave," Sa'galli said slowly, sitting up a little straighter. "I presume the crate you mentioned has some special significance for you, *Sahib* Gardner?"

---

1. Holy men—the *is-sada*—are regarded as sons of the Messenger of God because of their claim to descent from the Prophet Mohammed. In exchange for their services in lending religious sanctification and merit to tribal activities, the *Sada* are supported by the tribespeople.

"The case contains special weapons," Camellion said. "Weapons I prefer for my own personal use."

Yadollah I'Zoir's eyes lit up with interest. Omar Uruq, Ali Sa'galli's other lieutenant, peered intently at Camellion, his teeth showing whitely against his dark brown skin.

"Those special weapons," began Yadollah I'Zoir, a cagey look in his dark eyes. "They are a part of this Operation Camelback that *Sahib* Huwair mentioned? What is that plan? It is time you tell us!"

The Death Merchant placed the handleless cup on the rug and pulled the blanket closer around his shoulders— *Here's where Clayton, Bin Maktum and the others get a big surprise. That includes the Mossad agent, whoever he is. . . .*

"Operation Camelback is based on the element of surprise and on doing the totally unexpected," Camellion said, directing his explanation at a solemn faced Ali Sa'galli, a "son" of the "Messenger of God." "*Sada* Ali Sa'galli, how many men can you put into the field?"

Hopelessness dropped over the face of Sa'galli. "We have only 196. Such a small number is like a drop of water in a pond compared to the 15,000 men in Colonel Shaabi's army. I am including in that number the 4,000 members of the *al-Yemen i'Qrali.*"

"Half of Shaabi's Mig fighters are already destroyed," Colonel Bin Maktum said, sighing. He turned sideways and faced the Death Merchant. "How can you and—how can anyone expect a hundred and ninety-six men to fight even a small army?"

"Operation Camelback will involve 200 professional mercenaries," explained Camellion. "They will combine with the Sons of the Falcon to form a strike force that will be assembled in these mountains and transported to Aden in helicopters. We will strike at the heart of the capital, at Government House."

The Death Merchant got the reaction he expected. The eve before doomsday! The dawn before Armageddon! Ali Sa'galli and his men stared in silence at Camellion. The men of the Death Merchant's own group turned to him in amazement, Sa'id Al'amman and Rashid al-Khaima's mouths half open."

"*Rahmat Ullahi!*" grunted Ahmed Shukairy. "The wind is blowing and it is entering in every crevice."

Marlon Clayton inhaled loudly, a slight whistling sound coming from his nose. "Ridiculous!" he exclaimed sharply. "Why such a strike would cost fifty million dollars and the sheer logistics boggle the mind. Whoever thought of such a crackbrained scheme?—"

"I did!" Camellion said evenly. "I did and the plan was accepted. The logistics are really very simple. Within the last two weeks, fourteen French Super Frelon helicopters have been moved to a secret base south of Riyadh. Each chopper can carry thirty men. That's a total of 420 troops. The entire force will leave from these mountains and strike directly at Government House. With coordinated speed, we can destroy the heart of the South Yemen government."

"Shaabi still has almost a dozen jet fighters," Clayton said roughly, his blazing eyes of Camellion. "And fighters can fly circles around helicopters."

"Ten Westland Lynx helicopter gunships, armed with Sparrow and Sidewinder missiles, will accompany the Super Frelons. Even by the time Shaabi and his cutthroats realize what's happening, it will be too late." Camellion's voice became firm and determined." Shaabi's remaining Migs won't have a chance against the gunships, even if they get off the ground at the Wusadi—and I doubt if they do."

"And why wouldn't they?" Rashid al-Khaima asked dumbly.

The Death Merchant hooked his hands on the edges of the blanket. "General Abdulla Ibn Zarikid's North Yemen fighter-bombers will coordinate an attack on Shaabi's Wusadi's air base with our attack on Aden. All of Shaabi's aircraft will be destroyed on the ground, much in the same manner that the Israeli Air Force destroyed the Egyptian Air Force during the Six-Day War of 1967."

Camellion was very serious, and nothing about him indicated that he was not telling the truth, that his every word was a lie. He couldn't tell them the truth; he didn't dare. The Yemeni Royalist *Ibn'u Alib Saqr* would never appreciate, much less understand, such refined and polished deception. They were simple, direct men who would always be strangers to subterfuge. There would be a devastating air strike against Colonel al Bin Shaabi's air base at Wusadi in central South Yemen, but the British Hawker

133

Siddeley fighter-bombers, the same kind of aircraft used by General Zarikid, would not fly from the Yemen Arab Republic—North Yemen. Carrying North Yemen markings—three horizontal stripes of red, white, and black, with a green star in the center—the Hawker Siddeleys would scream in to the attack from Saudi Arabia.

"Who are the mercenaries?" Bin Maktum asked Camellion in a quiet tone.

"Major Michael Quinlan and his *Thunderbolt Unit: Omega,*" answered the Death Merchant, who, giving Bin Maktum a quick survey, was pleased at the Saudi agent's self-control. Unless he was abnormal, Bin Maktum had to feel some resentment over his own government's intelligence service having taken an American into its confidence while not revealing its plans to him, a trusted agent. At minimum, his pride had to have suffered some damage. If it did, he didn't show it, unlike Marlon Clayton whose every gesture and word betrayed antipathy interwoven with antagonism.

"I have heard of this Quinlan." Bin Maktum toyed with the handleless cup in his hands. "He is called 'Mad Mike Quinlan.' He is an ex-French Foreign Legionnaire." He looked up at *Sada* Ali Sa'galli. "Major Quinlan's men are the most expert commandos in the world. One of them is worth ten of Colonel Shaabi's men."

"They're killers and scum from all nations!" sneered Clayton, who then made unpleasant sounds with his lips. "They have the morals and the manners of lice."

"But they also have the killer instincts of a Great White shark," Camellion countered coldly. "Quinlan and his boys aren't coming for tea. Their mission will be to slaughter, and they're darned good at it."

Clayton, by now realizing that he had said the wrong thing to the wrong man at the right time, took another tact. "I can't deny you're right about Quinlan and his Thunderbolt boys. What I can't understand is why our people and the Saudis would trust you with information about this operation. If something had gone wrong in Aden, you could have been captured as easily as any of the rest of us; and don't tell me that any man, including you, can't be made to talk."

"A dead man can't even whisper," Camellion retaliated with a slight laugh. "Sure, fella. I could have been taken a prisoner. I would have died instantly by biting down on an L-pill. That's the difference between you and me, Clayton. You might have hesitated."

At a loss for words, Clayton looked away.

Camellion turned his attention to *Sada* Ali Sa'galli, who, all this time, had continued to sit like some modern-day Buddha that refused to reveal its thoughts.

"*Sada* Sa'galli, the decision to help in this operation is yours to make," Camellion said diplomatically. "Without your help, without your Sons of the Falcon, the strike can't be carried out. Should you help us, know that many of your men will be wounded. Many of your people will die."

"I must know the details," Ali Sa'galli said tonelessly.

"The helicopters you mention, *Sahib* Gardner," said Omar Uruq, "they would land close to here, in the same area in which the airdrop was made?"

"Yes, provided the area is large enough," Camellion said, "or the choppers could sit down on the plateau where we landed Colonel Shaabi's plane."

"There is plenty of room where the air drop was made," said Uruq, who was a bearded man of medium height, with a high, narrow forehead.

"As for the details," said the Death Merchant, "it would require a week or so for the force to be assembled in Arabia. The twenty-four choppers would come in very low until they reached the mountains to fool any radar that Soviet technicians may have operating in the area."

In a pleasant, matter-of-fact voice, Camellion explained that, no matter what kind of security and precautions were utilized, there would be enormous risks. He pointed out that, in all probability, Colonel Shaabi's helicopters would soon be searching the Jabal Mahrat in an effort to find the stolen Soviet transport plane. Another possibility was that Shaabi, thinking that the attack on Aden Airport had been carried out by the Sons of the Falcon, might want revenge. He might again attack the rebels in the mountains. This was another reason why speed in organizing was essential.

"By that I mean that once the helicopters have landed with Major Quinlan and his men, your people will have to board very quickly so that the helicopters can become airborne as soon as possible." The Death Merchant paused and regarded Ali Sa'galli solemnly. "Of course, what I am proposing is academic. It cannot become reality until I know if you are willing to assist in Operation Camelback."

"A man has two reasons for doing anything—a good reason and a real reason," intoned Ali Sa'galli, speaking as though he were making a pronouncement. "The real reason you Americans want to overthrow General Shaabi is to protect your oil in the country you refer to as Arabia. Our reason is that we fight for freedom. Yes, American, we will help you in this Operation Camelback. It would be a moral crime against Allah to sit here when the opportunity to strike has presented itself. Yes . . . we will fight."

"That is good, *Sada* Ali Sa'galli," Camellion said. Relieved, he glanced for a moment at the old-fashioned kerosene lantern hanging from the center of the tent, then looked at Majik bin Huwair. "What kind of transceiver did you bring with you, my Saudi friend?"

Huwair cleared his throat while flicking ash from his cigarette. "A Yaesu FRG-7000," he said. "As you may know, it covers .25 to 39.9 MHz in 29 bands with direct digital frequency readout to 1 kHz on all bands. I also brought four 12V batteries. One for the FRG, one for the message pulse-condenser, and two spares. A loop antenna. We'll have to use it in conjunction with an all-band SWL trap dipole antenna. We can set up anytime you want."

"The sooner the better," Camellion said heartily. "I've a long report to make and—"

"And so have I," Bin Maktum said casually.

"We'll set up the FRG after this meeting," Camellion said. "We'll have to do some climbing to erect the loop antenna and the T.D.A., and then take both of them down after we've completed the message."

Yadollah I'Zoir spoke up. "There is not too much danger of Colonel Shaabi's helicopters finding us. These mountains are vast and cover hundreds of square kilometers. Helicopters could fly around for years and never find us in these caves."

"But you were attacked twice before," Ahmed Shukairy said with his typical bluntness. "This time he will be twice as determined. We wrecked Aden Airport."

"Those were different times when Shaabi's forces attacked us," I'Zoir said hastily, placing the heel of his hand on the handle of the dagger in his cummerbund. "We then numbered almost a thousand men and could not move easily without being seen from the air." He made a deprecating gesture with his left hand. "We are now less than two hundred. Even as it was, we inflicted terrible damage on Shaabi's forces. Both times they retreated in panic."

The Death Merchant joined in. "There are special detection devices that could help men in helicopters to locate us." Camellion stabbed a finger at the lantern hanging from the center of the tent. "The smoke from that lantern, the smoke from your cooking fires, all of it is carried in an updraft to the surface. Those special instruments could detect odors in the smoke. It's not likely, due to the strong wind. Yet it is possible. However," his odd icy-blue eyes darted back to Ali Sa'galli, "there is another matter that should be touched on. It concerns one of your valued members, Nuri Boustani."

"It was *Sahib* Boustani who informed us that Colonel Shaabi would be at Aden Airport," Rashid al-Khaima said, his tone heavy with speculation.

Smiles of satisfaction crossed the faces of Yadollah I'Zoir and Omar Uruq. Ali Sa'galli's expression didn't change.

His voice was gentle. "Did not *Sahib* Boustani tell you that the source of his information was a matter of security?"

Camellion, who hadn't expected a revealing answer, slowly nodded.

"We knew the information had to come from someone very close to that devil Shaabi." Marlon Clayton was stupidly candid. "We wondered who the man—or woman—was."

A slight look of annoyance crept into Ali Sa'galli's eyes.

"It is written that a clear loss is better than a possible profit far distant. To reveal the identity of our agent close to Colonel Shaabi would not help Operation Camelback in any way. To reveal his identity would only endanger his life."

"It's those special detection devices that worry me," Rashid al-Khaima said. "I tell you, my friends, if the world did not contain so many mechanical miracles, life would be less complicated."

"Very true," commented Sa'id Al'amman. "My grandfather would never have believed that the day would come when there would be nuclear weapons that could destroy the human race."

"You could blame it all on the Germans," remarked Marlon Clayton. "The atom bomb was based on mathematical calculations formulated by Einstein. But scientists would have unlocked the secret of the atom without Einstein, sooner or later."

"Einstein was a dirty jew," interposed Ahmed Shukairy. "Those Jews are the cursed of this earth."

Ali Sa'galli clapped his hands sharply for attention. "Gentlemen, let us eat the first meal of the day. The day is young and there is much to do."

Accompanied by half a dozen Yemeni *Ibn'u Alib Saqr*, who were carrying Heckler and Koch G3A3 automatic rifles that had been part of the airdrop, the Death Merchant, Bin Maktum, and Majik bin Huwair left the cavern, climbed to the top of the cliff and set up the loop and the criss-cross SWL trap dipole antenna. Once the two antennas were in place, Camellion and the others carefully retraced their steps on the deadly rocks, uncurling four insulated strands of wire behind them. They reentered the cavern and, just beyond the opening, attached the wires to the FRG-7000 and to the message pulse condenser, or the "Black Box," the device that could condense fifteen minutes of conversation into 2.6 seconds, the length of transmission far too short for any radio triangulation by the enemy. Since the transmitter and M.P.C. also contained a voice scrambler, Camellion reported for himself and Colonel Bin Maktum in English, speaking for almost ten minutes. The reply came back immediately and was instantly unscrambled. The entire process of transmitting and receiving, including the antenna hookup, had taken three thours and thirty-six minutes. It took another three hours to take down the two antennas.

The Death Merchant and the others promptly returned to Ali Sa'galli's headquarters tent and Camellion reported that Riyadh was very pleased with the destruction of Aden Airport and had congratulated the tiny force on its accomplishment and on its escape into the Jabal Mahrat. The "higher powers" in Riyadh were elated over Ali Sa'galli's decision to throw his men into Operation Camelback— "and Major Quinlan and his men are due to arrive in groups of two and three in Riyadh in a week from now. I was told that the helicopter armada will land here in nine or ten days."

"During that time, you will be in contact again with Riyadh," Ali Sa'galli said. "We must know positively when the aircrafts will land."

"We will," Camellion said, his voice sounding golden warm. "I'll contact the capital again in three days. In the meanwhile we can get out equipment in order and set up a tight watch for Shaabi's choppers. He could get lucky and find us. So let's make plans to give him a warm reception, just in case his choppers do put down in this area."

The days that followed were filled with feverish activity. The weapons in the airdrop had included two 3-inch mortars, four Bren light machine guns and six L4A1 light machine guns, all from the Royal Small Arms Factory in the United Kingdom. The mortars and the four Brens were set up around the landing site three kilometers southwest of the cave—placed in such a manner that the mortars could lob shells into any enemy choppers that might land and the Brens rake the area in a murderous crossfire.

The Death Merchant had several long talks with *Sada* Ali Sa'galli in private and was surprised to find that the leader of the Sons of the Falcon was a strange mixture of dogmatic Muslim morality and modern common-sense pragmatism. Although Ali Sa'galli was not an eleventh-century fanatic like the Ayatollah Ruhollah Khomeini, he was an old-fashioned hardliner who, if he had his way, would return all of Yemen to the steel-hard morality of the Sunni Muslims.

In contrast to those impractical views on morals and ethics, Sa'galli had an uncanny insight into world politics. During one long talk with the Death Merchant, he stated that the West had a way of rationalizing its own stupidity. A deliberate gullibility that would lead to its own destruction.

"We are told about Soviet dreams of expansionism," Sa'galli said. "This is true. Just as the camel must periodically drink water, so the Soviets must expand and also export terrorism. Yet it is not true that the Soviet Union is directly causing a proliferation of nuclear arms. The reason is quite simple: the USSR does not put monetary gain above political considerations. This is not true with the West, which places money before everything else. It is the greedy French who have sold a nuclear reactor to al Jumhouriya al Iraquia, or the nation you refer to as 'Iraq.' It is the Americans who made it possible for India to explode a hell bomb. It is the foolish Americans who will build reactors in Egypt."

The Death Merchant, much to his discomfort, could only agree with Ali Sa'galli. Camellion could only wonder what Sa'galli and the Saudis would think—and do!—if they knew that American soldiers and airmen were due to be employed in the danger zone of the war-torn Middle East? *It's more of D.C. stupidity, but it's fact*—that on July 18 and 19, of 1981, the Reagan administration special envoy, Deputy Under Secretary Leamon Hunt, had met in London with representatives of Israel and Egypt to approve and initial a new pact for the formation of an expeditionary brigade to secure the borders of Israel, that force to be initially garrisoned—later in 1981—in the Sinai Desert, creating a U.S.-occupied "security zone" for Israel's south flank.

"Words of great wisdom you speak, *Sada* Ali Sa'galli," Camellion said. "We have the same kind of irrational thinking within the borders of the United States, practically all of it due to the thinking of foolish people who insist that man is the passive product of his environment."

In a patient voice, Camellion explained that some Americans reject the concept of volition, of individual responsiblity, they feel that all human behavior is the manifestation not of an active free will, but of a reactive knee-jerk. Consequently, when they want to deal with some undesirable action, they concentrate on controlling the external "stimulus" rather than the actor himself.

Said the Death Merchant, "They maintain, for instance, that poverty 'causes' crime, that empty sacks and empty bottles 'cause' litter and that bartenders 'cause' automobile accidents. They make little distinction between the innocent and the guilty. Instead of devoting all their efforts to the apprehension and punishment of criminals, these half-witted individuals compel noncriminals to pay for massive 'antipoverty' and 'rehabilitation' programs. Instead of cracking down on people who litter, they force nonlitterers to pay deposits on beverage bottles to ensure their return."

Ali Sa'galli shook his head from side to side. "My friend, the people of whom you speak are as foolish children. Their eyes are veiled and their minds are clouded."

"So called 'gun-control' is another example," said the Death Merchant. "These 'liberals' would disarm all honest men and give the streets of our cities to the criminals."

"A firearm is only an instrument, such as a knife or a stone," Ali Sa'Galli said. "It is the person who possesses such an instrument who is responsible for how it is used. How can these liberals be so stupid, *Sahib* Gardner?"

"It's not that they're all that dumb," Camellion said. "They either ignore or twist facts." He then explained that firearms were especially effective in preventing rape, and sited a 1979 survey as proof—in Orlando, Florida—". . . a city in a state of the United States"—where 6,000 women were trained by police to use handguns. *The result was that the incidence of rape dropped 90 percent the following year! No other major U.S. city experienced such a decline.*

Four different times, Colonel Shaabi's helicopters flew over the general area close to where the cave was located. Twice three Mil Mi-8 helicopters flew over at a height of 4,000 feet. The third time one Soviet Mil Mi-8 *thump-thump-thump-thumped* over at only a thousand feet. The fourth time was the worst. Two Mi-8s flew directly over the intended set-down area at a height of only three hundred feet.

"Well, that's it," Clayton growled. "The crap's in the apple butter. If they have 'sniffers' aboard, they must know we're down here, only three kilometers away."

For the rest of that day and all that night and all of the following day, the Sons of the Falcon waited for the attack. It never came.

At 15.00 hours of the seventh day, the Death Merchant, with Majik bin Huwair at the dials of the Yaesu FRG-7000, and with Bin Maktum and Marlon Clayton anx-

141

iously looking on, again contacted the CIA station in the United States Embassy at Riyadh.

Camellion first made his report: Ali Sa'galli and his men of the *Ibn'u Alib Saqr* were as ready to fight and die as they would ever be.

When would the Super Frelons and the Westland Lynx helicopters arrive. "Give me the date and the time, and please confirm," Camellion said.

There was an 11.7 seconds pause, after which the heavy, worried voice of Burton Webb, the Company Chief of Station at Riyadh, came from the speaker attached to the Black Box: "The landing will take place at the designated spot at 09.00 hours this night." Webb then gave the date, repeated the time and added, *"There has been a change of plans.* I repeat: there has been a change of plans." Webb paused. He then continued, speaking slower, his voice faintly excited.

"The attack on Aden is aborted. I repeat: *the attack on Aden is aborted.* We have very reliable information that Colonel al Bin Shaabi and Major Abdul Jahiz know your location. The helicopters used East German Klausen H-W sensors. At this moment, Shaabi, some of his top people, and three GRU advisers are at the headquarters camp of Rabadh Yahya Tabriz and his Dasni killers, in the Jabal Hadramawi, the 'Fingers of Shaitan' mountains."

Dumbfounded at the sudden change of events, the Death Merchant and the other three men listened to Webb give the details—Colonel Shaabi, and Tabriz's Dasni intended to attack the Sons of the Falcon camp with a force of 600 men, using 18 Mil Mi-8 helicopters to transport the Dasni to the area.

"Shaabi intends to attack your camp at dawn tomorrow," Webb said. "The plan is to first saturate the area with napalm and rockets, after which the Mils will put down. Gardner, give me your thought on on Shaabi's plans. Could Ali Sa'galli's men withstand such an assault? OVER."

A disgusted Camellion picked up the mike on its coiled rubber cord and nodded to a stunned Majik bin Huwair who flipped the TRANSMIT switch and adjusted the RF GAIN dial.

"Is the Pope of Rome an Eskimo?" Camellion asked rhetorically in a cold but calm voice. "Of course we couldn't withstand such a napalm and rocket attack. You said that Shaabi's choppers found us with heat wave detectors. In that case, he's eighty-five percent certain where we are. A dozen missiles could bring the entire mountain caving in on us. Not only that, but the terrain is not suitable for us to take on an enemy force of six hundred, even with the help of Mad Mike and his mercs. The enemy would have the advantage in that it would be making the attack. Later on, they could come at us in a three hundred-sixty degree approach. It would be as disastrous as fighting a large force on the desert. Another thing—"

"The helicopters!" butted in Clayton ponderously. "Tell him that if the Soviet Mi-8 whirlybirds catch our Frelons and Lynxs on the ground, they'll blow them all over these bleak mountains!"

"The Russian gunships could turn our egg-beaters into a million pieces of junk," Camellion barked into the mike. "Another thing, you said out ships would be here at 09.00 hours. Are we to assume that Frelons and the Lynxs are coming to lift us out? Or, is Mad Mike and his Mercs coming along? Over."

There was a 7.2 seconds pause.

Webb's voice: "Major Quinlan and his men will be with our helicopters. Over."

Colonel Bin Maktum wiped his forehead with a handkerchief. "Why doesn't that pencil-pushing idiot quit stroking us and say what he really wants?" he whispered angrily, balling his hands into fists.

Clayton grimaced as though he were tasting bitter water.

The Death Merchant pressed down on the mike's button. "Webb, none of us are in Arabia to teach the natives to toot or tap a triangle. Why don't you come right out and say that you want us and Mad Mike to attack Shaabi and those devil-happy halfwits at Tabriz's main camp? Over." Camellion did some rapid mental calculations.

Pause—9.6 seconds.

Webb's voice, low, almost mechanical. "The decision to attack Rabadh Tabriz's main camp is one you must make. Will Ali Sa'galli go along with your decision, should you decide to attack? Before you reply, let me tell you that the distance from your present position to Tabriz's camp in the 'Fingers of Satan' is only slightly shorter than the distance from your present position to Aden. However, there is an advantage to attacking Tabriz's camp. From his camp to Arabia is only a short distance in air miles—on the assumption that all of you are not terminated in the conflict. Over."

"Terminated in the conflict!" That paper-pushing pea-brain! The Death Merchant looked down at a tight-lipped Majik bin Huwair. "Are you positive that the 'Black Box' and the scrambler are in perfect working order?"

Huwair didn't have to think twice. "Yes. The green lights are on and the meters are at full strength. The entire apparatus is operating at peak efficiency."

Pressing down on the button, Camellion held the mike close to his mouth. "Webb, the 'very reliable source of information' that tipped you to Colonel Shaabi's plan: is it the same base source that has been supplying the Sons of the Falcon with top secret information. Over—and switch to the special code."

Pause—34 seconds. Words in the Mohawk Indian language, formed by the voice synthesizer of the computer, came through the speaker of the short wave transceiver.

"Oh, Goddamn! That crap again!" huffed Clayton in disgust.

The Death Merchant instantly translated the Mohawk words as they came from the speaker. "The identity of the source of information in Aden is on a need-to-know basis. We'll give you the identity of the source after you are back in Arabia. Are you going to attack Rabadh Tabriz's camp? Over."

The Death Merchant replied, "Affirmative. I repeat: affirmative. We will definitely attack Rabadh Tabriz's camp. We will take off from this location the moment the helicopters arrive at 09.00 hours. Important. Is the source in Aden connected in any way with the Israeli agent I must terminate? Confirm adknowledgment of attack agreement. Over."

A 13.6 seconds delay.

"Your attack plan confirmed." The words came in Mohawk, in a mechanical, robotlike tone. "The source in Aden is not related to the Mossad agent you must terminate. Do you have any clues to the identity of the man? If so, do not give his name in transmission. Over."

144

"Affirmative as to his identity. He will be dead before dawn. If there isn't anything else, give me an AR.[2]

"Out."

Camellion hung the mike on the case of the FRG-7000 and nodded to Majik bin Huwair who switched off the transceiver.

"Well, damnit! Do we or don't we attack Tabriz's camp?" demanded Clayton, reaching for his cigarettes.

Camellion smiled placidly. "We do. Of course, as W.C. Fields used to say, 'I'd rather be in Philadelphia.' "

The Death Merchant was happy for another reason: He was ninety-five percent certain of the identity of the Mossad agent.

The sands of his life have just about run out. . . .

☐ TWELVE ☐

The cloud cover made the darkness complete, a blackness that made Ali Sa'galli's unsophisticated rebels afraid that the helicopters would crash against the mountains and explode in flames. They became halfway reassured that all would go well when they were told that the Super Frelons and the Westland Lynx helicopters would land with the aid of infrared night vision devices by which the pilots could "see" in the dark.

Dressed in clothes that had been included in the airdrop, Camellion and the men who had escaped with him from Aden Airport were armed to the eyeballs with automatic weapons, side arms, and frag grenades. The Death Merchant, Bin Maktum, and Marlon Clayton wore regular OD Sateen fatigue caps, field jackets, U.S. Special Forces mountain boots, and TAWGS—Trousers-all-weather-Gore-Tex developed for UDT/SEAL special war-

2. In communications this means: *This is the end of my transmission and no answer is required.* AR is the prosign.

145

fare and for use in mountain, coastal or maritime operations. Ahmed Shukairy and the other Arabs, including Ali Sa'galli and his Sons of the Falcon, preferred to fight in the clothes of the desert, clothes in which they were the most comfortable.

All of them waited for the helicopter armada from Saudi Arabia.

At first, there was only a faint whispered sound from the north, an almost imperceptible buzzing that increased in volume to a steady *thump-thump-thump*. Rapidly the sounds grew louder and, with each second, still louder. In only five minutes the reverberation became a roar similar to the racket made by an approaching tornado that had touched down. This was normal. There were fourteen French Super Frelon helicopters and ten Westland Lynx choppers, the fourteen Super Frelons flying like geese in a wedge. Five Lynx gunships were spread out above the formation. The other five Lynx were spread out below.

The biggest and the heaviest helicopter yet produced in quantity to a West European design, each Super Frelon had three 1.630 hp Turbomeca Turmo 111C turboshaft engines and a main six-blade rotor that was 62 feet in diameter. When fully loaded, maximum speed was 182 mph. Service ceiling: 10,340 feet. Each craft carried on its nose a Sylphe panoramic radar housing. There was no armament.

The much smaller Westland/Aérospatiale Lynx (built in the United Kingdom, in partnership with Aérospatiale, France) had two 900 shp Rolls-Royce GEM 1001 three-shaft turbines, a four-blade main rotor 42 feet in diameter, could fly at a maximum speed of 207 mph. Carrying a crew of five, these specially outfitted Lynxs were the most maneuverable helos in the world, without outstanding smoothness and performance. They could be looped and rolled over at 100 degrees per second and flown backward at 80 mph.

Then ten Lynxs had been turned into flying arsenals, into the deadliest helicopter gunships in the world. Each Lynx had two pods on each side of the fuselage. One pod contained two long range Sparrow missiles; the other pod was filled with four short range Sidewinder missiles. On both the port and the starboard side of each chopper was a General Electric M134 multiple-barrel Minigun that fired 7.62 x 51mm NATO ammunition at a cyclic rate of 6,000 rpm and at a muzzle velocity of 2850 fps (869 mps).

The five Westland-Lynxs forming the lower guard came down first, slowly and very cautiously, landing toward the east side of the large area. One by one the giant Super Frelons set down until all fourteen of them were spread out in the center of the region. The other five Westland Lynxs remained overhead, "riding herd," just in case any of Colonel Shaabi's jets came along and tried to butt in with missiles and 20mm cannon fire.

Cradling an FN 5.56mm automatic rifle in his arms as he walked forward with Camellion and the other men, Rashid al-Khaima remarked, "Those drums attached to the sides of the smaller helicopters. They contain extra fuel?"

"You got it," the Death Merchant answered. "Without that extra fuel, the Lynxs would never be able to get back to Saudi Arabia."

Added Marlon Clayton, "That fuel is highly inflammable. They took a hell of a chance in flying from Arabia."

The Death Merchant had his eyes on one of the Super Frelons, only twenty feet away, from which someone had blinked in Morse code with a pen light—HEADQUARTERS CRAFT HERE. "It wasn't all that much of a risk," Camellion said. "Those long range Sparrow missiles are radar guided and radar sensored. They could have spotted any of Shaabi's Migs before the pilots of the choppers could even hear or see the jet fighters."

By then, Camellion and some of the others were up to the Frelon, whose six-bladed rotor was slowly revolving. Major Michael Quinlan, ex-French Foreign legionnaire and the leader of the world's most deadly group of mercenaries, was the first to get out of the chopper.

A well-muscled man in his middle thirties, who had a pleasant face, "Mad Mike" wore a black wool beret, a camouflage parachutist jump smock, NATO pattern camo combat trousers and black *Fallschirmspringerstiefel* German paratrooper boots. Two Safari Arms .45 MatchMaster auto-pistols were in shoulder holsters. Around Quinlan's waist were buckled two more MatchMasters. In his left hand he carried a Czech 68 Skorpion machine pistol with an extra-long 34 cartridge magazine. In his right hand was a 35″ long officer's Blackthorn walking stick.

Quinlin and Camellion had worked together several times before on highly secretive missions, and each time the Death Merchant had used a different name. Highly intuitive, Quinlan knew almost nothing about Richard Camellion, except that he was a very special independent operator who worked for the Central Intelligence Agency, an in-the-field operations expert who stayed alive and healthy for two reasons: he had a natural talent for subterfuge and for personal survival and, Quinlan suspected, to prevent his having an "accident" to insure his silence, the tall, lean man had secrets about the Company hidden away. The highly intelligent Quinlan also suspected that the man now standing before him was the infamous Death Merchant. A realist, Quinlan couldn't have cared less, one way or another. He did know that people who crossed the Death Merchant had a strange way of meeting with misfortune.

In contrast, the Death Merchant knew all about "Mad" Mike Quinlan, who was the black sheep of a wealthy New England family. Operating from Palma, the capital of Spanish Majorca, Quinlan, within forty-eight hours, could assemble the most expert killers from all over the world to fight in his *Thunderbolt Unit: Omega*, a force that never numbered over 200 men, a force that could strike with the swiftness of a lightning bolt and whose targets always met *Omega*—the *End*. That *End* was always death.

Not a sign of recognition passed between Camellion and Quinlan as the Death Merchant said, "I'm Gardner (As if you didn't know!). You and your men have already been briefed. You know where we're going and whom we're going to hit."

"Down to the last detail," Quinlan said agreeably, his voice calm and cultured, his eyes darting over the curious faces of the men around Camellion. "As soon as the gunships are refueled and Ali Sa'galli's men aboard the Frelons, we can talk. Who's who around here?"

"Names are not important," spoke up Marlon Clayton. "Getting the job done is all that matters."

Quinlan stared for a moment at Clayton, his lips curved in a whimsical, yet somewhat terrible smile. Then he chuckled and turned to the Death Merchant who was giving Clayton a disdainful look.

"He must be a Company desk man," Quinlan said to Camellion, referring to Clayon. "Is he lost or was he sent to South Yemen to be punished?"

"I'm here to do a job, Quinlan," Clayton said angrily. He thrust out his jaw and hooked his thumbs in the wide cartridge belt supporting two Smith & Wesson 9mm autoloaders in open leather holsters. "I've the same iron guts and steel backbone as you—and don't you forget it!"

"Yeahhhh, only I don't rust when it rains!" joked Quinlan.

Before a surprised and insulted Clayton could respond, Camellion began introductions, starting with Muhammad al Auf and ending with Ali Sa'galli, Omar Uruq, and Yadollah I'Zoir, the latter three of whom had walked up to the group.

Major Quinlan, speaking perfect Arabic, proved himself as much a diplomat and psychologist as he was a tactician in death.

"Peace be on you, *Sada* Ali Sa'galli. My men and I have come to assist you in ridding this land of a terrible evil. By the time the sun rises on a new day, that evil will have been destroyed."

Replied Ali Sa'galli, "Together, we will either succeed or fail, *Sahib* Major Quinlan. May Zahigrud[1] pass over you this night. . . ."

Quinlan proceeded to introduce the four other men who had deplaned with him from the Super Frelon. There was Manfred Werner Rohde, a giant West German whose face looked as if it had just recovered from a collision with a battering ram.

A squat, built-like-a-blockhouse man was named Georgious Trypanis. A Greek from Athens, he was a merc who had fought in Angola, South Africa, Algeria, and some banana republics in Centeral America. Trypanis had a beard that ran in all directions and wore what looked like a pair of old-fashioned aviator goggles across his eyes, the goggles held in place by a strap across the back of his

---

1. The Muslim demon of Death. Belial, from the Book of Revelation, is the Christian counterpart. Like Belial, Zahigrud is the cosmic power of evil, the Cosmic Lord of Death.

head. The goggles were his "fighting eyeglasses." The Greek was so nearsighted that, without eyeglasses, he wouldn't have been able to see the Rock of Gibraltar—three feet away.

Dimitur Zlatev, a Bulgarian who had fled his native land in his early twenties, after killing a dozen Gorzi—members of the Internal Security Directorate of Communist Bulgaria. Well over six feet, narrow in the shoulders but wide in the hips, the pear-shaped Zlatev—the Strangler as he was nicknamed—wore tiger-striped fatigues, German para boots and was loaded down with weapons. He acknowledged the introductions with a grunt.

Camellion and everyone else stared at Marcello Salamo, the fourth man. A Sicilian from Messina, Sicily, "Big Sal," only 42 inches tall, was a dwarf with bowed legs and short but massive arms. Clad in special made rip-stop poplin camo fatigues and wearing two holstered .357 Astra magnum revolvers around his waist, "Big Sal" Salamo had a large head, a tiny mustache, a small goatee and long sideburns fluffed out at the bottom, so that it appeared that two gray-brown powder-puffs had been pasted to the center of his cheeks.

Carrying a French Pistolet Mitrailleur MAT-48 submachine gun, Big Sal looked positively comical as he glared viciously at the Death Merchant and the other men and piped in a high voice, his words thick with accent, "Let's get something straight right now! I'm not a 'Cousin It,' or a goddamn midget. I'm a 'Little Person.' I'm the paymaster of Thunderbolt Omega. I'll blow the mutherfukin' head off any sonuvabitch who calls me otherwise."

Even the Death Merchant, who wanted to laugh out loud, sensed that the "Little Person" meant exactly what he said.

It required an hour and a half for the ten Westland Lynx helos to refuel and for the Sons of the Falcon to get aboard the Frelons that were already occupied by Major Quinlan's mercs. The Death Merchant and his seven-men group, as well as Ali Sa'galli, Yadollah I'Zoir, and Omar Uruq, rode in the command Frelon with Major Quinlan and his aides.

The last big Super Frelon lifted off at 23.00 hours. Filling the night and the cold mountain air with a thunderous roaring that seemed to crack clouds and sky, the twenty-four helicopters headed northwest, their destination the Jabal Hadramawi, the Fingers of Satan Mountains where Rabadh Yahya Tabriz and his Dasni had their main camp.

The Death Merchant leaned back against the padding in the Frelon and thought of a conversation he had had with Quinlan while the two men had watched the Sons of the Falcon boarding the Super Frelons. Mad Mike was convinced that the Middle East was doomed to explode in war, his opinion the same as that of U.S. intelligence analysts who believed that Israel would become more isolated and intransigent during a second Begin term. As a result the Israelis would stage more military strikes against the Arabs with even less concern for international opinion.

"You have more and more of the world going left and Israel going right," Quinlan had said. "That means trouble for the Arabs and for Uncle Sam. With Israel in the Middle East, it's like having a goat guard the cabbage patch."

"Not necessarily." Camellion had disagreed only to draw out Quinlan's views. He knew the man was right. *By 1990 there would not be an Israel.* "Begin did make peace with Egypt and he did withdraw from the Sinai. If he can somehow rationalize away his theological notion of Samaria and Judea, who knows—maybe he can work out the West Bank, too?"

"Dream on, my friend . . . dream on. . . ."

Either way, concluded the Death Merchant, it was all relative—*like evil.* Evil did exist, but it was only motion and could have its context only in the survival pattern of an individual, or in the species. If the sun turned into a nova and the world became a burned out cinder, that would be "evil." To a ten-headed Blz-D-iii from another planet, not knowing the world was inhabited, the frying of the planet would be only a passing spectacle. *Yeah . . . evil is when its going to get you, not when you're going to get it.*

Camellion relaxed and listened to the roaring of the Super Frelon's three Turbomeca Turmo 111C turboshaft engines. He had planned for every contingency—except dropping dead! In which case, victory or defeat wouldn't matter.

Yet there was always the possibility that something could go wrong. There were times when a crowbar couldn't break a cobweb. At other times, a leaf could start an avalanche.

Camellion did have one worry gnawing at the back of his brain—*Do we really have the element of surprise! If we do not, we'll need a miracle to whip the Dasni....*

☐ THIRTEEN ☐

While the Death Merchant knew that failures are divided into two classes: those who thought and never did, and those who did and never thought, his main worry was Factor-X—the unforseen/coincidence/the fickle-finger-of-Fate Fate was like a dictator; and all tyrants believe passionately in freedom—*for themselves*. Fate was also a hypocrite.

Factor-X, the twin brother of Fate, was one-third against the Death Merchant and his force. Colonel Shaabi did not have any radar installations in those grids of South Yemen crossed by the Super Frelons and the Westland Lynx helicopters. They had crossed the border from southern Saudi Arabia into nother'n South Yemen without being noticed, except by Yemeni tribesmen who couldn't have cared less. To them, a plane was a plane.

But a single South Yemen Mig-23 fighter jet, whose pilot was on a routine patrol, spotted the Death Merchant's twenty-four helicopters after they had left Ali Sa'galli's stronghold and were only nine minutes from Danikil, Rabadh Yahya Tarbriz's main camp in the Jabal Hadramawi, detected the enemy air armada on radar. Not wanting to believe what the radar scope revealed, the frantic pilot contaced the main air base at Wusadi and reported his terrible discovery.

Air Force General Bait Bazun bin Natrun, the commander of the South Yemen air base at Wusadi, hastily conferred with Major Arseni Rasseikin, the Soviet advisor. Following Rasseikin's advice, General Natrun then ordered the Control Tower to radio instructions to the pilot: *Keep your distance and follow the enemy helicopters. Report back to us every few minutes and inform us of your position. We are sending seven more jet fighters to assist you.*

The Control Tower then reported the approaching enemy air armada to Colonel al Bin Shaabi and Major Abdul Jahiz, both of whom were at Danikil, Rabadh Yahya Tabriz's main camp in the Jabal Hadramawi. With them were sixteen *al-Yemen Bayyi'l'ali* agents and three members of the *Glavnoye Razvedyvatelnoye Upravleniye*, or Chief Intelligence Directorate of the Soviet General Staff—Soviet military intelligence, or the GRU[1]. The Russians present in the *majlis*, or sitting room, of Tabriz's house in Danikil were General Yuri Leonid Kasmanovisky, Colonel Maskim Oosukhov, and Major Vasili Tarasov. They were just as stunned at the news as the Yemenis present.

Rabadh Yahya Tabriz glared like a demon at Colonel al Bin Shaabi. A fleshy man in his sixties—who looked forty—Tabriz had long black hair, curly at the ends, a short beard, skin that was the color of bronze, and eyes that were mere slits. Dressed in a black gallabiya and black boots, he had a Russian Stechkin machine pistol strapped around his waist and a short *stinviq*, in a leather scabbard, was tucked into the wide black sash underneath the gunbelt.

"How can this be?" Tabriz demanded angrily of Colonel Shaabi. "How can dozens of aircraft, with blades on their tops, be approaching this village? Colonel Shaabi, you assured me that we would be attacking Ali Sa'galli's stronghold in the Jabal Mahrat. Instead, he is attacking us!" His right hand made a sweeping motion toward the three Soviet GRU officers. "It is their advice you followed, the idiot words of those pale-skinned foreign devils from north."

"Don't be ridiculous!" Colonel Shaabi shouted, losing

1. The GRU is an acronym and not the initials of the deadly organization. In Russian the pronunciation would be *Geh Eh Ru*—"Gay A Rue."

his temper because he was really angry at himself, sensing that something was very wrong and that his carefully laid plans were about to collapse. "How could that damned Ali Sa'galli and his traitors be in helicopters? It can't be Sa'galli."

"It's the Saudis or the Americans," General Kasmanovisky declared, an acrid tone in his low voice. "Somehow they have learned of our attack plans." He turned coolly to Colonel al Bin Shaabi. "Colonel, somewhere within the higher circles around you, there is a spy."

Shaabi and Major Jahiz's eyes went wide with surprise and anger. Neither man had time to protest though. Major Vasili Tarasov, who was cocking his head to one side, hissed, "Listen! Do you hear that noise in the distance? Those helicopters are only ten minutes way from this village."

"They will have cannons," said Colonel Maskim Ossukhov, deep fear in his voice. "These stone huts with wooden roofs will not protect us."

General Kasmanovisky snapped in Russian, *"Likaya ini i estven'naya malen'kom gorode osaz debbaya!"* ("All we can do now is save ourselves and hope for the best".)

"To the temple," snarled Tabriz. "To the temple of Melek Taus. There we will be safe. Melek Taus,[2] the god of this world, will protect us.

The leader of the Dasni turned and strode to the thick wooden door.

The Death Merchant and his attack group were aware that their presence was known to the enemy. The radar of the Super Frelons had detected the single Mig-23 fighter at the same time that the South Yemen pilot had spotted them. At first, Camellion & Co. could not be certain of de-

2. Malek Taus—Satan—is considered the "god of this world." Ironically, the name DASNI means "God-worshippers." Melek Taus, is regarded as the chief of the angelic hosts. He suffers punishment now but will eventually be restored to his former high station. The Dasni regard the Devil as the creative agent of the Supreme God and try to propitiate Melek Taus as the source of evil. They do not worship him in the sense that a Christian worships God.

tection, one way or another, not knowing if the Mig carried radar. They became convinced that the Mig did have radar and had detected them when it changed course and started to fly on a course parallel to their own, yet keeping a distance of 36.3 air miles.

"It won't make any difference," the pilot of the command Frelon said, speaking through an intercommunication system to Major Quinlan and Richard Camellion, each of whom wore a RS-200 Boom mike-and-head-set with a push-to-talk button. "We're only a skip and short jump from Danikil. Even if they lifted their Mi-8 birds off the ground right now, we could still bring 'em down with missiles. I've put the other pilots and gunners in the Lynxs on full red." (Full alert.)

Remarked the Death Merchant to Mad Mike, who was sitting next to him, "He's right, but only from the point of view of a pilot. The truth is that our being spotted makes a tremendous difference. Colonel Shaabi and all his trash will have time to take over."

"There's only one refuge against our miniguns," Quinlan said. "The Temple. We could blow that mess of heavy stones apart with missiles. We can't. You know why, Gardner."

Camellion didn't comment. Sure, he knew why. His own orders and Mad Mike's were to make sure that Colonel Shaabi ended up as a cold cut in the market place. They couldn't ID his corpse from the air—*and we'll do damn well to find it on the ground!*

He looked at the Seiko on his wrist. It was almost time.

Only a few minutes had passed when the pilot's voice came over the three speakers in the rounded roof of the Frelon:

"ATTENTION. ATTENTION. WE AND THE OTHER FRELONS ARE GOING UP TO WAIT. FIVE OF THE WESTLANDS WILL BE GOING IN. WE'RE ARRIVED AT THE TARGET."

The attack plan was predicated on helicopter tactics perfected in the bloody mess that had been Vietnam, the well-trained, experienced American pilots knowing exactly what to do. While the fourteen Frelons started to gain altitude, five of the Westland Lynx gunships *below* the Frelons began to descend in a swing-around banking maneuver. The remaining five Westlands also began to climb the sky and gain altitude.

155

Stretched out for almost half an air-mile, the fourteen Super Frelons hovered at an altitude of 9,000 feet, 2.6 miles southeast/south of Danikil. Three thousand feet above the Frelons were the five Westland Lynx choppers. Just let any of Colonel al Bin Shaabi's jets show up!

Only five of the gunships would attack the main village of the Dasni—and five was more than enough to do the job. Three of the Westlands came in from due south. They would rake the village from an altitude of 300 feet. The other two Westlands would come in from the southwest and scatter death at an altitude of only 150 feet.

The three Westland Lynx guns ships from the south made the first slaughter-run, all in a row, one right after the other, their GE M134 Miniguns, sticking out of port and starboard, roaring a hideous symphony of execution—six terrible weapons that, combined, could spit out an incredible 36,000 rounds of 7.62mm projectiles *per minute.*

Quick, instant Death descended on Danikil, thousands and thousands of spitzer-shaped steel-cored slugs stabbing downward, a cloud of metal as thick as an intense hail storm. Many of the frantic Dasni—men, women and children—had managed to reach the jumbled rocks surrounding the village. Most had not. Hundreds of them were killed within seconds, the slugs butchering them, many of the corpses falling in pieces to the blood-soaked ground.

A triple Apocalypse! Goatskin tents by the dozens exploded into thousands of bits and pieces of hair fabric, their supporting poles turned into giant splinters. *BLAM! BLAM! BLAM!* There were scores of tiny flashes and explosions on the ground—like strings of firecrackers—as 7.62 NATO rounded exploded grenades carried by terrified Dansi devil-worshipers who were frantically trying to find cover.

Seemingly a constant tongue of flame, a foot long, remained in front of each Minigun as thousands of projectiles jumped from the muzzles, each one searching for a victim. The thin wooden roofs of hundreds of one and two room huts were dissolved into splinters, the same slugs exploding pottery, ripping through furniture and bedding and killing Dasni women and children who had not had time to flee from the rocks.

The 18 Soviet Mil Mi-8 troop-transport helicopters were

bunched together on the east side of Danikil. Projectiles from the gunships found the Soviet flying eggbeaters. *ZIP-ZIP-ZIP-ZIP!* Hundreds of projectiles ripped into the gray and white whirlybirds. Almost as a single unit, four of the huge four-bladed helos exploded into big bright balls of fire, parts and pieces of each craft soaring into the air, the big *WHOOOSSSHHHHHHH* of the explosions followed by thick black smoke crawling rapidly toward the clouds.

The gunners of the first three Westlands didn't bother to waste precious ammo on the immense stone temple of Melek Taus. The temple, which was 400 years old and had taken almost six years to build, had walls ten feet thick and a stone dome, of interlocking stones, five feet thick.

The run completed, the three Westland Lynx gunships zoomed up to the north and began to bank to starboard, the gunners secure in their holding straps, putting the ends of fresh belts of ammunition into the Miniguns.

The two other Westlands now attacked from the southwest, roaring in at an altitude of 150 feet, 300 feet apart from each other. The four gunners, wearing Vedex sound protectors over their ears, opened fire and began to sweep the terrain below with thousands of slugs. The gunners didn't have any difficulty in seeing the targets. Not only had hundreds of campfires been burning when the Westlands had attacked, but the 7.62mm projectiles, ripping through roofs and triggering various explosions, had generated more fires. More than a hundred houses were burning, dirty gray and black smoke boiling skyward. If anything it was the smoke that impeded the vision of the pilot and the gunners. More Dasni men, women, and children died, slugs ice-picking into their bodies. Arms and legs were torn off by slugs, heads exploded, shouts and screams of agony lost in the thunderous roaring of the Miniguns and the constant *thump-thump-thump-thumping* of the rotor blades cutting through the hot, smoky air.

The portside gunner of one Westland Lynx and the starboard gunner of the second gunship concentrated for ten seconds on the remaining Soviet Mi-8 helicopters, two of which were lifting off the ground, their pilots, lacking basic common sense, thinking that they could move the helos to safety. The damn fools might as well have tried to float a feather in the center of a tornado.

The first Mi-8 exploded when it was only twenty-five feet

off the ground. A big *WWWHHHOOOSSSHHHHHH*, a brief flash of fire and smoke, a flaming shower of aluminum and it was all over with.

The pilot the other Mi-8 was only slightly more successful. It had risen to seventy-five feet when hundreds of projectiles riddled the craft and sent fuel dribbling all over its hot engines. *BLAMMMMMM!* Another huge flash of flame and parts of the Mi-8 were tumbling to the ground, to mingle with the wreckage of the other Soviet transports and giving off thick smoke that might have been drifting into infinity.

Spotting the twenty-foot tall metal peacock rearing upward from the vivid red dome of the temple, one of the minigunners made an instant decision. He triggered a long burst of 7.62mm slugs at the point where the rod, supporting the gaudily painted peacock, protruded from the dome. In only seven seconds, hundreds of projectiles stabbed into the dome, the terrible impact tossing up thousands of stone chips and "digging" the brace-support free of the roof. For a moment, the peacock tottered back and forth, as if unsure what to do. Then it fell forward, crashed on the west side of the dome, slid down the stones and crashed to the ground with a loud noise.

Their work of destruction completed for the moment, the two Westland gunships grabbed altitude, banked to starboard and started to make the swing around, their movements permitting the three other Westland choppers to come in. The gunners of the three birds had reloaded and were anxious to complete the job. This time, however, the three Westlands used different tactics. Only one screamed over the burning village, its two Miniguns roaring. The other two—on orders transmitted by the Death Merchant—roared past the outer edges of the village, one moving clockwise, the other counterclockwise, all four Miniguns roaring. Again, thousands of projectiles streamed downward, this time zipping through budar trees and bushes and chopping up plants. One long scream erupted from almost constant ricochets, from slugs striking stones, many after having stabbed through the bodies of Dasni. Blood, gore, bits of flesh and bone, tiny pieces of clothing and other debris dripped and fell onto yellow *raqmah* flowers, white cranesbills, and tall purple plants the Arabs called *qaf'a.*

158

Each Westland Lynx slug-sweeping the perimeters took special care on the south side, swinging back and forth and criss-crossing the area, the GE Miniguns hosing down the entire area.

After some ten minutes the three Westlands moved upward and the two other Westlands came down as though to make a run. This time, however, the two birds did not make a west to east sweep. They came in and hovered, one to the east, the other to the west, swinging back and forth and moving slowly in a wide circle while their four Miniguns raked the ground with streams of projectiles.

A quarter of a mile to the south, the Super Frelons began to descend, their goal a large level grassland relatively free of rocks, the Thunderbolt Unit Omega fighters relieved that finally they would be getting into action and doing what they could do best—kill. Ali Sa'galli's men were even happier, but for a different reason. They had not been comfortable flying through the air, feeling that to ride in mechanical contrivances was positively unnatural.

Colonel al Bin Shaabi, Major Abdul Jahiz and the three Russians, as well as Rabadh Yahya Tabriz and over 130 of his killers had reached the Temple of Melek Taus, the last of the Dasni rushing in as the first Westlands streaked in for the attack. Miniguns had begun roaring as a dozen of the Dasni were closing the large double doors . . . massive doors, two feet thick and seventeen feet tall.

Consumed with hatred and helplessness, Colonel al Bin Shaabi crouched against a wall. All he could do—all any of them could do—was wait out the attack and hope that fighter jets arrived in time. Occasionally, Shaabi and some of the others would look up at the curved inward dome whose center towered 116 feet above them. To a man they knew fear when the Minigun opened up on the brace and the peacock crashed against the dome and slid down the roof.

TRAPPED! And everyman inside the temple knew it.

Standing next to Colonel al Bin Shaabi, Rabadh Yahya Tabriz said in a loud voice, "We have nothing to fear. Machine gun bullets cannot penetrate these thick walls."

Colonel Maskim Oosukhov, who considered all Arabs lice, took delight in saying, "What do you think missiles could do to this pile of stones? Only one enemy missile could bring that dome down on us."

Tabriz did not reply. No one else spoke. There wasn't anything to say. Not only had the entire plan to attack Ali Sa'galli collapsed, but—far worse—Danikil itself was being attacked. Every man had his own thoughts, but eventually every man's worried mind came back to square one: what would they do if the enemy attacked the temple. The large temple was bare, except for rows of stone idols, various altars, and stone benches.

One by one the Super Frelons started to descend and began to land. No sooner had each one touched ground than port and starboard doors were flung open and Thunderbolt mercenaries jumped to the ground and, automatic weapons in their hands, flung themselves to prone positions around each helicopter whose sides bore the markings of North Yemen, or the Yemen Arab Republic: red, white, and black horizontal stripes and a green star. Working with lightning speed, some of the mercs set up Heckler and Koch light machine guns—HK21s, HK11s, HK21AIs. Other mercs began to scan the rocks to the south and the west through night vision devices.

The command Frelon was the eighth helicopter to land, the Death Merchant and his seven men (who had expressed a desire to remain with him) and Major Quinlan waited while the other men left the chopper.

As Manfred Rohde, Dimitur Zlatev, and some of Mad Mike's other men brushed past Clayton, the CIA agent, looking perplexed and confused, turned to Quinlan, "Aren't you going to give them any orders, Major?" he asked.

"Why should I? They know what to do." Quinlan braced himself by hanging onto a handhold. "Twenty-five of my men will remain with the Frelons. The rest will be formed into squads of ten, each squad with a sergeant who will keep in contact with Manfred, Georgios, and Dimitur. They'll keep in touch with me and Big Sal. Big Sal monitors and tapes all communications for my records, for future analysis."

"Don't you also mean that your men will also report to Camellion and me?" snapped Clayton. He glanced toward the rear of the craft where "Big Sal" Salmao had set up a small folding table and had placed on it a Rank Telecommunications VHF 2-way "Pocket Phone" System, to which was attached two tape recorders.

"I mean to ME. I'll report to Gardner." Quinlan's eyes were suddenly as hard as diamonds. His voice carried a direct warning. "Get something straight, Clayton. As far as I'm concerned, you're not even here. Don't get in the way."

Clayton was thunderstruck! "Listen, Major, you are being paid by the Central Intelligence Agency. I happen to be—"

"That will be quite enough!" The Death Merchant's sharp voice had all the stopping power of a .44 magnum slug. "You're forgetting your own instructions, Clayton. You are subject to my orders. As of now, I'm ordering you to stay here with Big Sal. You don't have enough battle-and-kill moxy go with us. You stay here. That's a direct order."

Clayton was too stunned to speak.

"He'll either do what I tell him or I'll blow his mutherfuckin' head off!" squeaked Big Sal. "I'll do the monitoring. He can act as a guard."

Knowing that he had lost even the short end, Clayton didn't protest.

Once the Death Merchant and Major Quinlan had left the command chopper, they and the rest of the attack force lost no time in moving in toward the burning village. One concern they didn't have was the efficiency of the Thunderbolt Omega mercs, or, for that matter, the merits of Ali Sa'galli and the Sons of the Falcon. The rebels were highly experienced guerrilla fighters, having gained their experience the hard way, in fighting for years against Colonel Shaabi and his troops.

The advance was in the shape of a trident. Half of Ali Sa'galli's men moved to the west (to the left), the other half to the east (to the right). The mercenaries formed the middle prong of the trident. They moved straight from the south.

The orders were simple: kill anything that moved. Women and children? The women and children were

161

doomed, if for no other reason than Ali Sa'galli and his men firmly believed that a devotee of Melek Taus represented pure evil and must be killed, this conviction extending to even the wives and children, as well as the animals belonging to the devil worshipers. For evil can contaminate. A harlot does not repent, and water in a jar does not become sour milk.

The three prongs of the trident raced across the open area to a region of small boulders that lay between the village and where the Super Frelons had put down. The force stopped and began to proceed with extreme caution when they reached the rocks, the remains and partial exfoliation of a granite mountain that had been worn away for millions of years. It was not very likely that any Dasni were concealed in the rocks. The fire of the Miniguns had been too intense. But who could be certain?

In small groups, ones and twos, they moved through the rocks, more than ready for the enemy but finding only dozens of dead bodies riddled and bloodied by 7.62 millimeter projectiles. And they found men and women who were gravely wounded and moaning. The moans were quickly silenced with a variety of knives, especially *stinviqs,* the 19-inch short swords carried by the Sons of the Falcon.

The stink was terrible, not from the fresh corpses but from the burning village. The wind was blowing from the northeast and with it came the stench of burning wood and materials of various kinds: cotton, wool, leather and goatskin; of burnt metal, rubber, plastic, copper, jet fuel, and that peculiar smell that comes from stones subjected to intense heat. And from another odor, the not-un-pleasant smell of frying meat, a detached could have thought a barbecue was in progress. Cooked human flesh has the aroma of a good grade of pork (except in a modern crematorium, where nothing alive is inside the "oven" to smell it!).

Even while the dying village was still hidden by masses and slabs of granite, some of the rocks lying end-on-end like giant gray dominoes pushed over, the Death Merchant and the other men could see the bright fiery glow pulsating red against the low clouds, and see large sparks and burning embers being carried by the wind.

Camellion moved forward. He was ready, an Ingram

MAC-11 machine pistol in his left hand, the .44 Alaskan Auto Mag pistols snug in their holsters around his waist. The straps of bags, filled with grenades, blocks of high explosive and spare ammo, were tight against his shoulders, the bottoms of the bags secured by straps around his legs. To his left was Major Quinlan, to his right, Colonel Bin Maktum. Slightly behind him were Rashid al-Khaima, Muhammad al Auf, and the three other Arabs of the group that had been with him in Aden.

The only real puzzle facing Camellion was the Israeli Mossad agent. The Death Merchant was almost positive that he knew the identity of the Israeli intelligence agent. Yet he wanted to be certain. He didn't want to terminate the wrong man—*Assuming he isn't knocked off by the Dasni or some of Colonel Shaabi's boys. How can I be certain? A test? Uh-huh? What kind of test?*

Equally as perplexing was why the Company and the Saudi intelligence directorate wanted the Mossad agent dead. The Mossad spook couldn't be working for Colonel Bin Shaabi. The man had taken his risks like everyone else—*Which doesn't prove a damn thing. That would be part of his job, part of his cover-up. He has to be one of the six Arabs. Clayton is not the type. He's a bureaucrat and a pain in the butt; that's all he is.*

Ah . . . the X-Factor again. Could the Mossad agent be a double? Was it possible he was also working for the GRU or the KGB? *Or is he really a KGB officer? Even so, why klll him? Why not take him in and try to turn him?*

The Death Merchant's group, that is, the "middle trident," was a mere twenty yards from the south side of the village when all the men heard Colonel al Bin Shaabi's jet fighters in the distance. The six Mig-23 fighters when two of the Westland choppers, hovering far above the village, fired six long range Sparrow AIM-7 missiles at the Migs.

Currently one of the most important missiles in service with NATO air forces, the Sparrow is an all-weather all-altitude weapon with tremendous maneuverability, this making it an efficient "dogfight" weapon. Powered by a Hercules Mark 58 Mod O solid-propellant rocket motor, the 12-foot long Sparrow guided and controlled by a Raytheon semi-active Doppler radar homing system with control by movable wings. Its maximum speed was over Mach

163

3.5. Its maximum range: 44 km (28 miles). Its warhead, 88 lbs. of cyclonite, was actuated by a proximity fuse.

The six Sparrow missiles streaked toward the six Mig-23 enemy fighter planes whose Russian pilots fired off 10 AA-6 Acrid missiles a split second before they broke formation and began to roll. The largest outboard antiaircraft missile in the world (21-feet long; range 15.5 miles; speed: almost Mach-4), the Acrid was deadly. There were ten of them in the dark sky, and all ten were streaking toward the ten Westland Lynx helicopters whose frantic pilots now fired off 18 Sidewinder AIM-9 missiles. Nine feet in length, the airframe of each Sidewinder was a slim cylindrical aluminum body, with a glass hemispherical nose, powered by a solid-propellant rocket motor and controlled and guided by an infrared homing guidance system. Speed: Mach 2.5. Range: slightly over two miles.

BLAMMMM! BLAMMMM! BLAMMMM! BLAMMMM! There were four beautiful balls of brief, bright fire as four Sparrows hit four Mig-23 fighters and reduced them to a flaming aluminum shower. The last two Migs rolled and dove in an effort to escape the two Sparrows streaking right behind them.

A micromoment later there were eight more explosions, each one an instant of shimmering light, a fleeting flamboyant brilliance that momentarily lighted up the black sky. Eight of the Sidewinders had made contact with eight AA-6 Acrid missiles.

The echoes of the 12 explosions were still crawling around in the clouds and the ten Westland Lynx gunships were maneuvering frantically in an effort to dodge the last two Acrids when six of the Westlands shot off four more Sparrows and the last two Acrid AA-6 missiles found two of the helicopters. *BLAAMMMMMMMM-BLAAMMMM-MMMM!* Then, far to the northwest were two more faint concussions and two ephemeral winks of red, like rare old wine spilled on a dirty gray tablecloth. Two of the sparrows—from the first batch of six—had found the last two South Yemeni Mig fighter jets.

The explosions of the two Westlands and of the two Acrid missiles seemed extra loud and the instantaneous bursts of light intensely dazzling, but only because the choppers were directly overhead, over Danikil. Burning wreckage and dismembered corpses began tumbling

164

through the hot sky to the burning village thousands of feet below.

A third Westland helo began to spin in circles and to swing crazily from side to side, the pilot fighting the collective and throttle and the cyclic and the trim controls. His efforts were useless. Large chunks of metal from one of the exploded Westlands had struck the tail rotor and one of the blades of the main rotor. The chopper was doomed. The blades were out of pitch, the gears falling apart in the gearbox. Coming down at a steep angle, shaking violently, the Westland Lynx careened wildly to the east, headed straight for destruction. It seemed that the craft would have to slam into the west side of the temple's dome. It didn't. Missing the temple altogether, the Westland crashed and exploded sixty feet behind the east wall of the temple. A big bang. A flash of flame and a lot of smoke and that was the end of it.

"Three out of ten isn't too bad," commented Major Quinlan who had moved over to the Death Merchant. "We'll be able to get back okay, but only if the skies remain clear of enemy fighters."

"If more jets show up, I reckon that would worry me a'plenty," Camellion said, slipping deliberately into a Texas accent. Came the instant change. He was all business, all professional, his voice low and firm. "Major, you had better check our column and the other two. Once we're positive everyone is set, we'll move in."

Muhammad al Auf, who had moved up to him and Quinlan with Ali Haddi, said very seriously, "Remember, *Sahib* Americans, many of those dwellings have deep cellars that could protect many Dasni from helicopter machine gun bullets. We cannot take any chances with a dwelling whose roof and contents have not burned."

"Grenades will do the job." His smile not particularly nice, the Death Merchant pulled a Tadiran PRC-601 Palm-Held FM/VFM transceiver from its plastic case on his belt. He pulled up the telescoping antenna, turned on the set and pressed the channel-4 button. Four feet away, Quinlan turned his PRC-601 and held the device close to his mouth. He pushed the TALK button and held it down. "*Sahib* Ali Sa'galli—"

Ali Sa'galli, in charge of the Sons of the Falcon to the west, reported that his column was ready to move into

Danikil and that "the blades of their *stinviqs* are thirsty for the blood of the evil servants of Shaitan. There has not been a change of plans?"

"No, there have not been any changes. You and your people will handle the village. We will close in on the temple," Quinlan said. He then contacted Yadollah I'Zoir and Omar Uruq, who were in charge of the *Ibn'u Alib Saqr* to the east. I'Zoir reported impatiently that all the men to east were anxious to go and "cut the filthy throats of those slime still breathing."

"Move in," Quinlan said. He looked over at the Death Merchant and grinned, his meaning very clear to Camellion. Fanatical hatred was the best kind of stimulant. The bloodthirsty Sons of the Falcon would slaughter every Dasni in sight.

With hopes high and weapons ready, the Death Merchant and his force poured from the rocks and stormed into the village of Danikil.

Now there was only one Prime Rule: *kill or be killed.*

☐ FOURTEEN ☐

If Richard Camellion had been a pessimist, he would have believed that everybody was as nasty as himself and would have hated them for it—if he had been a pessimist. But in these kinds of fire-fights, he was a complete optimist who was positive that one ingredient of success was always a wide-awake, persistent, tireless enemy. With Colonel al Bin Shaabi, the GRU, and Rabadh Yahya Tabriz, the Death Merchant had enemies who possessed all these qualities.

The Thunderbolt Omega merc and the blood-hungry fighters of the *Ibn'u Alib Saqr* stormed into Danikil from the south, the east, and the west, the men running in a zig-zag, their eyes trying to be everywhere at once.

The region was thick with smoke, and stank with the fetid funk of destruction, the thick stench of Death. There

166

had been hundreds of stone or adobe brick houses and hundreds of tents, the space underneath some of the tents equal to that of a four-room house. Eight out of every ten dwellings were either burning or giving off smoke from hot ashes that had once been roofs or crude furniture. Not a single goatskin tent remained standing. Those that had not been half-burned into rubble lay crumpled, riddled with bullet holes, their support poles ripped apart by Minigun slugs.

Almost immediately, submachine guns began chattering and MK3A2 offensive grenades began roaring off as the Sons of the Falcon began the slaughter run from the east and the west sides of the doomed and damned settlement.

The Death Merchant and his own "personal" group of six, and Major Quinlan and his Thunderbolt Omega kill experts, racing in fast from the south, used the same technique. Don't bunch up! Keep as low as possible and run in a crooked criss-cross pattern to a dwelling, even those still on fire. Quickly now! Throw in two grenades that would demolish the stone or wooden floor, even if the floor was wood and was burning.

Using his Ingram MAC-11—set on three-round bursts—as an auto-pistol, the Death Merchant darted to the side of an adobe house and crouched down, humming softly, the words to the tune turning over in his mind: "This land is your land, this land is my land, from the off-shore oil rigs, to the strip-mined mountains; from the redwood saw mills, to the toxic land fills, this land is owned by industry."

Had he detected movement from inside the dwelling, from the other side of the wall. No, he had not—*but I sense it*. Someone is inside.

Ahead, to his left, he saw Sa'id Al'amman and Padraig O Riain (whose name in English would be Patrick Ryan), a merc from the Republic of Ireland, toss grenades through a window of a burning hut then crouch down and wait as the hand-thrown bombs exploded.

Camellion couldn't see them, but behind him and to his right, Quinlan, al-Khaima, Shukairy, and Basappa Ram Gokhale, an Omega member who was a Gurkha, were stitching down four goatskin tents that had fallen and were harboring the Dasni enemy, the goatskins jumping and undulating as 9mm and H&K 5.56mm projectiles found warm flesh and the Dasni cried out as slugs slammed them into eternity.

Camellion half turned when Brian Morris, a British merc, came up behind him and muttered, "We 'aven't all day to waste on these bloody beggars. Let's get off our duffs and do what we 'ave to do, straightaway."

With a small grin, Camellion, giving Morris a disdainful look, noticed that the man had a .45 Colt Long Slide autoloader in each hand. Each .45 had an extra inch of barrel protruding that was Mag-na-ported, two horizontal cuts EDM-machined into the top of each barrel.

"Don't let speed overcome your common sense," Camellion told Morris. "There's two or three of the enemy inside. I was about to toss in grenades when you arrived. This is a two- or three-room deal."

"Let's do it, then," Morris growled and started to shove one .45 long slide Colt into a shoulder holster.

"You toss," Camellion said. "I'll ice those the grenade misses. Before you toss one in, count to fifteen slowly. That will give me time to get around to the front. And listen, don't throw more than one grenade. You got it?"

"Yeah. One."

"Start counting." The Death Merchant ducked down, crawled underneath a window opening, stood up and hurried around to the front of the house. He saw that there were two more windows, one on either side of a door that was closed. He had ducked under the closest window and was racing past the door to the far window when the grenade exploded, the concussion bashing little bells in his brain.

Never turst an unknown quality. Camellion had no intention of charging into the room where Morris had tossed the grenade. Suppose the merc tossed in another one? Instead he moved to the front window of the adjoining room, raised the MAC-11, looked in and fired instantly at the four *al-Yemen Bayyi'l'ali* agents crouched against the east wall. The Ingram chattered, the 9mm hollow point projectiles tearing into the bodies of the South Yemeni intelligence agents. Just in time Death Merchant spotted two more Yemenis rearing up from a heap of rubble in the southeast corner of the room and duck to his left to avoid a stream of nine-millimeter slugs splitting from the barrel of a Czech-25 submachine gun. He reacted instantly. The

168

next step of the two Yemenis would be to toss grenades through windows. What else could they do.

Camellion raced around the northeast corner of the house, came to a window, jumped in front of it and fired at the same time that the grenade, tossed through the front window by Hudo Dualeh, exploded. Abdul Shadada, the second Yemeni, had just pulled the pin from a Soviet RGD-5 grenade when six of the Ingram's 9mm projectiles chopped into his chest, tearing off bits and pieces of his uniform which fluttered to the ground as the impact knocked him backward and the grenade fell from his hand and exploded. By then, Camellion had dropped below the window and was moving back toward the front of the house. Reaching the front, he called out to Brian Morris, "It's clear. Come ahead."

It took only eighteen minutes for the Death Merchant, Major Quinlan and the other men of the "South Trident" to get within 150 feet of the monstrous temple of Melek Taus, which, due to the shadows cast by the various fires, appeared more hideous than usual.

The attack was going as scheduled, Ali Sa'galli, Omar Uruq, and Yadollah I'Zoir reported that their respective forces were meeting little resistance from the pathetically few survivors who had escaped the rain of death from the Westlands' Miniguns.

From around the edge of a stone wall that was part of a two room dwelling, Camellion, Mike Quinlan, Colonel Bin Maktum, and Rashid al-Khaima surveyed the Bunyanesque temple whose large stones were black with the age of centuries. Ahmed Shukairy, the three other Arabs of Camellion's "personal" group, Georgios Trypanis, and Marcel Lecanuet studied the temple structure from several windows. Lecanuet, a Frenchman and an exmember of the French Foreign Legion, had a habit of talking to his British 4.85mm "Individual Weapon" assault rifle, which, for some weird reason that only he knew, he called *Le Chinois*, "the Chinaman," although he thought of the weapon in the feminine gender. When asked about *Le Chinois*, the bearded, round-headed Lecanuet would say, "She is my best friend. She has saved my life more than once. She keepts me warm at night and she cannot become pregnant." Then he would roar with laughter.

"We have enough RDX packets to turn that temple into a rockpile," Quinlan remarked to the Death Merchant, his brown eyes scanning the double behemothic doors of the temple's main entrance. "When you get down to the bottom line, we don't even know for sure that the scum we want are inside."

"They're there," Camellion said moodily. "Unless Colonel Shaabi was never here, the logical place for him and his goons and Tabriz is the temple. Where else would they seek sanctuary from the Miniguns?"

"On that basis, you're correct," agreed Mad Mike curtly. No matter how we do it, we're going to have to use explosives to blow those doors. What are your ideas?"

Bin Maktum, a Beretta autoloader in his right hand, interjected, "There should be some way for us to push the odds in our favor. That building could hold five hundred men." The Saudi intelligence agent glanced to his right, at Marcel Lecanuet who, hunched over, was moving over to Quinlan.

"Mon Major, it would be no trouble for me to plant explosives on the doors," suggested Lecanuet, patting *Le Chinois*. "*Oui*, it would be a simple *une balade*, a walkover. Blow the doors and storm the entrance."

"*Non. C'est dangereux, mon ami*," Quinlan said without emotion. "They'd cut us to pieces when we stormed the opening." He glanced at the Death Merchant, who was studying the giant temple. "Gardner, what we need is a diversion to knock the 's' and the 'c' out of suicide. I want our losses to be kept at a minimum."

"Three big bangs would be better." Camellion was casual, his eyes remaining riveted on the temple. Hideous in the sunlight, with its black, hoary stones and vivid red dome, the temple was even more bizarre at night, especially now with fantastic shadows, generated by the numerous fires, gliding over the walls and the dome.

"Three?" Quinlan's eyebrows raised. "Such as?"

The Death Merchant pulled the Tadiran PRC-601 from its case. "A pound of RDX will blow those doors to hell. Two more blocks in back, by the east wall, will make us another opening, wide enough for several tanks to go through."

"And the third explosion?"

The Death Merchant extended the antenna of the PRC-601 and pressed the channel-2 button, then the TALK button. "Big Sal, patch me in to Colonel Davis."

Back came Big Sal's high-pitched voice. "You dumb hay-head! How in hell can you talk to Colonel Davis? He's scattered all over the place. He was in one of the helicopters that stopped a missile."

"Okay, big man. Give me the head honcho who's now in charge of the Westlands," Camellion said, stiffling a laugh.

The Death Merchant was soon talking with Captain Adam Whitclee who was in one of the choppers that was landing close to the Super Frelons. Camellion had only one question: how much damage would a Sidewinder missile do if one was shot into the dome. A lot, replied Whitclee, depending of course on the thickness of the dome.

"A Sidewinder would blow a hole at least twenty feet wide in the dome," stated Whitclee. "I can't be sure. It's only an educated guess. But the explosion wouldn't destroy the dome. The dome's too big and the walls too thick."

"Fine. I don't want the dome destroyed," Camellion replied, a pleasurable feeling surging in his chest. "We only want a diversion."

Laughter floated out of the Tadiran PRC-601. "You'll get that, all right. I could have tons of stones fall inside the temple. Do you want me to go up now and slam a Sidewinder into the dome? Any particular side?"

"Go upstairs but don't fire one off until you get the order from me or Major Quinlan," instructed Camellion. "Hit the dome from the north side, say . . . about its center. And keep your channel open. AR for now. Sal, you there?"

"Big Sal?" screamed the dwarf. "You dumb mutherfucker! I'm *Big* Sal!"

"BIG Sal, keep me patched in to Whiteclee," Camellion said sharply, "and make sure the hookup is secure. A lot of lives depend on it—and knock off the smart talk. You got it?"

"I got it." The dwarf was serious, all his anger dissipating instantly.

Camellion switched off the transceiver, returned the set to its case and gave a long searching look at Quinlan who

171

was studying the temple through 8 X 33mm Zeiss bincolulars.

"You'll notice that there's not a single window or any gun ports," Camellion said. "Apparently those rows of square holes at the top are for ventilation. I don't think the holes are even a foot square, and they're sixty feet above the ground. The Dasni can't be that high, unless they're on stilts. Even if they were, what could they see through those thick walls?"

Mad Mike Quinlan lowered the binoculars. "How do you want to do it, Gardner?"

The Death Merchant told him. Ten minutes more and the two groups were ready. Camellion, Ahmed Shukairy, Sa'id Al'amman, and ten Thunderbolt mercs, led by Manfred Werner Rohde, would blow the double doors. Colonel Bin Maktum, Rashid al-Khaima, Ali Haddi, and ten more Omega fighters, led by Dimitur Zlatev, would race along the south side of the temple, then move to the east side and plant explosives at the bottom center of the wall.

Camellion visually inspected the men, checking them one by one. They stared back at him, silently telling him they were ready.

"May our wives not become empty due to this evil night," Basappa Ram Gokhale, the black turbaned Gurkka, said softly.

Claude Wicks, an American mercenary, gave the big, bearded man an odd look. "That's a helluva strange expression, Bas, old buddy. How come 'empty'?"

"In Sanscrit, the word for widow is *Pu-di*," explained Ram Gokhale. "It means empty."

"Let's do it and do it fast," the Death Merchant said. "We'll all link up on the south side of the temple. Quinlan, make sure your boys with the crossbows are ready."

"They will be," Quinlan said. "Just make damn certain we have the room."

Led by Camellion, who now had a .44 AMP in his left hand and an Ingram sub-gun in his right fist, the two tiny forces began the run across the short space, the sounds of gunfire, of shouts and yells and screams coming at them from the east, the west, and the north. The Sons of the Falcon were having their revenge with interest.

Camellion & Company zigged and zagged . . . just in case. To Major Quinlan and the others watching, the race to the temple resembled the flight of giant hummingbirds that dart first one way and then anohter. Not a shot was fired from the temple.

Camellion, Shukairy, Al'amman, and the ten mercs under the control of Manfred "Scarface" Rohde, reached the southwest corner of the temple and proceeded to move with chain-lightning speed to the double doors on the west side. Colonel Bin Maktum, Rashid al-Khaima, Dimitur Zlatev and the other ten Thunderbolt boys rushed up the south side of the enormous stone structure.

With the mercs—down on one knee, their weapons pointed outward—forming a half circle around him and the two Arabs, the Death Merchant removed two one-pound blocks of RDX from one of his Marine Corps cargo packs.

Ahmed Shukairy's dark face mirrored surprise. "*Sahib* Gardner, you are going to use two blocks. Such explosions will blow away far more than the doors."

Putting down the two blocks of RDX, Camellion reached into the bag and took out two remote control detonators, a roll of copper wire and a pair of wire cutters. "That's the general idea, Ahmed. Besides, each block is 33 percent wax[1]."

On his haunches, Camellion cut off two lengths of copper wire, wrapped them around each block of explosives, got to his feet, reached up and wrapped both ends of one wire, securing one block, around a square bolt head that, on the left-side door, was only a foot from the edge of the stones in the wall. He then pressed the prongs of the R-C detonator through the oily brown paper, feeling the metal slide through the powerful explosive, which had the consistency of a block of frozen butter. The last thing he did was pull the seal from the detonator and flip the switch, all the while wishing he could hear Liszt's *Les Préludes*—perfect music to kill by.

Camellion then repeated the process, with the second block of RDX on the door to the right. He was moving

---

1. RDX is Cyclonite and is composed of cyclotrimethylenetrinitramine. Sensitivity is appreciably reduced by the addition of wax.

the switch to ON with a forefinger when the PRC-601 began beeping.

The caller was Colonel Bin Maktum. "We're set on the east side," reported the Saudi intelligence agent, sounding nervous. "Six feet up and ten feet apart, as you instructed. Over."

"You're sure all is in order? Over."

"Positive. *Sahib* Rohde set the charges. He's a demolitions expert. He said at least fifty feet of the wall will go and that the trash inside will be lucky if the entire east wall doesn't come down. Over."

"Good enough. All of you get to the south side." The Death Merchant held the PRC-601 transceiver close to his mouth. "AR. Ten-four. And all that jazz." He paused for a moment and looked up at the sky, at the Delphian darkness tinged with flickering shades of red from the fires in the village. The cloud cover had lowered; the humidity was higher, and he could sense that the dew point—the temperature at which air becomes saturated and/or can hold no more water vapor—had risen. *The seasonal rains! We don't want the first shower before we're done with this night's work! The hell with it! ¡El olvido, la muerte de la muerte!* (To be forgotten is the death of death.)

Camellion spoke into the PRC. "Sal, did you hear all that?"

Marcello Salamo's childish voice popped out of the PRC's speaker, "I heard."

"Give me a P to Captain Whiteclee," Camellion ordered, his gaze catching Shukairy's. The north Yemeni Royalist stared back at him.

Captain Whiteclee was beginning to swing the Westland Lynx around by the time the Death Merchant and his group had reached the center south wall of the temple and were linking up with Bin Maktum, "Scarface" Rohde and the rest of the men who had been by the east wall of the enormous structure.

Many curious eyes were on the Death Merchant as—in response to Captain Whiteclee's beeping—he switched on the PRC transceiver.

"Gardner here."

"We're almost in position," Adam Whiteclee reported.

174

"By the time you count to forty, the missile will be on its way. Everyone in position? Over."

"Shoot—and out," Camellion said.

The other men, flattened against the long and high stone wall, had already pushed rubber ear plugs into their ears and were standing with their mouths open and breathing deeply as protection against the coming concussion.

The Death Merchant put away the transceiver and put in his own ear protectors. He was taking out the battery-operated "trigger" of the remote control detonators when Captain Whiteclee and Lieutenant Horowitz banked the Westland and turned on the electric gunsight, switched in over to the pods and turned on the computer. Seventeen seconds more and there was a whosh from one of the starboard pods. The deadly Sidewinder was on its way.

The missile streaked to the north side of the giant red dome, hit in the center and exploded with a thunderous crash that made the entire building shudder. Chunks and masses of rock and stone flew upward and out, the smaller pieces sailing several hundred feet from the center of the explosion. One 180-pound hunk of stone fell on one of the Rolls-Royce GEM 10001 turbine engines that had belonged to one of the Westlands that had been shot down. The R-R GEM 10001 had fallen 150 feet north of the temple's north wall and had half-buried itself in the earth. A vast shower of jagged rocks and stone chips rained down on the rest of the dome and on the tiled roof of the long section of the "T" shaped building. The huge clouds of dust had not even begun to settle as a feeling-good Camellion flipped the ON switch of the remote control device that controlled the detonators on all four blocks of RDX. Seeing that the signal light was glowing green, he glanced first to the left, then to the right. The men, in place, were waiting. His thumb pushed down on the red firing button.

BLAMMMMMMMMM-BLAMMMMMMMMM-BLA-*MMMMMMMMM-BLAMMMMMMMMM!* The four pounds of RDX exploded simultaneously, the monstrous blasts sounding like the salvo from half a dozen 18″ guns on a battleship. The south wall trembled so violently that for a shave of a second, Camellion and the men with him had the fleeting fear that the entire building was about to come down around them.

How about that! Camellion pulled out the PRC walkie-talkie, glanced to the left and saw that three of the mercs, one of them Scarface Rohde, were looking around the southeast corner of the temple. The PRC started beeping when six of Quinlan's men, 150 feet to the southwest, began shooting fragmentation grenades through the blasted opening where the giant double doors in the west wall—the front of the temple—had been. The mercs were using Barnett self-cocking crossbows, the grenades attached to the center of the arrows.

One after another the grenades exploded, throwing up more fragments of stone and dust.

The Death Merchant switched on the walkie-talkie and at the same time noticed that Sa'id Al'amman was running toward him. "This is Gardner. What does the west wall look like, Major. Over."

"A damn good job." Mad Mike sounded like he wanted to laugh and tap dance. "There's a hole forty feet wide and twenty-five feet high. What about the east-side wall?"

The Death Merchant was forced to pause by five more grenades that, winged inside on the arrows of crossbows, exploded. "Hold on a sec," he said, speaking into the walkie-talkie. He looked at Sa'id Al'amman.

The North Yemeni grinned, revealing big teeth. He put up his hands, holding them two feet apart. "A larger tear in the stones, *Sahib* Gardner. Fifteen meters wide and the same in height. All we can see is smoke and dust, and there is only silence from the inside of the evil place."

The Death Merchant barked into the PRC. "A hole, fifty feet in length and just as high. It's a wonder the wall's still standing. So let's do what we have to do. You take the west side. We'll take the east. We'll trap them in a crossfire. Any questions? Over."

"See you in church. Out."

Putting away the PRC transceiver, the Death Merchant saw that scores of mercs were already coming in from the southwest, zigzagging for the west wall. He took a deep cleansing breath, raised his right hand and waved it forward, the signal for the men with him to attack through the east wall. He took another deep breath, pulled the twin Alaskan .44 Auto Mags and, with the rest of the men, began racing east and psyching himself up for combat, calling upon the power of Chi—

176

The three walks of life:
to walk in the heavens,
to walk on the water,
but first to walk the way
of the Tao' Lin Tui . . . .

☐ FIFTEEN ☐

The exposion of the Sidewinder missile had not been unexpected by Colonel Qahtan al Bin Shaabi and his force;
they had anticipated some sort of blast. Nonetheless, the
explosion had done little damage. Tons of dislodged stone
blocks fell from the dome and crashed to the center of the
floor, burying the main altar and smashing a dozen tall-
as-a-man candle holders filled with black candles. Two
large brass incense burners were also flattened and buried
by rock rubble. But because Colonel al Bin Shaabi and his
men were crouched by the north and the south walls and
scattered next to mammoth square pillars in the long, per-
pendicular "T" section of the temple, not a single man had
been hurt. There was only an insidious ringing in their
ears and a vast awe, a surprise, an astonishment that they
were still alive.

The two explosions from the east and the two explosions from the west were very different. Not only had
they not been unexpected, but the blasts were worse than
deafening, the concussion an invisible wall of pressure that
even pushed at one's eyeballs. The terrific thunder-blasts
caused instant changes. Blocks of granite, black with age,
could not withstand the pressure. Blocks that weighed tons
and had not been disturbed for centuries were changed
into crushed rock, some of the snagged rocks as large as
old-fashioned vinegar barrels, others the size of basket-
ball—on down to hunks and chunks the size of baseballs,
marbles, and even smaller than BB shot. It was the smaller
pieces that did the damage. They stabbed inward from the

east wall and the west wall as though blown from shotgun barrels. The granite shrapnel chopped into a dozen men— ten Dasni and two al-Yemen Bayyi'l'ali agents—killing nine of them instantly.

Three Dasni were killed by the immense wooden doors exploding, doors that were turned into splinters, many of which—along with thousands of stones—stabbed inward. Two Dasni went down, the front of their bodies riddled and dripping blood. The third man went down with a two-foot-long piece of wood, the size of a two-by-four, sticking out of his chest.

But for the long length of the forward section of the "T" shaped temple, scores of men would have been riddled by the stone chips and the barrage of splinters. Even so, the enormous explosions had stunned the Dasni and most of the Yemeni intelligence officers into a mental limbo, into a prision of emotional shock. When they began to recover their sensibilities, they found there were torrential phantasms of fear floating across their minds, nameless horrors that, springing from some unknown nuclei of polypous perversion, screamed of approaching death.

His iron nerve unbroken, Colonel al Bin Shaabi yelled at the *al-Yemen Bayyi-l'ali* gunmen to cover the still smoking hole in the east wall, while a furious Rabadh Yahya Tabriz and his lieutenants, all dressed in black *gallabiyas*, screamed at the Dasni to prepare for the attack, to take positions behind and to the sides of stone altars and by stone idols of lesser demons resting on huge pedestals of black basalt. They would fight to the finish—"And we will win!" screamed Tabriz. "No power on earth can stand up against the power of Melek Taus!"

However, within all the smoke and dust and madness, there was some reality and four realists: Major Adbul Jahiz, General Leonid Kasmanovisky and the other two GRU officers. Jahiz coldly accepted his fate as a matter of course. At least death would be quick. The three Russians also knew they would never leave the temple alive, although they had a particle of hope. They knew that only a miracle could save them; and men who believed that Man was an "accident" in the universe and totally conditioned by his environment could hardly believe in miracles. The three GRU officers had even less faith and hope when the first arrow-grenades streamed in at an angle through the forty foot wide gash in the west wall, exploded, and sent more rock, already blasted from the wall, flying toward the east. And the grenades kept coming. When the arrows finally did stop darting through the opening, they were replaced by scores of Thunderbolt Omega fighters who jumped through the gash, firing submachine guns and assault rifles as they darted to support columns. Eight Omega fighters died in three seconds, riddled with 7.62mm AKM and 5.45mm AKS-74 projectiles.

For the first time in its long history of evil, the temple of Melek Taus was being invaded. Malignant moss-covered walls and demon arcades, some corners choked with fungous vegetation, were no long secure and under the protection of Hell. It was as if a vast purification had been unleashed on a loathsome tidal wave of corruption more devastatingly horrible than the mind of man could imagine.

Some of the fierce Dasni, not used to being on the defensive, ignored the orders of Rabadh Yahya Tabriz and scurried toward two large mounds of rubble, of broken stones, in the center of the largest portion of the floor. Directly above the two piles was the gaping hole in the north side of the dome. Many of the Dasni attempted to move to the east side of the mounds of rubble, since not a single shot had been fired through the enormous rent in the east wall.

Surprise! The atsonished Dasni were promptly cut to pieces by Manfred "Scarface" Rohde who started raking the area with a Heckler & Koch GMBH G3A4 automatic rifle. With the battered-faced West German, leaning around the broken and jagged wall stones at the south end of the rip in the east wall, were Rashid al-Khaima, firing an Igram sub-gun, and Carlos Luis Cerón, an Omega merc from Argentina, who was firing short, deadly bursts of 9mm Parabellum slugs from a Belgian Mitraillette Vigneron M2 chatter box; and while the three men saturated the area with streams of high velocity death, other Omega kill experts poured through the ugly gap and stormed forward, running in a crooked pattern. With them came the Death Merchant, ducking and darting, dodging and weaving, an AMP Alaskan in each hand. A 5.45mm AKS projectile spun by his head, only three centimeters from his left temple. Half an eyeblink later, a 9mm Vitmorkin machine pistol slug, fired by Major Vasili Tarasov, almost struck his wrist as his right arm was raised. Instead of hitting flesh and bone and almost tearing off his hand, the flatnosed slug struck the edge of his Seiko, shattered the wristwatch and sent the blown-apart mechanism to the four hot winds.

Two more bullets streaked close to Camellion's body, one barely leaving a burn mark on the outside of his TAWGS on his right leg, at a point where the tough material of the trousers was tucked into the U.S. S.F. mountain boot. The other bullet tore along the inside of his left arm, tugging at the cloth of his field jacket.

Only minutes had passed since Camellion and one group had stormed through the east wall and Major Quinlan and his force had charged inside through the west wall. But already the Death Merchant and the other men were engaged in an eyeball-to-eyeball shoot-out and a man-to-man combat with the devil worshiping Dasni.

Camellion had four rounds left in his right Alaskan Auto Mag and two .44 cartridges in his left AMP. Ducking, moving from side to side with fantastic swiftness, he fired coolly and calmly. A tall, bearded Dasni, about to aim down on Urho Sundqvist, an Omega merc from Finland, took a .44 magnum projectile in the chest. He was slammed back against a stone support column, his *galla-biya* dripping blood. Eyes rolled back in his head, he slid down the stones and fell on his face.

Two more Dasni cried out, jerked up short, and went down almost simultaneously. A .44 magnum slug had torn through the chest and the back of one man, had struck a vertebra on its way out, changed course and had hit the second Dasni in the stomach, as a third man—looking as if he could thrive on ground glass burgers—came at Camellion swinging a deadly *Stinviq* and screaming curses at him.

"Baby cakes, you're demoted—to dead!" Camellion laughed, swung the right AMP, and barely touched the trigger. Another great blast of sound from the Alaskan Auto Mag and a 265-grain bullet leaped from the twelve and a half-inch long barrel. It struck the Dasni low in the stomach, the terrible impact doubling over the dying man as effectively as if he had been hit in the gut with a baseball bat.

Camellion at once decided he was in serious trouble and about to have more difficulty than a mouse in a bucket of black buzzards. Dasni were coming at him from all sides! A big hand grabbed his left wrist. At the same time he ducked in time to avoid a *Stinviq* that, if the sharp blade had connected, would have lifted his head from his shoulders.

Damn! He felt steel-hard fingers close around his right wrist, and, from the corner of his eye, saw a man coming at him from the left.

Hi-ho, everybody! It's count-your-blessings time!

Having reached the end of a stone altar on the south side of the temple and having exhausted the ammo in his Skorpion machine pistol, Mad Mike Quinlan pulled two Safari Arms MatchMaster auto-pistols from his hip holsters and began firing, each silvertip .45 point slug bringing the worst kind of catastrophe to black-robed Dasni fighters. Shooting very fast but carefully, Quinlan was about to snuff two more Dasni when Pat Ryan darted in to the pillar, coming in behind him, and, getting down, began to reload his two nickel-plated Hi-Power Brownings, and said in a thick Irish broque, "Let's get to another support, me boy. This position is a wee bit too dangerous."

ZZZIINGGGGGGG! An enemy bullet sped by Quinlan's face, stroked the stone support and richocheted. Another projectile, this one from a 9mm Soviet Makarov self-loading pistol, zipped to the right of Ryan and burned through the highest part of Quinlan's black beret, tugging viciously at the wool material.

"Behind us! At eleven o'clock!" yelled Ryan and dropped flat.

Jerking around, Quinlan fired both S.A. MatchMasters by instinct and training, pulled the triggers simultaneously. One bullet missed Buk Zeid'q, the Dasni gunman. The second .45 silvertip bullet smashed into Zeid'q's chest and slammed him back against two more of Rabadh Yahya Tabriz's killers who were frantically trying to reload their Soviet AKS-74 assault rifles. Moments later, both men cried their last cry, jerked and started the short, quick slide to hell, their bodies the home of 230-grain Federal .45 projectiles presented to them by Brain Morris, who was

181

down on the floor behind several Dasni corpses. Morris never got the chance to direct his .45 Colt Long Slides to other targets. The final grain in the hourglass of his life had dropped. One of Major Jahiz's *al-Yemen Bayyi'l'ali* agents spotted the British merc and stitched him down the back and along the left side with fourteen 7.62mm AKM slugs. Morris's eyes went wide. He grunted, jerked, and was dead before he had time to realize he was no longer among the land of the living.

Quinlan didn't take time to reload. He shoved the empty S.A. MatchMasters into their hip holsters, pulled two more stainless steel MatchMasters from his shoulder holsters and thumbed off the safety catches.

"I keep telling you to use Brownings," admonished Ryan, his eyes darting all around. "More shells in a clip equal time saved."

"MatchMasters never jam," Quinlan said. "Move! Get going!"

Ryan jumped up and both men got—raced—to the next pillar ten feet to the south. They darted around to the south side of the immense support and found themselves face to face with half a dozen *al-Yem Bayyi'l' ali* agents!

The Death Merchant was having his trials and tribulations. What made him angry at himself was the fact he was becoming furious at the four Zaidi—or Dasni—tribesmen who had ganged up on him. The insane looking goon to his left was trying to twist the AMP Alaskan from his left hand; the stinking piece of low trash to his right, the AMP from his right hand, while the bearded, frog-faced freak in front was drawing back a *Stinviq*, preparing to run him through with the sharp blade. To command Camellion's misery, a fourth man, a *Stinviq*[1] in each hand, was rushing in at him from the left side.

Damn and triple fudge!

Thank God and determinism for fourteen years of training in the martial arts! The Death Merchant—three times as strong as he looked and twenty times more agile—executed a very fast and a very powerful Tae Kwon Do Hyung roundhouse kick, the tip of his right Special Forces

1. Pronounced STO-VU in Arabic.

182

boot smashing into the underside of Summi Ali Ranan's chin with a loud crunch. Broken teeth popped from Ali Ranan's mouth, and so did the tip of his tongue which the upper and lower teeth, coming together, had cut off. Knocked unconscious, his lower jaw broken three places, his upper jaw fractured in two, Summi Ali Renan dropped his *Stinviq* and, choking to death on his own blood, started to melt to the floor.

The three other Dasni didn't have time to adjust to the Death Merchant's tactics and prepare accordingly. Camellion jumped a foot into the air, came down, jerked back with his entire body and tugged with both arms, pulling Iskim Mur'q'ul and Mahdi Al-Tejir off balance. He turned slightly to the right and his right knee came up in a power-lift that connected solidly with Mur'q'ul's groin at the same moment that Mur'q'ul, now using both hands, succeeded in twisting from the Death Merchant's finger the Alaskan Auto Mag which fell to the stone floor. A look of surprise dropped over Mur'q'ul's face and an agonized "OHHHH!" jumped from his mouth. His fingers relaxed on the Death Merchant's right arm.

"I don't want your brain to rush to your head!" snarled Camellion, who, now that his right arm was free, spun to his left and, in as little as three-fourths of a second, executed a double maneuver. He used a Shito-Ryu karate *Ushiro Kekomi Geri* rear thrust kick that turned Mur'q'ul's intestines to bloody mush before cannonballing the Dasni boob backward.

At the same time that his right foot was burying itself in Mur'q'ul's guts, Camellion's right hand streaked out in a *Sangdan Chirugi* high punch, his knuckles slamming into the bridge of Mahdi Al-Tejir's nose. Stunned and in pain, Al-Tejir cried out, relaxed his hold on the Death Merchant's left forearm and staggered to the right. A thick left-legged *Mae Geri Keage* front snap kick by Camellion to Al-Tejir's stomach demolished the man and sent him flying back.

The Death Merchant now had what he wanted: the Auto Mag in his left hand. He still didn't have time to use it. He had calculated that Al-Tejir would slam into Milan Muhammad Dauistan, the slime-ball with a *Stinviq* in each hand. Wrong! Dauistan jumped nimbly to one side and, screaming curses at Camellion, swung one of the short-

183

bladed swords. All the Death Merchant could do was duck the sharp blade that missed the top of his OD Satteen fatigue cap by one half an inch. What saved Camellion was that Dauistan's right arm was carried forward by its own momentum. Before the Dasni could move the *Stinviq* in his left hand or try for another swing with the right-handed blade, Camellion, who was going down on his left hip, snapped up the Alaskan and pulled the trigger. Sounding like a baby cannon, the Auto Mag roared, the big .44 magnum bullet catching Dauistan high in the left thigh, the lead tearing through the Pectinus muscle, cutting through the common iliac vein and tearing away several inches of femur bone. His leg almost torn off by the savage impact, Dauistan yelled and went down, his head only several feet from the stones of the floor when the Death Merchant's next .44 projectile exploded his head into numerous pieces of bloody brain and bone fragments.

Camellion scrambled to his feet, looked around, reached down, picked up the other AMP and, knowing he didn't have time to reload, shoved both big auto-pistols into their hip holsters. Reaching down again, he picked up one of the *Stinviqs* and pulled a .22 Walther P-38K from the top of his right boot.

Ducking and darting, Camellion saw that everywhere men were locked in a death struggle, fighting hand-to-hand. He saw Muhammad al Auf go down when a uniformed South Yemen intelligence agent stabbed him between the shoulder blades with a short-bladed boot knife. The *al-Yemen Bayyi'l'ali* agent's triumph was short lived, lasting only a micromoment. He died when Claude Wicks, whose left shoulder and side were soaked with blood, put two Smith and Wesson .41 magnum revolver slugs into his hip. Wicks then collapsed across the corpse of a Dasni.

Ahmed Shukairy! Seeing the North Yemen Royalist duck behind a square stone support thirty feet ahead of him, the Death Merchant moved after him, his cold blue eyes moving from left to right as he jumped lightly over "cold cuts" on the stones. Four times on his way, he used the *Stinviq*, its blade dripping with blood, to terminate Dasni struggling with Thunderbolt mercs, and one with Colonel Bin Maktum, the Dasni doing his very best to bury a spike-bayonet in the Saudi's chest. The man gurgled like a fifty-year-old flush box when Camellion slid the blade of the *Stinviq* between his ribs and sliced through both his lungs.

"Thanks, *Sahib* Gardner!" panted Bin Maktum. "I—" But Camellion, already moving ahead, didn't hear him. Maktum then, quite by chance, spotted a face he hated, the face of a man with long black matted hair, a short beard and whose entire countenance reflected evil at its worse. Rabadh Yahya Tabriz was ducking behind a six-foot wide pedestal on which rested an idol of Mobippid, a power demon represented as a man with the face of a toad, horns, four legs, and two enormous arms that hung down to his feet. Determined to kill Rabadh Tabriz and the two men with him, Rifa al Bawi and Kemel I'Tourii, his two top aides, Bin Maktum pulled his backup weapons from the front cargo pockets of his TAWGS, two .380 ACP Beretta 70S pistols.

Ahmed Shukairy, at the other corner of the support column, turned and twisted his mouth, showing his dirty teeth, when the Death Merchant jumped down beside him.

"We are winning, *Sahib* Gardner," Shukairy said. "Soon this battle will be over and the evil on this peninsula destroyed. " He then turned away and shoved a full magazine into an Ingram M-10 .45 submachine gun. He was about to pull back the cocking knob when Camellion said, "*A makeh unter yenem's orem iz nit shver tzu trogen!*"

Hearing Camellion speaking Hebrew—"Another man's disease is not hard to endure!"[2]—Shukairy jerked his head around and stared dumbfounded at Camellion, alarm in his dark eyes. The Death Merchant could see the guilt and the trapped look, not only in Shukairy's eyes, but also in his expression and demeanor.

Without a word, Shukairy attempted to pull back the cocking bolt of the Ingram, then swing the very short machine gun toward Camellion. He had to know he would never succeed, but it was the only choice he had, the only chance available to him. There could be only one result. The P-38K Walther in the Death Merchant's hand cracked

2. Literal translation: "A boil under another man's arm is not hard to bear."

once, twice, three times, the .22 caliber slugs zipping into Ahmed Shukairy's right side. A long "Uhhhhhh" was jumping from Shukairy's mouth when the P-38K barked two more times. This time the two projectiles tore into the side of Shukairy's neck, a few inches below his right ear, the slugs leaving two small black-blue rimmed holes in the dark skin that quickly filled with blood, a thick, deep redness that began to flow. The dead Shukairy, blood also trickling from his mouth, fell to his back, his eyes wide open, fixed in an eternal stare.

Wondering if any of his own people had seen him terminate Shukairy, Camellion leaned down, reached over and pulled the Ingram from the Mossad agent's stiffening fingers. He cocked the submachine gun and was preparing to look around the corner of the support when he heard two MK3A2 offensive grenades explode 100 feet northwest of his position, one right after another. And with the explosions came high shrieks, screams of agony. He stepped over the body of Shukairy—*I wonder what his real name was?*—looked carefully around the corner of the pillar and saw a lot of light blue smoke drifting away from the west end of a twenty-foot long altar on which had rested numerous five-foot high gold candlesticks. The candlesticks now lay scattered on the floor, knocked there by concussion from the exploding blocks of RDX on the double doors.

Who had thrown the two grenades? All Camellion could see were bodies and men still struggling. He saw Ali Haddi shudder and die on his feet, the Arab's striped *gallabiya* jumping from the impact of the nine millimeter Stechkin M-P projectiles. Colonel Maskim Oosukhov's next burst of machine pistol slugs crawled all over Albert Loots, the professional merc from South Africa, and kicked him into eternity.

From his position by the corner of the support, the Death Merchant detected by instinct that the stream of slugs had come from the west end of the altar, from behind the altar's west end, although, because of his position and the forty-foot width of the altar, he could not see who was firing. His problem now was how to get behind the altar.

How do I walk on water?

Major Quinlan and Pat Ryan should have been killed on the spot when they found themselves face to face with the six *al-Yemen Bayyi'l'ali* agents, all of whom had either AKMs, AKs, or Soviet-made autoloaders in their hands. It was a matter of speed. Mad Mike and Ryan might snuff four or five, or even all six of the South Yemenis, but two or three of the Yemenis, at the same time, would almost certainly kill them. A Mexican standoff! Like two men facing each other with double-barreled shotguns—six feet apart.

What tripped the scales in favor of Quinlan and Ryan was Basappa Ram Gokhale, the quiet, philosophical Gurkha, and Mehmed Gursël, a giant of a Turk who had a chin like the cowcatcher of an old time steam locomotive. A singularly repellent man who always smelled of sweat and who combined the surliness of a shark with the hauteur of a King Cobra, Gursël had three talents: he could hold his booze, was a crack shot, and could throw a knife with an accuracy that was uncanny. These latter two abilities he had in commin with Gokhale, who didn't touch alcohol and thoroughly detested Gursël.

Concurrent with Ryan and Quinlan's moving to the pillar behind which lurked the six South Yemen intelligence officers, Gursël and Gokhale moved from a support—twenty feet to the east of the pillar harboring Colonel Shaabi's boys—and saw the six South Yemenis. Then saw Ryan and Quinlan. During that micromoment of truth, as well-trained as they were, Gursël and Gokhale knew that if they sprayed the backs of the six enemy agents with slugs, some of the projectiles might cut all the way through their backs and chests and perhaps strike Ryan and Quinlan.

There was one more factor that saved Major Quinlan and Patrick Ryan—the lightning speed of the two men. Both were a shade faster than the three startled South Yemenis directly in front of them. At the same time that Mehmed Gursël and Ram Gokhale fired downward at the booted feet of the *al-Yemen Bayyi'l'ali* gunmen, Mad Mike began triggering his twin MatchMasters; and Ryan, his nickel-plated Hi-Power Brownings.

Wipeout! All in 3.8 seconds! As 9mm Parabellum Browning slugs and .45 silvertip MatchMaster projectiles bored into the chests and stomachs of three of the Yemenis, Gokhale's 5.56mm X 45 Colt "Commando" sub-gun slugs and Gursël's 9mm Spanish Star machine gun bullets chopped off the feet of the three enemy fighters to the rear, some of the projectiles setting up a crescendo of ricochets as they struck the stones of the floor.

The six South Yemeni agents flopped like fish out of water, screamed for only an instant and fell as Quinlan and the three other Thunderbolt mercs pumped more slugs into their bodies. The six corpses lay twisted on the stones, streams of blood crawling from underneath their bodies.

Linking up, Major Quinlan and the other three moved from pillar to pillar, darting to the north, noticing that there was less and less firing and that for every commando alive or wounded, ten to twelve Dasni were dead.

Quinlan and the other three mercenaries jumped to a pillar harboring Manfred Rohde and Marcel Lecanuet, the former of whom was spraying the top and the west end of a long altar to the north. As Quinlan and the three jumped between Rohde and Lecanuet, the French merc tossed a grenade toward the altar. He was tossing a second grenade when Rohde muttered, *"Verdammt verflucht!"* ("God-damn it!") and pulled back.

Colonel al Bin Shaabi himself had reared up from be-hind the altar, at its center, and had triggered off a short burst from an AKS-74 assault rifle. One of the 5.45mm projectiles had cut across the outside of Rohde's left arm, cutting through the sleeve and digging a half-inch deep ditch in the biceps.

"Get over here, Manny," ordered Major Quinlan. "I'll take over your position. He reached out and took the H&H G3A4 automatic rifle from the German's right hand. As Rohde moved back, Quinlan stepped to the corner of the pillar, then quickly ducked back as a dozen more 5.45mm slugs struck the stones and screamed off into space.

Mehmed Gursël placed his Star submachine gun flat on the floor, pulled a large adhesive bandage, a tube of Efod-ine Ointment and a nylon cord and stick tourniquet from an LC1 Paratroop first-aid kit on his belt.

"Here, Dutchman," he growled in a thick accent. "Clean wound, and bandage I will."

The Death Merchant, the Ingram SMG in one hand, a reloaded AMP in his other, moved like a very crooked streak from pillar to pillar. Finally, ducking slugs the last seven feet, he reached the side of a support column only 30 feet southeast of the east end of the altar and got down with Arturo Guido, Dimitur Zlatev, and Urho Sundqvist. Almost immediately, Camellion detected that the only firing was from behind the long altar, another pillar to the west and from behind the pillar to which he had just moved.

Arturo Guido was at the corner of the pillar, the corner opposite Camellion's position, the little Sicilian firing an *Oberkommando der Wehrmacht MP 38 Erma Maschinenpistole,* which, ever since World War II, had been incorrectly called a "Schmeisser" (after Dr. Hugo Schmeisser who didn't have a thing to do with the development of the Erma MP 38).

Guido would wait a moment, count to five, then lean around the corner and trigger off a short burst of 9mm slugs, just to let the enemy know he was still in action. He would then quickly pull back.

Dimitur Zlatev, shoving a full magazine into a Galil ARM assault rifle, gave the Death Merchant a quick glance of inspection. "All Arab trash dead," he smirked. "All *neposti!* As you say, finished forever. Behind that altar, the only ones left. We make them *neposti* soon, damn quick!"

His back against the pillar, Camellion flinched involuntarily as a dozen projectiles tore into the side of the stone support near the edge of his position. *Zing-Zing-Zing-Zing!* Slugs glanced from the stones with loud whines. Dust and pieces of chipped stone fell on his left sleeve.

The narrow-faced Urho Sundqvist pushed the Ranger Patrol cap back on his head, blinked at Camellion who was taking the PRC-601 from its case, then said to Zlatev, "It will take a while. We can't rush them without flirting with the god of suicide. There's no cover between here and that altar."

Pulling up the antenna of the Tadiran walkie-talkie, Camellion heard a series of low, deep rumbles from outside the temple, to the west. *Thunder!* The first seasonal rain was on the way. *Damn it!*

He switched on the W-T and pushed the call button. In

a few seconds, Major Quinlan was speaking from behind a pillar to the west.

Camellion told him what he had in mind—". . . provided one of your boys has a weapon with a grenade projection adapter."

"I was thinking along the same lines," Quinlan's steady voice came out of the transceiver. "I have a man here with me who has a grenade adapter. The trouble is, the GPA will only fire an M31 shaped charge, an antitank deal."

"Yeah, I know the kind. It's a HE charge. How many does your man have?"

"He's carrying four." Mad Mike (called "Mad" because of his daring) sounded surprised. "But you realize what HE charges will do to the wall above the targets? Hundreds of pounds of rubble will come down."

That's the idea, old buddy!" Now it was the Death Merchant's turn to sound perplexed. "So what's your worry?"

"Rohde got a look at one of the dog-drools behind the altar. It was Colonel Shaabi. I was thinking that maybe you wanted that son of a bitch alive—and did you hear the thunder?"

"I heard it. That's another reason why we have to hurry—the seasonal rains. Some of these rains can be real downpours. As for Shaabi—we terminate him and everyone with him. The last thing we do is blow up this temple. Listen carefully, here is what I want you to do. . . ."

The first M31 antitank grenade whizzed from the adapter on Marcel Lecanuet's British "Individual Weapon," struck the north wall twenty feet above the altar and exploded with a crashing roar, the blast digging a large hole in the granite and throwing out hundreds of fragments, some, very sharp, a foot long and weighing from ten to fifteen pounds.

While Quinlan and Gürsel raked the top and the west end of the altar from the corners of one support, and Arturo Guido concentrated on the east end, a happy Marcel Lecanuet placed another antitank grenade in the adapter attached to "The Chinaman." Moments later. Lecanuet fired. The 25-ounce grenade shot upward, struck the wall above the altar, and the 9.92 ounces of Composition B exploded with a bright flash and a crashing noise.

An M31 high explosive antitank rifle grenade has the capability of penetrating 25 centimeters (10-inches) of homogeneous steel armor or 50 centimeters (20-inches) of reinforced concrete; and this second grenade did what it was intended to do: it exploded a huge hole in the wall, the blast causing hundreds of fragments to rain down behind the altar.

BLAMMMMMMMM! The third antitank HE charge scattered more sharp chunks of granite, the hundreds of pounds of stone particles falling on Colonel al Bin Shabbi, Major Jahiz, the three GRU officers and two *al-Yemen Bayyi'l'ali* agents, the latter two of whom wishing that they had gone with Rabadh Yahya Tabriz and his killers.

The seven men protected themselves as best they could, hunched down by the back of the altar, their heads almost to their waists, their hands over their heads.

Jeddah A'baghlan yelled in pain as a sharp piece of granite fell and stabbed him in the right hand. The South Yemen intelligence officer reached the breaking point. He stood up and, with arms over his head, rushed west through the rain of falling granite, figuring he would have better luck ducking a slug. He didn't. A'baghlan was only a few feet from the west end of the altar when Major Quinlan cut him to pieces with a dozen H&K A-R projectiles.

BLAMMMMMMMMMM! The fourth and the last antitank grenade exploded, setting up another shower of stone, and telling Camellion it was time—kill-time.

The Death Merchant left his position by the support column and sprinted northwest toward the east end of the altar, ducking several falling stones on the way. Right behind him came Dimitur Zlatev with his Galil assault rifle.

Camellion reached the outer corner of the altar, took a deep breath, moved to the inside corner and jumped to the rear. Colonel al Bin Shaabi and the men with him were trapped, caught flat-footed. The ant had walked alone into the nest of scorpions and the scorpions had not expected him.

Shaabi was holding an AKS-74 over his head and was turning to the left when he saw the Death Merchant only thirteen feet away. Richard Camellion was the last man on earth he saw. The little Ingram chattered and a dozen 9mm projectiles dissolved Shaabi's face, stabbed into his neck and showered the front of his dust-covered silver-gray uniform with blood and tiny chunks of flesh and bone. Resembling nothing human, the corpse fell against the back of the altar and slid to the floor.

In desperation, Major Abdul Jahiz, the three Russians, and Mali Joo'iq tried to get their weapons into action. But the five only had time to realize they would be dead in the length of time required to take a deep sigh.

The Alaskan Auto Mag roared once, twice, and the Ingram continued its noisy *duddle-duddle-duddle-duddle*. Major Abdul Jahiz was trying to stand up when a .44 AMP magnum projectile stung him in the left side, tore through his lungs, blew off part of a rib on his right side, took its exit and stabbed into Major Vasili, who, at the time, was standing up and turning around. The .44 magnum bullet caught the GRU officer low in the chest and stopped half an inch from his heart at the same time a nine-millimeter Ingram projectile popped him just to the left of his nose and two more nine-millimeter slugs sliced into his throat and dug bloody tunnels out the back of his neck.

Mali Joo'iq tried to fall flat on the floor—for all the good it did him. He jerked once when a full metal jacketed .44 bullet cut apart his spine, stabbed into his intestines at an angle, left his body and hit the stones.

Colonel Maskim Oosukhov and General Yuri Leonid Kasmanovisky left life together, horrible looks of fear on their dust-covered faces. The two Russians had only an instant of awareness before the slugs tore into them. One .44 AMP bullet hit Kasmanovisky high in the forehead and made his blond hair jump. Another .44 projectile speared into his chest and knocked the corpse back off its heels.

Death grabbed Maskim Oosukhov. His body jerked, jumped, and did a five-second dance of death as the last six 9mms from the Ingram stitched him perpendicularly from his penis to the nape of his neck. Stone dead, the Soviet GRU official twisted and spun, resembling a kind of barber pole, with blood twirling around him. He flopped to the floor and lay still, his head propped up by a piece of stone.

The hot Ingram and the hot, heavy AMP in his hands, Camellion looked with satisfaction on his work and smiled

very slightly. Albert Einstein maintained that there was only one absolute in the Universe: the speed of light.
Albert was wrong. There's the power of money!
The third absolute was Death. . . .

☐ EPILOGUE ☐

Riyadh: the capital of *al-Mamlaka al'- Arabiya as-Sa'ud-iya.* The Embassy of the United States of America.
14.00 hours.

Burton Webb, always nervous in the presence of high CIA officials from D.C. but never showing it, continued to twist the signet ring on his finger, his calm eyes on Joel Considine.

Sitting to the left side of the desk in a chrome, nylon upholstered lounge chair, Considine peered at Noah Gardner.

"Then you are unequivocally certain that Colonel al Bin Shaabi is dead?" he said, stroking one side of his large mustache. "There isn't any way that the Marxist in South Yemen can connect our government and the Agency with the operation?"

Many times over the years, Camellion had given reports to representatives of Courtland Grojean, the boss of the Company Covert Operations Section. It was always the same: tell the story in detail. Then repeat it. Then repeat it again. The same questions. Always the same answers.

"Colonel Shaabi is dead," Camellion said flatly. "I personally performed brain surgery on him. He's dead, and the dead don't rise from their graves." He held up a hand for silence when he saw that Considine was about to interrupt. "Rabadh Tabriz is dead. Colonel Bin Maktum killed him and two of his top men. Unfortunately, one of them buried a *Stinviq* in Maktum. We found all four after the

193

battle was over. Now ask me again about Ahmed Shukairy, the Israeli Mossad agent."

Considine presented the Death Merchant with a large, friendly smile. Half-bald and of medium height, he was a pudgy man with a too-large brown mustache, almost no chin, and an affable manner. This time he was traveling as a representative of ARAMCO, the Arabian-American Oil Company. When he wanted to, he could ooze personality.

Considine's smile vanished; a glint came into his eyes.

"We still can't be absolutely certain that Ahmed Shukairy was the main target, the Mossad agent. I realize that certitude and absoluteness can't extend into infinity. However, we must do our best to determine all the facts."

"I gave you the facts," Camellion said, pleasantly enough.

Considine thought for a moment, moving his tongue around in his mouth in a probing expedition.

"Your speaking in Hebrew to Shukairy isn't indicative that he was the Mossad target who had to be terminated. Your speaking Hebrew could have indicated to him that you were an Israeli. I presume you've considered that possibility?"

"You're putting the wagon half a block in front of the nag," the Death Merchant mused. "I didn't decide the target was Shukairy by flipping a coin. I didn't have any evidence against him until he made a slip, not only of the tongue but of logic, his logic, which represented his own personal moral culture. That's how he tripped himself."

"Tell me again."

Camellion sighed and leaned back on the couch. "We were discussing the atom bomb, and the Nazis. Marlon Clayton remarked that the math for the bomb had been worked out by Einstein."

The Death Merchant explained that Shukairy had made a fatal error in referring to Albert Einstein as a "dirty Jew." While it was normal enough for the average Arab to hate an Israeli or a Jew—"And an Israeli doesn't have to be Jewish!" interjected Camellion—it was very unlikely that a Yemeni Arab would call a German a "dirty Jew." ". . . even if the Kraut was Jewish," Camellion said. "The Arab mind doesn't work that way. The Jewish mentality does. A Jew, who identifies with Einstein, would consider Einstein a Jew first and a German second. That was enough for me to think of Shukairy as being Jewish; and to be in the Mossad, you must be Jewish. Shukairy, in keeping up with the pretense that he was an Arab, wanted to show his hatred of the Jews. That was reasonable. It was totally out of character for him—as a supposed Arab—to refer to Einstein as being Jewish. Why, the average sand crab has never heard of Einstein. But any Jew or Israeli has. The Jews identify with Einstein."

"I don't see your point." Joel Considine continued to play the role of the devil's advocate. "After all, Einstein was Jewish."

Camellion didn't reveal his irritation. "You listened but didn't hear! Only a Jewish-Israeli, pretending to be Arab, would call Albert Einstein a 'dirty Jew.' Of course, there's one chance in a million that even a totally uneducated Yemeni could have heard of the scientist and would know he had been Jewish. That was not the impression I got from Shukairy. At the time, from his intonation, it was apparent to me that he was well aware that Einstein was a German-Jew. That made the difference. Anyhow, at the last, guilt was written all over Shukairy's face. Take it from me. Shukairy was the Mossad target. He's dead. Now it's your turn."

"My turn?" Considine looked curiously at Camellion.

"Your turn to tell me why the Mossad agent had to be silenced. The reason, what's behind it?"

"That's quite impossible." Considine drew back, a frown of concern creasing his forehead. "The information is sensitive compartmented information. I don't even have it. Even if I did, I couldn't reveal it. I'm surprised that you should ask."

Camellion, his eyes blue fire, turned his attention to Burton Webb, who cleared his throat.

"It's part of Gardner's contract," Webb said casually, avoiding the direct gaze of the astonished Considine, who had turned in the chair and was staring at him, "and I do have the information and Mr. Grojean's permission to give it to him."

"I'll be damned." A startled Considine glanced from Webb to Camellion. "Such procedure is unheard of!"

"We don't know what Shukairy's real name was," Webb said to Camellion. "We only knew that an agent of Mossad was among the Royalist rebels and might be a member of your force. We couldn't be certain. We were positive that the mission of the Mossad agent was to find out the details of how Colonel Al Bin Shaai and Colonel Muammar Kaddafi of Libya were going to use a nuclear device they planned to steal.

"An agent-in-place within the Mossad," Camellion said. "That's the only way you could have known that the Israelis were onto the plot."

He watched Webb's eyes to see if his guess was correct. It was!

"Our man didn't know the identity of the agent," Webb said. "He doesn't have that kind of security clearance within Israeli intelligence. He did learn that, somehow, the Mossad agent—Shukairy, if you're right—learned the details of Shaabi and Kaddafi's plan to involve the Middle East in a full-scale war. What we think happened is that Shukairy, in keeping with his work as a North Yemen Royalist, had to go along on the operation you handled before he could make his way back to Israel."

"Do you know how he managed to infiltrate the Royalists?" asked Camellion. "But if you knew how he did it, you'd probably know his real name."

"Exactly. We must give the Mossad agent credit. He was very clever."

"Another question," inserted the Death Merchant forcefully. "Does the Israeli agent have any remote tie-in with how the Company was tipped off that Shaabi and the Dasni were going to attack Ali Sa'galli in the Jabal Mahrat? I know your source of information was not the same as the source of the information to the Sons of the Falcon. Another agent-in-place?"

"Not exactly." Webb seemed thoughtful as he took a Barclay cigarette from a pack lying on the desk. "We haven't the faintest idea who was supplying the Sons with data. Our origin was a member of the GRU stationed in Aden. He wants to defect and wants us to help him get his family out of the Soviet Union. Don't ask me his name. That wasn't part of the deal."

Freshly shaved and dressed in an off-white shirt and cream trousers, Camellion crossed his legs, the lines around his eyes and mouth not betraying any emotion. "I couldn't care less about his identity. It's ironic though. He could be dead. He is if he was one of the Russians at Danikil."

"He wasn't." A sly look had crept into Webb's eyes. "He was at the South Yemen air base at Wusadi when the battle was going on. That's all I can tell you."

"What matters is that the operation was a success," Camellion said. "You wanted a job done. I did it. A hundred grand was sent to my special account in Swissland—correct?"

"Deposited yesterday, right after you and the force returned to Arabia," Webb said. He finally lighted the Barclay with a desk lighter that was a tiny model of an armored car, blew out smoke and leaned back in the swivel chair, the Death Merchant detecting that something was on his mind.

"I'm afraid that the job is only half over," Webb finally said. He glanced at Considine, then stared at Camellion and added quickly, "Hold on! It's a whole new ball game and another one-hundred-thousand dollars for you. You see, we think that Colonel Kaddafi succeeded in grabbing not one but two nuclear devices. It happened in West Germany two days ago, and it's your baby. You leave tonight."

His thoughts tumbling around, the Death Merchant did not speak. Sooner or later it had to happen.

It had!

A hellbomb had been stolen by terrorists!

CELEBRATING 10 YEARS IN PRINT
AND OVER 22 MILLION COPIES SOLD!